A HOUSE TO DIE FOR

A Selection of Recent Titles from M R D Meek

POSTSCRIPT TO MURDER
THIS BLESSED PLOT
TOUCH AND GO

A HOUSE TO DIE FOR

M.R.D. Meek

This first world edition published in Great Britain 1999 by
SEVERN HOUSE PUBLISHERS LTD of
9–15 High Street, Sutton, Surrey SM1 1DF.
This title first published in the U.S.A. 1999 by
SEVERN HOUSE PUBLISHERS INC of
595 Madison Avenue, New York, N.Y. 10022.

British Library Cataloguing in Publication Data

Meek, M. R. D.
      A house to die for. - (A Lennox Kemp mystery)
      1.   Kemp, Lennox (Fictitious character) - Fiction
      2.   Lawyers - Fiction
      3.   Detective and mystery stories
      I.   Title
      823.9'14 [F]

      ISBN 0-7278-5442-9

Typeset by Palimpsest Book Production Ltd
Polmont, Stirlingshire, Scotland.

Printed and bound in Great Britain by
MPG Books Ltd, Bodmin, Cornwall.

One

The house in Albert Crescent bought by the Kemps on their marriage two years ago had a pleasant air of superiority about it. As well it might, because Newtown Council in their wisdom (something of a rarity in that chamber of local worthies) had decided it should become a listed building. There were few other contenders in or around Newtown when the dread word 'heritage' travelled up the Lea and made councillors look about desperately to find buildings worth preserving.

Number Two Albert Crescent wasn't such a bad choice. Although hardly a gem of Victorian architecture, it had nevertheless been built in a good period. The 'very dry stone and well-baked bricks' – as set out in the original specification – had weathered to a soft yellow-beige which looked particularly fine in early morning or late evening light. Also, it had fared better over its 150-odd years than any of its neighbours, for it had housed only two families in that time and they had cared dearly for its appearance. Other properties in the Crescent had suffered damage both social and material through having had too many changes of ownership, in some cases even the final slur of multiple occupancy. Façades shaken by the bomb that had landed near the station had been patched up in post-war penny-pinching years with more haste than taste, and now plaster had peeled and old scars gaped afresh.

Mary Kemp was unconcerned about the down-at-heel look of its surroundings; she fell in love with the house the moment she entered its doors.

"It has been cared for by my family," murmured the elderly vendor, a Mrs Channing, last of her line and now destined for

1

an Eventide Home, ". . . and by the Threadgolds before us. It was built by their Grandfather, a railwayman . . ."

Mary didn't think for a moment that he'd shovelled ballast on the line. She had nursed in families down on Long Island where the 'old money' prudently accumulated from last century's railway bonanza was still considered classier than the new.

"I shall look after the house as if it were a child of my own," she said, startling Louisa Channing by the extravagance of the language. Her old eyes peered more closely at this woman who, although a solicitor's wife and therefore in Mrs Channing's view a person of some merit, was an odd creature, short in stature, plain of face and not particularly well dressed.

The words used seemed a trifle high-flown in the banal circumstance of a mere house-sale, but the slight Irish accent of Mrs Kemp underlined rather than diminished their sincerity. "I'm sure you will," murmured Mrs Channing, rather taken with this prospective buyer. She had not wanted to sell, but had been forced to it by age and a meddlesome family, so she had been grumpy with house agents and viewers alike. "Not treat it the way some do," she went on, "those people next door, now . . . Letting out rooms indeed . . ."

She makes it sound like a thieves' kitchen, thought Mary, slipping unconsciously into the other woman's idiom. Really, this lady needs lessons in salesmanship, no wonder the place has been so long on the market. She was determined to have the house and knew the price she and Lennox were prepared to pay was over the odds. "Then it'll just make it the more interesting getting to know the neighbours," she said, cheerfully.

Surprised at this novel approach, Mrs Channing had softened and remarked that it was not poor Miss Weston's fault that she was reduced to taking in lodgers, she was understood to have fallen on hard times.

That conversation had taken place years ago and by now Mary Kemp had found out more about poor Miss Weston than Mrs Channing – still occasionally visited in her comfortable nursing home – would ever have wanted to know. The Channings had always considered themselves of a better class than any of their neighbours in the Crescent, and had therefore never mixed.

"They lost out on a lot of the fun in life," Mary remarked to her husband one night over supper. "This street is your whole class system in microcosm."

"What on earth have you been reading? It's all these sociology classes you've been going to. And you've been in next door again."

"Prim asked me to mind the child this afternoon when she went shopping – and Miss Weston, too, of course."

"And how is the old lady?"

"Speechless, as usual. If only she could talk . . ." Gwendolyne Weston had suffered a stroke some years ago which had left her a semi-invalid and unable to speak. She was cared for by Primrose Sutton who seemed to be some kind of relation. Prim Sutton herself was an unmarried mother with an infant daughter.

"I like Prim," said Mary, piling plates and taking them into the kitchen. "I think she's straight."

"But not above earning a little on the side that's not shown at the benefits counter," said Kemp to her retreating back.

"I'm talking about straight in character, not necessarily straight with the authorities." Mary came in and put fruit salad on the table.

"And there's a difference?"

"You know there is. Though it's not like you had the experience of it. Do you want cream?"

"As much as you'll let me have. You've got a soft spot for people in Prim's circumstances. She makes you think of when you were a girl."

"Oh, no . . ." Mary sounded as horrified as she was. 'I don't think of it that way at all. Anyway, there's really no comparison."

Kemp had to admit she was probably right; no matter how far it had fallen in the social scale, the house next door would be a palace compared to the shack in Vineland, Pennsylvania where the young Mary Blane had played little mother to a flock of ne'erdowell siblings. She'd had to protect them as much from their own follies as from the heavy hand of her drunken stepfather and the unwelcome weight of local welfare agencies.

"I'm trying to live it down," she said now with a smile as she followed his line of thought. "I never tell people, you know, and I've never been one for reliving the past. The present's fine by me. I love my house, I love Newtown, I love England, and I love you. There, does that not satisfy you?"

It was only later that she brought up once again the subject of the people next door.

"Prim Sutton would like you to do her a favour, Lennox."

"If I can, I will. What is it?"

"It's not really for herself, though she might benefit. It's for Miss Weston. She's never made a Will, and folk think she ought to . . ."

"What folk?"

"Well, it's not Prim herself. In fact she's the one who's hesitant about the whole thing. But the old lady has been listening to some of the others and getting into a state. Do you know Gregory Venn?"

"There's a young clerk of that name who works for Roberts the Solicitors down by the station. I've met him a few times."

"He has the top flat next door. He sees quite a lot of Miss Weston and he's been talking a lot of legal jargon to her."

"What sort of legal jargon?"

Mary should have known that when she used a vague term like this to Lennox he would want her to be more precise. She tried to give verbatim the gist of the conversation she'd had with Primrose Sutton.

The subject had arisen through Gwendolyne Weston's enthusiasm for the National Lottery. It had become a source of joy to her and really, as Prim said, there was little else could bring that into her life, the poor soul stuck in a wheelchair from morning till night with a helpless right hand so that even household tasks were beyond her. It had been young Gregory Venn who said to her one evening, half-joking, "What if you won a million or two, Aunt Gwen?" Everybody called her Aunt Gwen though only Primrose seemed to be any kin to her. "What would you do with a million, eh?" he had gone on in his teasing way. There was nothing wrong with Miss

4

Weston's hearing, and she had laughed like they all did at the very idea.

Prim had described where they had all been sitting and as Mary had often been in the big, untidy living-room of the house next door, she could see them in her mind's eye: Prim on the sofa with Liza-Jane, the toddler, between her and Blanche Quigley who was helping the little girl to thread beads. Gregory Venn was still at the supper table finishing off a shepherd's pie, watched by Jaz Quigley who was often about the place although he did not live there—

"Hold on," said Kemp at that point, "can you sort these people out for me?"

"Gregory Venn has the top flat. Sometimes he cooks for himself but more often than not Prim makes him an evening meal. I suppose he pays her extra, and she certainly needs every penny of it. Jaz Quigley's a mate of his, and his sister Blanche is one of Prim's little army of volunteers who look in on the old lady from time to time, and baby-sit for Liza-Jane when Prim gets a waitress job in an evening. All these people troop in and out of Number Four at all hours – I think Prim likes it that way, and of course it provides a diversion for the old lady." She stopped and looked round the dining-room where she and Lennox were sitting.

"The house must have at one time been like this, but now it's quite different because it's divided into flats. The whole of the ground floor seems to be this one great living-room with a kitchen and bathroom extension out on the side away from us. Where we have our big kitchen and this room there's Miss Weston's bedroom, and there's two small rooms at the back that make up Prim's own room and a nursery for Liza-Jane. Upstairs is a whole flat with kitchen and bathroom, and I think one bedroom though I've never been up there because the last tenant left about six months ago and the new one has only just moved in. I have met her. Her name's Grace Juniper and she's a schoolteacher."

"And was she part of this crowded scene you were telling me about?"

"I don't think so. She's probably not yet integrated into the household. Prim didn't mention her, and I'm only repeating what Prim told me was said and why the question of a Will came up at all. Gregory's friend, Jaz—"

"Jazz as in the musical genre?"

"Only one zee. I think its short for Jasper – isn't that a rather old-world English name? Anyway, this Jaz asked Gregory Venn what would happen if somebody's numbers came up on the Saturday night and they were dead of shock by Sunday morning. Gregory said it would be in that person's estate and go under the Will. Then he picked up the conversation he'd had earlier with Miss Weston, and called out to her: 'Hey, Aunt Gwen, I hope you've made a Will . . .' Although it had all been in a spirit of fun, according to Prim, the old lady became very agitated, and Prim had to go over and calm her down. She told the young men to shut up – they were obviously upsetting her aunt."

"How well can Miss Weston let her wants be known to those caring for her?" Kemp asked.

"Um . . ." Mary gave the question her serious consideration. "From what I've seen, Prim understands pretty well when the old lady mumbles something and makes gestures with her good hand. But, then, its mostly practical things like she might want to go to the bathroom, or she needs her cardigan. How it would be if a serious discussion were required, I really wouldn't like to say . . ."

"But you've had experience with patients like Miss Weston."

"Yes. I learned that it takes a deal of patience, a lot of time and some professional knowledge. Primrose Sutton hasn't any of these – that's why she needs help."

"In what way?"

"Well, it looks as if her aunt does want to make her Will. Somehow she indicated to Prim that she had never made one, and after those remarks were passed – even in jest – she got worried."

"And you would like me to see her?"

"Oh, yes, Lennox, if you would. Prim's in a difficult position. She doesn't want people saying she pushed the old lady into it; on the other hand, if she doesn't do something Gregory Venn will go around saying she did nothing because if the aunt dies intestate she'll get the lot because she's the only relative."

"He said that?"

"I've only Prim's word for it of course, but apparently since that first conversation young Venn has kept on about it, and told Prim that her aunt ought to have legal advice and he'd be glad to arrange it with his firm."

"Not the first young man to try pushing business his way . . . What do you really know of Miss Weston's circumstances?"

"Not much. From surmise and observation I think it unlikely she has much to leave anyone – unless of course she did win the lottery. She seems to live on her pension, and some small allowance that comes in monthly, but where from I've no idea."

"But that house is surely worth quite a bit?"

"Ah, but it's not hers. She's only a tenant. I owe that particular nugget of information to Gregory Venn and I've no reason to doubt him. His firm – Roberts, isn't it? – acts for the owners, a property company to whom Miss Weston's father sold out years ago. One of the considerations of the sale was that she should be a tenant for life – is that the proper name for it?"

"Not exactly . . . but, never mind, do go on." Kemp was always being surprised by his wife's talent for acquiring knowledge and storing it, whether it came out of text books new to her, or from the gossip of neighbours; it was as if the tablets of her mind had been blank till now, uncluttered alike by education or received opinion, and only awaited fulfillment as a formidable database.

"Primrose knows all about the house. She never expected to get it anyway when the old lady dies. Prim's not very worldly at all. She says she's quite prepared to move on. She's never been a settled person – and I can appreciate that."

"Of course you can." Mary had moved around all her life until now. "But surely Primrose has the child to think of?"

"She says that when they had Liza-Jane they were travelling, and she will go on travelling. She looks on Four Albert Crescent as a temporary oasis."

"Her words or yours?"

"Hers, of course." Mary was indignant. "I don't use other people's images. I was trying to give you some idea of

7

Prim's way of living. Her hold on it I should call fairly loose."

"OK. Now, exactly what relation is she to Miss Weston?"

"Ah, you have me there. She's never said. I think – but it's only an idea of my own – that it's through her husband . . ."

"I thought she was an unmarried mother?"

Mary felt uneasy; she had given this aspect of Primrose Sutton much thought but without reaching any conclusion. "Perhaps I got the wrong impression when I met her first," she said, slowly. "That, oddly enough, was at the college, not next door. She came to some of the early sociology sessions, then she seemed to sort of drop out. But she'd already made her presence felt as a bit of a trouble-maker. She complained about the timetable, why didn't they have a crèche, why were the hours all wrong for mature students with children – that kind of thing. She spent a lot of time arguing."

"But I thought that was what sociology was all about," Kemp remarked, innocently: "tossing arguments around . . ."

Mary eyed him severely. "I go to classes to learn," she said, "but I could see that Prim and others like her had a point. Prim saw herself as deprived because she hadn't any qualifications and was trying to get some. To be honest, I don't think she'd the head for it. Anyway, she left. Then I found that she lived next door."

"Has there ever been a husband?"

"Once I got to know her better she talked as if there had been. At the college with the other students, some of them about her age, she wore the unmarried mum thing like it was a badge for valour – particularly after that man in Parliament had gone on about them. I think it suited her to be one of an oppressed minority, it got her kudos with her mates."

"I'll bet," said Kemp. "There's nothing sociology students like better than a member of an oppressed minority; it shows up the system as unfair."

"Well, those youngsters don't like any system that's unfair," said Mary, allowing herself to stray momentarily from the subject of discussion. "I'm partial to a bit of rebellion myself . . ."

"I could say that's the Irish in you," said her husband, grinning, "only it wouldn't be true. You knew what it was

8

like to be really poor, and deprived. You didn't rebel against the system, you just set about tidying it up in whatever ways you could – some of them pretty ingenious and a lot of them downright illegal. Come on, my sweet, you and I know this isn't an ideal society. I'm all for justice and fair play, and I try in my job to get as near to these concepts as possible, but perhaps life was never meant to be fair for any of us, not just unmarried mothers. We have to take the world as it is not as we think it ought to be."

Mary put her head on one side and looked at him with her pale, opaque eyes, just short of mockery. "Yeah, boss," she said, "we have to accept the status quo. Mr Carlyle said as much."

"Mr Carlyle? A lecturer at your college?"

"No. Thomas Carlyle, a Scotsman of strong views. When told that some woman called Fuller had said she accepted the universe, he said: 'By Gad, she'd better . . .'"

Kemp stared at his wife. "You know, Mary," he said, "you have the knack of pulling plums from the driest of literary pies. Where on earth did you find that one?"

"Dusting your books. They haven't been opened since Lincoln was a lad."

"I don't know what I can do to keep up with you."

"You can do as I ask and make an appointment to see Miss Weston about her Will."

Kemp had found out by now that his wife nearly always got her way if she was set on it. Perhaps it was time to take his wits out and dust them down. It was all very well thinking he was keeping up-to-date by attending the odd course on those aspects of fiscal law continually being interfered with by a Government that bumbled along like a drunken bee, but how long was it since he had read one of those classics Mary was going through at the rate of two a week? What did he know of this 'Structuralism' she'd mentioned, and he'd been too wary to ask her what it actually meant?

He smiled when he thought of Mary; she always did that to him. Something had come in his middle years – he was fifty – which he never imagined could happen. He'd found the love of his life.

Two

Although it didn't get the afternoon sun, the huge sitting-room of Number Four was surprisingly light when Primrose Sutton pushed the door open and stood back to allow Kemp to go in. Miss Weston was strategically placed halfway between window and fireplace in an armchair but with her wheelchair against the wall behind her.

"Shall I leave you?" asked Prim, awkwardly.

"Of course not." Kemp went over and shook the old lady's hand, the good one which she raised from her lap for him to take. "I shall need you, Primrose." All these new friends of Mary's seemed to use only first names; in any case he didn't know whether Prim was Miss or Mrs, and he hardly knew how to pronounce Ms – though he'd been told often enough by his staff.

"I hope you keep well, Miss Weston. Although we are such near neighbours, I'm afraid you and I haven't met before."

She smiled, nodded and looked pleased. Indeed, her face, which was a healthy pink, and moon-shaped, registered her passing feelings and her thoughts rapidly so that an alert watcher had instant clues to the effect people's words and actions were having on her. This mirror, as it were, took the place of what in another would have been rejoinder, explanation or, by change of tone in the voice, perhaps remonstrance or argument.

Her eyes which were bright, though almost swallowed up in folds of wrinkled skin, never left Kemp as he took the seat beside her proffered by Prim.

"Well, then," she said, "I'll just sit over here, and if you want me . . ."

10

She sat down on the other side of the fire which was burning small spluttering logs.

The interview was not as difficult as many Kemp had had with elderly clients where age had dimmed the eyes or dulled the hearing. Miss Weston's stroke had indeed been a disastrous one, as Primrose explained. She had been left with little or no power of speech, and one side of the body was completely paralysed so that the right hand had curled into a useless claw, and the leg and foot were misshapen and incapable of sustaining weight.

"At first, she went for physiotherapy to the hospital," said Prim, "three times a week for over six months. You didn't much like that, did you, Auntie?"

Miss Weston grimaced, turning down the corners of her mouth.

"Then I think they gave up on her. They'd had that leg in a caliper to stop the foot turning in, and there were all those exercise she had to do with the hand . . . You did try, didn't you?"

Kemp noticed the way Prim made sure the old lady heard, and could, if she wanted, take part in the conversation. Now she was nodding vigorously and making clutching movements with her good hand.

"But it wasn't any good. They as good as said there'd be no more improvement."

"Were you here then?"

"No." Primrose got up and put another small log on the fire which had been burning brightly enough. "I came later."

As she volunteered no further information, Kemp turned back to Miss Weston. She signalled approval as he brought out notebook and pen and pulled towards him a small pie-crust table with a leather top. It looked a good piece to Kemp. He had been learning about antiques through Mary's sudden interest in what to her was a peculiarly English phenomenon. The little table on which he now set out his pad was one of the few bits of furniture in the room worth a second glance. The rest was like the house itself, a mishmash of the shabby old and the tasteless new.

With the help of Primrose, but never without getting an

11

approving nod or other sign from his client, Kemp took down the formal details.

She was Gwendolyne Ann Weston of 4 Albert Crescent, Newtown. When he repeated the address she gave a little laugh, raised her good arm and turned her eyes on the ceiling.

"She means she was born here, in the bedroom upstairs," said Prim.

Kemp waved aside the question of age as unimportant but Prim whispered: "She's proud of it." And went to a desk in the corner and brought out a birth certificate. The old lady's face flushed with pleasure as she took it and held it close to her eyes. "Do you want your specs, Auntie?" Prim asked, but she shook her head and gave the flimsy piece of paper to Kemp.

"Daughter to George and Adelaide Weston . . . July, 1908. You are an Edwardian, Miss Weston, you were born in a good period of history."

Her eyes, which he could now see were a faded blue, sparkled; it may have been that they just caught the firelight, but there was no doubt that she was beaming a smile at him as though she liked what he was saying, so he continued on the same lines while Prim went into the kitchen to make tea.

Watching the responses running like waves across the old lady's face he realised how much she was relishing the attention given her, how the talk of days that were long gone – and to him the stuff only of other people's memoirs – was effectively quickening a mind half-asleep but by no means senile.

After a while it was the clatter of cups that seemed to return her to the present. Before Primrose could enter the room Miss Weston put her hand on Kemp's notepad and brought it down twice in emphasis. At the same time she turned her head towards the kitchen door.

"Primrose?" Kemp queried.

A vigorous nod, a spread of the fingers over Kemp's notes in a gesture of openness.

"You want it all to go to Primrose Sutton?"

A shake of the head, and a frown of irritation. Miss Weston raised her arm, let it fall over the arm of her chair, and held it out as if to measure a height a few feet from the floor.

"The child? Is it Liza-Jane?"

Once more the beaming smile, and the nod of acceptance; he had understood.

Kemp spoke carefully of the need for a trust until the little girl was eighteen. It would be a simple matter, no necessity for it to be complicated. Did she want the child's mother to know? The answer was in the affirmative.

"Then we can make her one of the trustees," said Kemp. "And there should be one other. Have you any relatives, Miss Weston?"

It was then he lost her for a moment. She turned her eyes towards the window, the lids drooped and the lines of her face took on a sullen air. She made impatient movements with her shoulders, and thumped the good hand in her lap as if pounding dough.

"Oh, dear, she's got herself into a tizz." Prim left the trolley she was wheeling into the room, and went over to her Aunt. "You mustn't upset yourself. Look, I've brought you a nice cup of tea and some of those nice scones from the bakers . . ."

The old lady's face brightened. "T-t-tea . . ." She managed to get the word out, and it seemed to cheer her.

"It's practically her only word," said Prim, apologetically. "They had to give up on the voice therapy as well."

"I was only asking her if she had any relatives," said Kemp. "She seemed to take it badly . . ."

"She's not got any," said Prim, shortly. "She's probably just tired. When she concentrates for long it tires her out."

The small table had to be cleared for the old lady's cup and plate where the good hand could reach. As Kemp gathered up his notes he said: "I won't need to trouble you any further, Miss Weston. I've got all I need. Would you like me to tell Primrose?"

She had still not recovered but her eyes met and held his as she nodded.

"She would like everything she owns to go to your daughter," he said to Primrose.

"Oh, but that's sweet of you, Auntie Gwen." Prim rushed over and kissed the old lady's cheek, and gave her a hug. "I'm glad I bought you these scones." She laughed and had Miss

13

Weston laughing with her. "Now my Liza-Jane's an heiress
. . ." Prim went back to the trolley and poured Kemp's tea.

"You know there isn't much?" He told her. "Miss Weston
informed me that she doesn't even own the house, and the little
money that comes in every month is an annuity which ends
with her death." When he said Miss Weston had informed him
he felt no ambiguity in the phrase; he had put questions, she
had answered by the only means still available to her, but her
understanding was sound, and she knew what she was doing.

"Oh, I know all that," said Prim, handing him his cup and
a buttered scone on a plate, "the house went years ago. And
what comes in monthly doesn't amount to much, though it
pays me. But it's nice she thought of Liza-Jane. It's the thought
that counts, isn't it? But I'll not bring her up to have great
expectations . . . Hey, we did that at school."

"You may well have done," said Kemp, "but your aunt is
no Miss Havisham. You're much too sensible, aren't you?"
He turned to the old lady with a smile, but this time she was
slow to take the allusion, her mind preoccupied. He suspected
she might have difficulty supporting two lines of thought at the
same time, partly as the result of age but more likely because
of her enforced isolation. Now she was sipping her tea, her
eyes dark and brooding.

"I'll need to have your daughter's full name," Kemp said to
Prim, "and yours too of course. Is it Sutton in both cases?"

She was putting hot water into the teapot at the trolley and
had her back to him. "Of course it is. I'm Primrose May – God,
what was my Mother thinking of? She must have had delusions
of gentility. Anyway, that's me, Primrose May Sutton. When it
came to the baby I went double-plain. Well, I was in a student
acting thing up in Liverpool, a bit of a Lancashire play we
did in one of those old warehouses they were doing up for
the tourists, full of Annies and Nellies. I was Eliza-Jane, and
it sort of stuck, like . . ."

Kemp did not ask whether the father was also from
Merseyside, but the thought prompted him to observe that
it was good of her to care for the old lady even though she
wasn't a relative.

Primrose nudged another log further into the fire with the

side of her boot. Her face was red when she came back and
sat down but whether because of the implied compliment in
his remark or the heat of the fire it was hard to tell. "I told
you she's got no relations, didn't I?" Prim sounded huffy as
she went on: "Everybody calls her Auntie Gwen. I get paid.
Not a lot but it's a roof over our head, me and Liza-Jane, till
something better comes along."

There was a pause, the only sound the crackling of the logs.
"Under the Will," said Kemp, "you'll be named one of the
trustees for your daughter. Miss Weston's agreed to that. A
member of my firm can be another trustee, and we'll keep
the whole thing simple."

Although he was speaking directly to Primrose, he made
sure Miss Weston could hear him, and as he glanced at her
he saw that she did.

"Then I'll take my leave of you," he said, getting to his
feet. "Thanks for the tea, Primrose. In a few days I'll bring
the Will for you to sign, Miss Weston. Do you understand?"

Her hand responded to his when he took it, and she smiled
at him as if pleased by what he had done.

In the hall on his way out he told Primrose Sutton that he
would bring one of his clerks to witness the signature.

"Good," she said. "I'd not want some of them in this house
knowing too much."

The remark sounded ill-natured. She had a tendency to alter
her tone of voice abruptly, one moment spontaneous and frank
and at the next brusque as if words themselves could be a
snare. Kemp wondered if she was as straightforward as she
seemed.

"Witnesses are only required as to signature," he said,
mildly. "They needn't know what's in the Will; the contents
are confidential. I gather from my wife you have rather a full
house here."

"Oh, it's all for the benefit of the wonderworld of Acne
Property Services. They pull in the rents." Prim gave a wide
grin which emphasised the laughter lines round her brown
eyes, and instantly made her more likeable. "It's the Acme,
of course. Didn't they use to make mangles?"

"Which you're much too young ever to have seen."

"Don't bet on it. My aunt had one. My real aunt, that is. They clung to th'auld ways up in the North . . ."

Kemp had to laugh at the accent into which she slipped so easily.

On the doorstep she thanked him for coming in to see Miss Weston.

"I cleared the decks of the others so that you could see her alone, even sent Liza-Jane out to tea with a friend. There's none so nosy as folk when the talk's of money . . ." She made it sound like a line from a play – perhaps it was the one she'd been in up in Liverpool. "It worried me, you know," she continued, "her not having the right sort of advice about a Will. There's some would say it's no concern of mine, me being no relation and getting paid, like, but it was the lottery thing made her anxious. I'd say she's always been one for keeping things tidy."

"I agree with you there." Kemp too had surmised that Miss Weston had a tidy mind.

"Folks round here say she helped her father in the building business and if he'd let her do the books instead of just the typing he'd never have gone broke. Leastways, that's what I've heard . . . but of course I wouldn't know, I've only been here a few years."

"How did you happen to get the job?" Kemp was genuinely interested.

Primrose Sutton's mouth pursed tightly, and she turned away as though she had not heard.

"Bye," she said, over her shoulder, and she closed the big front door smartly in his face; so might she have dismissed an importunate salesman.

16

Three

Kemp was intrigued so he put the same question to his wife that evening.

"Do you know how Primrose Sutton got the job of looking after the old lady next door?"

Mary considered. "Rumours vary, and there are plenty of those. Prim herself says it was through some domestic agency, the kind that advertises for housekeepers, but then I heard her tell the new tenant in the flat upstairs that she got it through *The Lady* – that's a magazine, isn't it? Mind you, I think she only said that because it's the kind of thing Grace Juniper reads. Prim tends to vary her signals to suit those she's talking to."

"I'd noticed," said Kemp, drily. "So where's the truth?"

"Somewhere between the two, I think. On the other hand, Louisa Channing says Primrose Sutton came there because of her husband who was some sort of kin to the Westons."

"You do surprise me. She shied off any mention of husband with me, and she was dead against any suggestion that she was related to Aunt Gwen, as she calls her."

"Everybody calls her that," said Mary, absently, "even the delivery boys. Aren't we having the right old gossip?"

"We are, and I find it interesting." Kemp would not have told her – and, indeed, Mary knew better than to ask – anything about Miss Weston's Will, but there seemed no harm in discussing the persons involved.

"Of course, what Miss Channing says is coloured by her own view of how things ought to be." Mary was thinking aloud. "When a young couple with a baby came to live next door she would naturally assume they were married – all her nieces and nephews who have kids are neatly spliced and set up all over the home counties. Perhaps it was Miss Weston

17

herself who hinted at the kinship rather than admit the couple were just in off the street."

"But surely she wouldn't have taken in people like that . . . ?" Kemp had difficulty himself following Mary's line. "You really are going down into the depths."

"Lone spinsters like Gwendolyne Weston can sometimes be desperate for someone to look after them if they get ill. She'd had that stroke before Primrose came there. She'd been in hospital and then a nursing home, but she apparently wanted to be in her own home. Care in the community, as I learn it's called in this country, wouldn't stretch to the extent of full day-and-night attendance. Prim took that on."

"She said it gave her a roof over her head."

"That's probably true, and only the child made her stay. Prim herself's the restless kind. She told me she'd always been one of those with no stake in the future. Possibly she recognised another of the same."

"I think the phrase was yours in the first place."

Mary didn't deny it. At times she felt that some liberty was now withheld from her because she had staked a claim by marrying and settling in a house. She understood Prim Sutton better than her husband ever could.

He, for his part, was thinking that whatever negative views her mother had, the infant Liza-Jane already had her stake in the future. He was also aware that there were a lot of Prim Suttons about these days, a whole sea of them, lapping the shores of society at all levels, unable – or unwilling – to find a hold. They stirred the fringes of more conventional lives like waves tugging at seaweed, withdrawing as tides do and leaving only faint impressions on the sands behind them.

He had met a few becalmed from time to time in his office as they kicked their heels against some particular legal process into whose net they had swum and been caught. He had found them wary of authority and given to needless lying, as if the truth were too precious a commodity for daily use.

"Does the uncertainty about Prim's position in the household next door make a difference to your advising Miss Weston?" Mary asked, catching his line of thought.

"Not in the least," Kemp assured her. "That's all taken care of. I like the old lady, and I'm sure your company is good for her, so don't stop going in there."

"I wasn't going to. I'd be a right prig if I told you I only went in because of Miss Weston – I think I've got past the stage of good deeds. I just find they're an interesting lot next door, and I don't mind being manipulated by Prim. She's got a fine old band of workers since she started to take on more waitressing jobs."

"I'll pretend I never heard of those," said Kemp, thinking of the income support Primrose Sutton was undoubtedly claiming. "Has she managed to enrol Miss Juniper yet?"

"Oh, yes, Grace Juniper hadn't been in the house five minutes before she was taken on as assistant baby-sitter. I would have thought she'd enough of kids during the day but apparently she's a specialist teacher of some kind and only part-time. She hasn't a television of her own so she comes down in the evenings and sits in with the old lady."

Mary had found Grace Juniper a lady much to her liking. For one thing, she was well educated. Of course, other women of Mary's acquaintance, wives of her husband's colleagues, local friends she had made in Newtown, most of them were well educated; what she admired in Grace was that it showed. Miss Juniper was a serious minded, somewhat austere person who lived for her work in the education of young children, particularly those with learning difficulties, but she also had a wide-ranging intellect which took her far beyond the confines of these duties. It was this aspect which attracted Mary who had never been properly taught in school where her attendance had been scrappy, dependent on the health of her mother, the temper of her step-father and the demands of her siblings.

Now that she was coming up to forty, Mary found that she had a predatory instinct for the thing denied her in girlhood: she was hungry for knowledge. But with the years had come discrimination. The chatter at dinner parties, coffee-table discussions of the royals, politics or the shortcomings of the transport system could not satisfy her mind; only someone like Grace Juniper could fill her in on the use of coincidence in the novels of Hardy, or metaphor in the works of Shakespeare.

Grace had a good classics degree. She had been engaged to

a university lecturer but he had died young, and no one had come along to replace him. Lack of means had thrust her out of the groves of academe, and she had become a teacher. Now semi-retired she did supply-work, visiting local schools when her special skills were required, and doing research projects of her own at leisure. She was still not completely at her ease in the turbulent household at 4 Albert Crescent but her interest in Miss Weston herself was evident, and Primrose Sutton in her inimitable way was already making good use of that interest.

A few weeks after Kemp's visit, Mary went to return some books lent her by Grace and found all the members of what she thought of as Prim's little band grouped in the big sitting-room as if on a stage set. Primrose herself, dressed for the street, was moving rapidly between kitchen and table, throwing off remarks in a voice high enough to be heard even when bending over the stove. Gregory Venn and his friend, Jasper, lounged at the fireplace keeping the warmth from Miss Weston in her armchair at one side, while Blanche Quigley and Grace Juniper shared the sofa with the child and looked as if they were in competition for its favours.

A furious argument was going on, and everyone appeared to be uncomfortable.

It sounded like one of those rows which start off mildly political but end up strongly personal. As Primrose emerged from the kitchen with a small casserole young Venn shouted: "Call yourself a socialist? Don't make me laugh . . ."

Prim dumped the dish on the table so that its lid danced and a drop of the savoury contents spurted out on to the tablecloth. Mary had to admit the smell was mouth-watering.

"Pay me, but don't insult me," said Prim with some hauteur. With an eye on her audience she was obviously reining in a more pungent comment. "You owe for two suppers already this week, and there's none of this for your mates." She glared at Jasper who must have been on Gregory's side in the argument. He shifted uneasily and looked across at his sister.

"If we're not welcome here, we'll go . . ."

"Speak for yourself," she retorted. "Prim asked me to baby-sit, didn't you, Prim?"

"But this is my night for sitting in," Grace Juniper observed, quietly. "I don't suppose Primrose wants all of us . . ."

Gregory came over to the table and pulled out a chair. "Oh, come on, Jaz, for God's sake. There's enough here for two. And there's the bloody lolly you keep on about." He took out his wallet, abstracted two ten-pound notes and threw them down on the cloth. "You're a right little money-grubber, Prim Sutton. Where'd you be if it wasn't for the likes of us?"

Primrose aimed the slap at his face but as he was sitting down when it landed it caught him on the side of the head, making his ear sting. "You – you stupid bitch!" Temper flared in his face.

Fortunately Miss Weston was in her usual seat on the far side of the fireplace and practically out of earshot, but she could hardly have missed the scene by the table. Mary caught the glance of horror on her face and went quickly over.

"It's all right," she said, "they're just at a bit of the play-acting."

The old lady smiled and let Mary take her hand and sit and talk to her for a few moments, ignoring the hubbub round the table which had also upset the child so that she set up a crying.

Mary handed the books she had brought to Grace who was trying vainly to placate the little girl. But Liza-Jane was too frightened by the uproar to be solaced. She broke free from Blanche and Grace and ran, howling, across to her mother who comforted her till the wailing stopped. Mary had noticed that the child was a spunky little thing, used to vicissitudes and not disposed to keep up a mood if there was no gain in it. Prim placated her daughter with a chocolate biscuit and carried her back to the sofa.

"I really have to go. I'm on at the Castle at eight." She looked harassed, but apart from that smart flip of the hand she'd aimed at Gregory she was in control of herself. "I don't mind which of you stays. Aunt Gwen will be ready for bed after she's watched *The Bill*, won't you, Auntie? She's had her supper and so has Liza-Jane, but there's some trifle left if you want it, Blanche."

"I'll stay," said the girl, eagerly. "There's a programme I

want to see later on the box, anyway." She turned to Mary. "Sorry about the behaviour of the brother. He follows Greg like a little dog. Been like it ever since school."

Mary had guessed the friendship to have been of that nature; when together, the young men larked about as if still boys, egging one another on to ruder utterances, sillier tricks. So they must have goaded their teachers, bullied the smaller fry, a team of two bent on mischief. Gregory had the edge, the quicker wit, the better job – conveyancing clerk at Roberts and possibly hoping for articles – but Jasper had the looks and, judging from what Blanche had let drop about her own private schooling, a better social background. Mary had been finding the English class system a fascinating subject. She wondered why early anthropologists had bothered to go as far as Samoa or Fiji for material when they might just as well have been unravelling caste and kinship of the British islanders on their home ground.

Primrose was rushing about, stuffing things into her hand-bag, finding a pair of high-heeled shoes from a cupboard overflowing with everything from stilettos to flip-flops, until at last she stood at the mirror and gave her hair a last pat. All the while the young men at the table had continued to act laddishly, keeping up a flow of remarks about the hard-fistedness of landladies and, from Gregory in retaliation for the slap on the ear, a scarcely veiled reference to other means of earning money at the Castle Hotel which was why Prim was taking so long checking her appearance in the mirror. Despite this running commentary, Mary saw that the two males had scoffed the contents of Prim's casserole with relish.

Finally satisfied with her hair – reddish-gold this evening, though it had been known to vary – Primrose snatched up the notes from the table, cuffed Jasper adroitly on the back of his head on the principle of equality all round, and was gone with a slam of the outer door.

Her exit was followed by a stagy silence, except that on a real stage the curtain would have been lowered by now to avoid the awkward gap in conversation among those remaining. Eventually, Gregory Venn and young Quigley started up some low-voiced boy-talk about motor cars from which they shut everyone else out. Mary would like to have listened but because she had only just passed her driving test they regarded her as strictly a non-starter in the automobile stakes. Little did they know that she had been driving beat-up old trucks on the turnpikes of Pennsylvania when they were in their cradles. She'd not had a licence of course – the Smith family weren't strong on any documentation which might lead officialdom to their door – and she was now rather proud of the one just achieved. The test had been a walkover; she had more than enough mechanical skills, plenty of road sense and had gone at the highway code as if it were an honours degree. Now all she wanted was a car of her own and had the occasion been more friendly she might well have asked either of the young men for advice.

As it was, she got up and went to say good-night to Miss Weston whom she always treated as the proper hostess in this house. Despite the currents flowing round and over her, it was the invalid who was at its centre, the reason for them all being there.

"Don't go yet, Mary," said Grace who had also risen. "Come upstairs and I'll see if I can find you another book. No, not that way . . ." as Mary went towards the hall and front door, ". . . we can use the back staircase."

"I didn't know there was one," said Mary, following her into a dark passage at the back of the room. "This house is sure full of surprises."

"I suppose it was originally for the use of the servants, though I would think by the Westons' time there'd only be a little maid of all work." Grace had opened a narrow door disclosing an even narrower flight of wooden stairs. "Primrose keeps that door shut because of the draught but there's no light. Usually when I come down I have a torch."

She lifted the latch of a door at the top of the short flight, and they emerged into the hallway of her own flat. "It was all closed and the doors nailed up when the house was divided into separate apartments, but trust our Primrose to find it and open up the stairs. I must say it makes all the difference to me when I baby-sit or want to keep an eye on the old lady."

"Did the tenant before you use these stairs?" asked Mary, who was genuinely curious.

"It was a he, and I don't think he fitted into Primrose's scheme of things. He couldn't be utilised as either carer or baby-sitter."

Mary grinned. They seemed to share the same view of Primrose Sutton.

"She does tend to manipulate. Are you minding that?"

Grace turned from the bookshelves. "Not really. I suppose I use her as she uses me. I wouldn't do it if I didn't want to. I like Miss Weston, her past interests me and I don't find it as difficult to communicate with her as others do. The child is not difficult, and seems to have affection for me . . ."

Mary guessed that in that last sentence lay the root of the matter: to be a teacher of young children you would like to get a positive response; it would be doubly welcome if it came freely.

"Are you ready for some more difficult literary criticism?" Miss Juniper changed the subject, and handed Mary a book. "It might not be a bad idea to read the deconstructuralists now you're coming to all these great works with an open mind."

"H'm." Mary wasn't sure but she took the rather forbidding-looking volume with the title she didn't understand but would come to at her leisure. "If you call them 'great works' then surely there can't be any doubt?"

"You'd be surprised," said Grace, grimly. "There's some of the opinion that all such books are only called so to keep the ruling classes in position at the top, and the proletariat where they belong." She laughed when she saw Mary's expression. "Sorry, I do tend to run on. I forget you're new to all this academic mayhem."

"Don't apologise," said Mary, hastily, "I'm very much in favour of a bit of mayhem. It's just that I didn't know it spilled over into literature. I guess I look on what are called classics as if they were a lot of sacred cows . . ."

Mary had got thus far with her account that evening when her husband put down his knife and fork and observed that if the steak had come from a sacred cow it had been a well-fed one. "Dinner and entertainment both excellent. You really are getting the most out of your visits next door – neighbourly gossip and intellectual stimulus all at the same time."

Mary sighed. "I do sound like a bored housewife in a sitcom. But, you know, it's probably the first time in my whole life I have absolutely nothing to do . . ." She reflected for a moment. "No, I'm wrong about the sitcom. There's those heroines of Ibsen's . . ."

"No," said Kemp, firmly, "there'll be no shooting-off of guns in the dining-room. Why can't you sit at home stitching samplers or darning my socks?"

"I don't think I'm the type," said Mary.

Four

Lennox Kemp and Mary were away the weekend Grace Juniper died. A young friend of Kemp's was being married in Edinburgh and they flew up for the wedding, and stayed over till the Sunday. The occasion had been a happy one, although Mary reserved judgement on 'The Athens of the North', finding the east wind had a particularly penetrating chill. Also, in preparation for the visit, she had tried to read *The Heart of Midlothian* (in her husband's opinion, Mary's approach to literature was childlike in being both naïve and calculating) and had found it impossible.

"I thought it was about a riot," she exclaimed, "but getting there was like wading through jello in flippers. Besides, it's not written in recognisable English." She had not uttered this last gem of literary criticism while they were still north of the border.

Arriving back late at 2 Albert Crescent after their drive from Heathrow, Mary could not shake off the bleak air of Princes Street. The first thing she did was turn the central heating up to high. "It seems much colder than usual," she said, next putting on the kettle, "and the place so dark when we came in . . ."

"Well, I'd rather that than have it ablaze with burglars at ten o'clock at night," said Kemp, reasonably.

"When you were putting the car away I noticed it was all dark next door as well. That's most unusual for a Sunday night. Those two front windows of theirs are always well lit up from outside even with the television on. It's because the drapes are too skimpy."

Primrose had said often enough that they ought to have heavier curtains rather than the summer-weight floral cottons but, like much else that Primrose suggested, nothing was ever done about it. Lack of money, Mary supposed.

"Perhaps everybody's away for the weekend, like us," said Kemp.

"That can't be so," his wife pointed out. "Gwen Weston can't go anywhere, neither can she be left. I hope it doesn't mean she's had another stroke. That would explain it, she's in hospital . . ."

"Whoah there. Don't look on the gloomy side . . ." But he could see that Mary would not rest easy without some further investigation. "I've got to go back to the car to get my overcoat. When I'm out at the garage I'll see if there are any lights on at the back."

There was one. The top flat had a fairly large window which looked out over the gardens at the rear. Although the blinds were drawn, it was obvious someone was at home.

Kemp made more noise than he need have done closing the garage door. As he turned away he heard the clatter of feet on the outside staircase of the other house.

"Is that you, Mr Kemp?"

The young man had by now reached the foot of the steps and was peering into the darkness of the side passage which separated the two houses. At one time there had probably been a wall or fence but the necessity to provide entrances to the upstairs flats at Number Four had meant that side being taken up by the stone stairway while on the Kemps' side there was width enough for a driveway to their garage.

"I heard a noise . . . I thought it must be you and Mrs Kemp coming home. All I can say is I'm glad to see you."

That was a lot to say, for a stranger to me, thought Kemp, but the young man had been polite though his voice sounded agitated.

"You're Gregory Venn?" He said. "Is something the matter?"

"You'll not have heard, you being away. There's been an accident . . ."

Young Venn had come up close to Kemp and there was such compelling urgency in his attitude that Kemp felt he was about to be grabbed by the lapels.

27

"Miss Weston?" Kemp queried, for this seemed to him the most obvious explanation.

"No, no . . . not to Auntie Gwen. It was Miss Juniper . . . the lady in the middle flat. She's dead."

Kemp drew in his breath sharply. "I'm sorry to hear it . . . Look, young man, let's not stand out here in the cold. Come inside, and tell us what happened. I'm afraid my wife's going to be very upset at your news."

"I'll just run up and shut my door. I was waiting, you see. I didn't know when you'd be back." He darted up the staircase. The first flight consisted of stone steps but after the small landing leading into the middle flat the staircase was of metal like a fire escape – which it may well have been originally.

"Mary's in the kitchen," said Kemp when Gregory rejoined him. "We'll go in the back way."

She was in fact standing by the open door which led out into the rear garden. "I heard voices," she said. "Has something happened?"

Kemp waited until the closed door shut out the cold night air before he answered her.

"Bad news, I'm afraid. This young man tells me that Miss Juniper has been in an accident . . . has died."

It was a tale quickly, though not easily, told. Listening, Mary felt her heart lurch, then be still. After all, she had hardly known Grace Juniper. For how long? Barely three months . . . Lots of people whom she had known for years had passed on – as the emollient phrase has it – and their passing had not moved her. Early in life she had seen death in the raw, through poverty of circumstance and from deprivation, in hospitals she had watched the inexorable march of disease through wasted bodies; but, apart from her mother to whom death had come as a blessed release for both of them, Mary had never known the effect of a particularly sudden cutting-off, and it now flooded her being.

It was Kemp who made fresh coffee for them all as they sat round the kitchen table. Mary wanted all the details, Gregory Venn gave all he seemed to have, her persistent questioning only making him the more nervous, the more confused.

Watching him, Kemp thought the young man had the face

and bearing of a London clerk, and was surprised that such an idea should spring to his mind. Once there, however, he could not shake it out. There seemed to be a type, and Gregory fitted it: the thin, sharpish features, a pasty complexion just out of adolescent acne, carefully arranged hair which did not grow becomingly, the whole manner of one desperately keen to be thought well of and yet with an underlying swagger as if to say to hell with those who did not appreciate his effort.

Although he had apparently not been present when Grace Juniper was found – by Primrose about eight o'clock that morning – he was anxious that his own performance should be seen in a good light.

"I insisted that Prim and Liza-Jane didn't spend another night there – not in view of what had happened. I arranged they should go and stay with Blanche Quigley for a few days. That's why the house is empty. They left once the police had finished . . . Not that there was much to do. I mean an accident like that . . ."

It seemed that some time on the Saturday night Miss Juniper for some reason had attempted to come down the inner staircase, and had fallen, hitting her head at the bottom.

"Although of course there will have to be a post-mortem," said Gregory, knowledgeably, "there doesn't appear to be any doubt that she died from that fall on her head. I wouldn't be surprised if she didn't break her neck. She was all twisted up when Prim found her, you know how narrow the space is in that staircase."

It was Kemp who asked for details of the interior stair itself, but Mary only answered absently. Gregory Venn described it, and gave his opinion that it was dangerous, particularly in the dark.

"But Grace said she used a torch if she came down at night," Mary exclaimed. "Was a torch found?"

As to that, Gregory couldn't say. He had only arrived on the scene at ten in the morning, having been away for the night, and by then the place had been swarming with police and paramedics.

"Prim had the screaming ad-dabs," he recounted with some

29

satisfaction, "saying it wasn't her fault and silly things like that."

"At least she had the good sense to call an ambulance right away," Kemp observed, mildly. "Didn't you say it came within minutes of her finding Miss Juniper?"

"Yes, so I was told. I think Prim did all the right things," Venn conceded. "It was only afterwards – I suppose she got to thinking about it – well, she got a bit hysterical."

Mary doubted that Prim was the hysterical type. "And she managed to get Miss Weston herself into a nursing home?"

"Well, she could hardly stay in that house, not with all those policemen marching about, so Prim phoned one of the nurses at the Centre and between them they got the old lady in. She can stay there for a few days, at least until things get back to normal."

His voice trailed off. Evidently he had run out of steam.

"I'd best get back," he said, getting to his feet awkwardly.

"Yes, of course," said Kemp. "You look as if you could do with a good night's sleep." Indeed, the young man was quite white.

"And, thank you, Gregory, for putting us in the picture," said Mary. "When you see Primrose will you tell her how sorry I am about what's happened, and if there's anything I can do . . ."

"I'll tell her, Mrs Kemp. Good-night."

"What an awful thing," she said to Kemp when he came in from showing the young man out, "and for all his zeal in reporting I think Gregory was most shaken up by it."

"Tell me a little more about this hidden staircase," said her husband, "sounds like a real death-trap to me."

Mary tried to point out to him in their own house where the extra stairs had been but it looked as if the Channing family had disposed of them long ago to provide a modern kitchen and bathroom, and had opened up any such dark corners.

"The main stairs next door must have been removed when the division of the flats took place," she surmised, "and what was their hall became part of that enormous sitting-room, and where the stairs were there's a passage and then Prim and Liza-Jane's bedrooms."

30

"So they are on the opposite side of the house from the hidden stairs? Would that explain why Primrose didn't hear Miss Juniper fall?"

"That's what I was thinking," said Mary, but with hesitation. "If it happened in the middle of the night or early in the morning, what on earth was Grace doing on those stairs at all? Prim was home – there wouldn't be any need for Grace to be listening for the little girl or Miss Weston."

"Who says Primrose was at home? It was a Saturday night. Isn't that when she does a stint at the Castle? That's when they have Rotary dinners and such, and the call goes out for waitresses."

"Oh, no . . . I can't believe that . . ." Mary looked aghast. "You mean Prim might not have been there? But from what Gregory said, Prim was in the house all night . . ."

Kemp shrugged. "How would he know? He wasn't there himself. Look, darling, perhaps I shouldn't be so suspicious – it's just my natural reaction . . ." He could see that Mary was hurt by what he was implying against her friend. However, she was tough enough minded to recognise that Primrose Sutton's domestic arrangements were sometimes loosely tied. Would she really leave a small child and a disabled old lady alone all night, the only other person in a flat upstairs? From what Mary had learned through other baby-sitters their hours stopped strictly before midnight. Yet, Grace had inferred that she did sometimes use the back stairs. Did that mean that she could be 'on duty' as it were for longer on occasions?

"Gregory said it looked as if Grace had been in bed . . ." Mary was almost talking to herself.

"I noticed he had difficulty with the word 'nightie'," said Kemp, drily. "I think in the end he called them 'night-clothes' as if he were in a Victorian novel." Once more the impression of an earnest young clerk returned, a youth fresh from a home where there had not been much talk of anything never mind ladies' night attire. Kemp realised that if his mind was going to wander like that it meant he was tired.

"It's no use our speculating on what happened," he said as he took the cups to the sink and began rinsing them, "we've both had a long day and it's time we were upstairs."

"I know," she agreed, wearily, "it's silly to talk when we've probably only got half the story anyway."

"Tell you what. I'll have a word with John Upshire tomorrow. It'll be too early for the full report on the accident, but at least the station might have more of the facts than young Venn."

Five

The station did indeed have the facts and they did not differ in any degree from young Venn's version. An ambulance had been called at seven thirty on the Sunday morning, but when it was found that the lady was dead the police had been informed. The ambulancemen had moved the body no further than was necessary to establish death.

Sergeant Mort – Kemp had had to look again to make certain this was the name – and a policewoman had gone immediately to the house. They had called Dr Albury whom Kemp knew to be the pathologist attached to the local force. He had arrived a little after nine, and made an examination on the spot; his findings would be available after the post-mortem, but initially he had said to Sergeant Mort: "that it looked as if the deceased had struck her head a severe blow against the bottom step when she fell, and there was also an indentation on the base of the skull where she might have cracked it against the wall of the staircase." Albury had gone on to say that the stairs were a death-trap, particularly at night when there would be no illumination whatsoever.

It seemed that Primrose Sutton had gone on the defensive right away. She said the stairs were never meant to be used. She had heard nothing. She had got up at seven because that was the hour when Liza-Jane normally woke and wanted juice. Primrose had noticed as she made her way to the kitchen that the door to the staircase was slightly ajar. She had pushed it open and discovered Miss Juniper. She had phoned immediately for an ambulance. Had she realised Miss Juniper was dead? No, she had only touched her shoulder, the head had lolled over and she thought Grace was unconscious.

The unhappily named sergeant had noted that Mrs Sutton

33

had been 'co-operative though naturally upset.' Details of the household were obtained from her. She had no knowledge of whether the tenant of the top flat, Mr Gregory Venn, was present or not, but within the hour that question was resolved by his turning up and wanting to know why there was a police car at the door.

When Lennox Kemp conveyed this information to his wife the following evening, she was quiet. She had given much thought to her late friend; the death had left her with a sense of waste, an emptiness, an unfulfilment. She wished now that she had seen more of Grace Juniper, called on her more often, not hesitated of an evening to go to the flat next door for fear that the older woman might be tired after work, or found it tedious to be forever asked for knowledge. Too late now the realisation that the bond had been a good one – between one eager to learn and the other who had a natural gift for teaching.

During the next few days she was irked by this sense of loss which would not be shaken away and had assumed a bitterness foreign to her nature. When she spoke of it to Lennox he did his best to be understanding.

"You had not known Grace long but one's appreciation of a person as a potential friend needn't depend on the length of time one's known them. Your friendship would have deepened had she lived, that's the loss you're feeling."

"H'm. Could be . . . There's certainly a lot of the 'if only' about it." Mary was grateful to him for not dismissing out of hand her preoccupation with the death. Even when the medical report became available it did nothing to ease her mind – rather the reverse.

Grace Juniper had died as the result of a fall downstairs, more precisely from the haemorrhage into the brain which had occurred after striking her head with considerable impact on the wall of the staircase. Other contusions indicated that she had again struck her head on the lower step edges before finally coming to rest against the bottom door.

"That's where my sergeant noticed the blood. Not a lot," said John Upshire, "but enough to show the lady had come down hard. Young Mort did a thorough job, he's a good note-taker, and let me tell you it's all paperwork these days."

"And that's why the door was slightly pushed open as Mrs Sutton says." Kemp was taking advantage of an old friendship by invading Inspector Upshire's office to look at what was to the police a routine accident report, and now that the coroner was satisfied, one that could be safely filed away. "I notice Mr Harvey had some testy comments to make on that staircase. I suppose it's up to the property company to see it's nailed up before they let the flat to another tenant. I'll let Mary know the contents of this." He handed back the medical report. "Though it's not going to make her feel any better about the death of her friend."

"Another thing Sergeant Mort noted was that bit of curled-up linoleum at the top of those damned stairs. Looks like that's where she caught the heel of her slippers . . ."

"Mules, they're called. And they don't have heels."

"Well, whatever. The lady fell, and came down a fair cropper. I'm sorry about it, but that's it. I hope Mary hasn't got a bee in her bonnet?" Upshire added, somewhat apprehensively; he'd had to do with some of Mary Kemp's hunches in the past.

"Oh, no, nothing like that. Just that she's lost a friend."

"Well, that's all right, then." John Upshire closed the thin file and put it on the floor where someone would pick it up and lose it under 'no further action'. "I'm afraid she died from a fractured skull – falling downstairs is just one of those domestic accidents that are so common nowadays, Lennox."

And also, Kemp reflected, one of the easiest and least traceable methods of getting rid of someone, the suburban equivalent of a handy cliff, a boiling sea below and a deserted coastal path. He did not voice this thought; he realised it had crept in from his past experience of a shadier world than the blameless Miss Juniper could ever have known, and was therefore quite irrelevant to her death.

"But was her torch found?" Mary queried, rather irritably.

"Nothing about it in the report I read, and that fell sergeant was most meticulous, lived up to his name in fact." Kemp was rather proud of the small conceit but Mary was not to be put off by any literary showing-off which she didn't understand.

"She would never have attempted those stairs without some

kind of light. Either the door at the foot was open, or she carried a torch."

"It's possible Primrose picked it up if it had rolled down the stairs."

"I'll ask her," said Mary, determined not to lose something already fixed in her mind's eye.

But Primrose Sutton, once she had returned to the house next door, proved elusive for over a week. She was taking Liza-Jane to play-school, or collecting her from there, she was shopping, she was visiting Miss Weston in the nursing home, she was just vaguely 'out' whenever Mary tried to see her.

Only when the old lady was at last pronounced fit to return to the house – and returned looking rather better for her sojourn in a place where she had more regular meals and proper bedtimes – did Primrose say, yes, she would be pleased if Mary called one afternoon when they would all be at home.

It was a Sunday afternoon about teatime, and indeed Miss Weston was already stting with the small table at her elbow on which there was a cup, saucer and plate. Prim deftly slid a piece of chocolate cake on to the plate as Mary talked to the old lady. "Auntie liked it in there," Prim said. "All that attention. They made a fuss of you, didn't they?" But Miss Weston would have none of it. She shook her head, laughed and waved her good hand in denial. "You'd rather be here at home with us?" There came a vigorous nodding, and the eyes seemed to brighten as they looked at Primrose. There was no doubt as to where Miss Weston preferred to be, and whatever anyone might say, it was Primrose Sutton who made the place home.

"Of course it was a shock," she said when Mary raised the subject of Grace's death. "But we hadn't got to know her that well. It's not like she was family . . ."

Since none of those present, Gregory, both the Quigleys, Mary or even Primrose herself were related, the term had to be taken in its widest sense; it had an all-embracing air, like a lot of Prim's expressions.

"Did she not have a light with her?" asked Mary, bluntly, "that stairwell's so dark . . ." Primrose gave her a sidelong glance and it occurred to Mary, but too late to withdraw the question, that perhaps not everybody knew about the second staircase.

"I've never heard of a stairwell before," Blanche chimed in, "sounds real spooky."

Primrose went on cutting up chocolate sponge cake. "Want another slice, Jasper?" She called out to the young man on the floor in front of the television watching a match with the sound turned down. Jasper scrambled to his feet and came over, surprised to be granted this favour.

Despite this diversion, Mary repeated her question. "Did Grace not have a torch with her?"

"I found it on the stairs." Prim's tone was brusque.

"And was it working?"

"How should I know? I just put it back in her room." Prim clattered the teacups and marched off to the kitchen with the tray.

Later, when Mary told her husband about the conversation he looked thoughtful. "I wonder why she would do that?"

"Habit, I think," said Mary. "Prim's a great tidier-upper – she has to be in that house where everyone leaves things about. Anyway, I couldn't go on about the torch, the subject was closed as far as Prim was concerned."

And there it looked as if the matter should be allowed to rest – but uneasily for Mary, who put her own unsatisfied feeling down to the loss of a friend rather than the manner of her death.

"I still have two books belonging to Grace," she had told Primrose.

"Well, I'll let you know when her sister's coming to sort out the things in the flat. She's the one who arranged for the funeral to be in Yorkshire where they both came from. It was much too far for any of us to go, and anyway we hadn't known her that well . . ." Prim was repeating herself as if by doing so she was further distancing the dead woman from the house. "The sister's a Mrs Prentice. She has the keys to upstairs and said she would ring me when she's coming to clear out the furniture. As soon as that's done the agency'll want to let it again soon as possible. Catch them losing any rent they can get . . ."

It was Mrs Prentice who knocked on the Kemps' door one evening in the following week. She looked exhausted and was glad to sit down and have a sherry.

"I've managed to clear the flat," she told them, "but I'll stay there overnight for it's a long drive back to Barnsley. The men from the auction rooms are coming tomorrow morning. I've only taken a few small items of family stuff. Fortunately Grace travelled about a lot and she was not a hoarder, thank goodness."

Mrs Prentice was an older and homelier version of Grace Juniper and seemed a person of much practical good sense. "My sister wrote to me about you, Mrs Kemp," she said to Mary, "and that's why I've come. There are so many books in the flat . . ."

"And I've got a couple more here," said Mary, laughing.

"We've always been a bookish family," Mrs Prentice sighed. "And now my husband and I have retired to a small bungalow, well, there just isn't the room for more. I'd like you to have all Grace's books . . . No. I mean it," she went on, seeing Mary's instinctive gesture of refusal, "you'd be doing us a favour."

"And we've bookshelves in the study simply waiting to be filled," put in Lennox. "I'm sure anything that your sister had will be of enormous value to Mary – she's on a proper reading binge."

"That's what I gathered from Grace's letters. And I've always hated the thought of books ending up on those awful shelves in auctioneers like unwanted pets looking for a good home. I've already put them up in cardboard boxes but I'm afraid they're very heavy. Perhaps Mr Kemp . . . ?"

Kemp jumped to his feet. "Of course, I'll carry them in. Be glad to." He didn't say he would also be glad to have the opportunity of looking at that inner staircase before the property agents sent in the builders to nail up the doors.

Mary had invited their visitor to stay for dinner but she refused; she needed an early night, and had brought her own sandwiches. "Mrs Sutton offered me a meal, but I told her the same. Seems to me that young woman's got her hands full anyroads. It's a rum household she's got there."

Mary did not know how much about the Sutton menage

may have passed in letters between the sisters so she kept quiet.

When they had briefly talked of Grace's death, Mrs Prentice seemed to have accepted the verdict of misadventure without question. "That would be like our Grace," she said, sadly. "She was never one to look where she was going, and if there was a child in the house she'd be the one to hurry to it if it cried . . ."

With the departure of Mrs Prentice back to Yorkshire, and the removal van from the entrance to the house next door, it was almost as if Grace Juniper had never been – except for that still lingering sense of loss in Mary Kemp, and the three large boxes of books now waiting her attention in the study.

"You're like a child with a box of chocolates," Lennox said to her one night: "you're itching to get at them yet you're still looking on them as a treat to come."

"It's because I've never possessed as much as a paperback novel in my whole life. Not one of my very own. I used to read everything I could lay my hands on in the houses where I nursed – and very peculiar tastes some of those gentlemen had I can tell you – but they were never *my* books. I once pinched a Gideon Bible from a hotel room but I put it back the next day . . . it didn't seem right stealing a bible."

"And now with your college textbooks and those from Grace you've enough to start your own library. Seriously though, that was a nice thought of Mrs Prentice. A sensible woman. She didn't even blink when we both took a look down that stairwell."

"She said Grace had told her on the phone recently that she was going to have her eyes tested. Oh, if only we'd known . . ."

"Don't fret about it, Mary. Don't you see, it only strengthens the verdict at the inquest that it was an accident."

Six

With that she would have to be satisfied – at least for the present. The present in any case had its own diversions.

"What? No classes today?" said Lennox at breakfast.

"We're like kids at school. We've been given a day off."

"What for?"

"A visitation. Does that sound pompous enough?"

"Not royalty, surely?"

"I don't think the cause of further education is quite their thing; Newtown College is hardly the playing fields of Eton. Far from it – I'm told there's going to be some tomato-throwing."

"Not the sun-dried sort you get in tins, I hope?"

"More your squashy English kind from the back of the market. They're going to be waiting for the honourable member when he's done his tour."

"Ah, I've got it: Stephen Durward-Cooke is coming to town."

"Call me Steve, don't stand on ceremony – at least that's what he told the English department when they asked him to open their new library. Stand on ceremony, indeed. That lot wouldn't know a ceremony from a travelling circus. Some airhead on the committee even wondered if they could get out a bit of red carpet."

"Well, it might help to cover him when he runs the tomato gauntlet."

"I don't think the members of the committee of welcome and the tomato-throwing brigade are on the same wavelength. Anyway, I gather the whole thing is to be kept very low key. A cool shake of the hand, he pulls the string over the little plaque,

40

then it's tea and buns in the cafeteria. The council don't want to be caught throwing money around."

"Then I trust Durward-Cooke will appreciate the high cost of tomatoes. He's rather slumming it, coming to Newtown. He lives on a much more exalted plane, fairly well up in the Conservative ranks and marked out for further promotion. What your college is going to give him sounds like a Band of Hope outing . . . No," he went on, seeing her look of puzzlement, "I'm not going to explain, you can look it up in your sociology books under temperance. Just tell me, where do you get all this information about the visit? It seems to come in from both sides."

"I take coffee with the senior lecturer. He says it's good to talk with a mature woman – makes a change, like." Mary's imitation of Mr Bradshaw's flat Mancunian accent was kindly meant. "Then I have a beer in the pub at lunchtime and mingle at the students union . . ."

"You do get about." He had always admired Mary's possession of the common touch, a useful tool for an undercover agent, as he himself had found when forced into that occupation. "You make my office work sound like a boring old treadmill, but I suppose I'd better get on with it. Are you going to this college caper?"

"Wouldn't miss it for the world. Tell me, before you go, this Member of Parliament – you said he was up for promotion. I thought he would be in the doghouse because of that speech about unmarried mothers?"

"Good heavens, no. The backbenchers lapped it up. 'Onward, Durward,' they cried, fight for the family – particularly the English version with a wage-earning dad and mum in the kitchen where she belongs, or a salaried City-man with a wife in the drawing-room and a maid under the stairs. I mean it," he went on, seeing Mary's disbelief, "what in John Major is nostalgia for a lost England of warm beer and cricket on the green is to Durward-Cooke a vision of the future." Kemp proceeded to fill Mary in on the man's position within his own party. "If you stand centre and look away to your right, past the Army and Navy, the Palace and the Home Counties, there far out on the horizon you'll see the Honourable Member for Welchester West – trying to put as much distance as possible between himself and Europe. In the run-up to the election he'll be courted by the Referendum Party as a leading Europhobe."

Mary was having trouble with her "philes" and "phobes".

"You mean he doesn't like Europeans?"

"That's it. Especially Germans. The word 'kraut' has been known to cross his lips more than once – in private, of course. What I can't understand is why the chap's coming to Newtown at all. We may be on the edge of the Home Counties but we're hardly Tory heartland."

"Oh, I know why he's coming," said Mary as she cleared the table. "I got it from Louisa Channing. Mr Durward-Cooke, she tells me in that prim way of hers, comes from these parts. His family on his mother's side were local gentry."

"That's true, but he opted for a safe Conservative seat years ago. The folk who came out here to our new town after the war were products of the London boroughs – and Labour supporters to a man. Durward-Cooke could never have coped with that. I suppose this visit of his is just an opportunity to show his face around – a bit of early electioneering. I understand he's very ambitious."

"I'm looking forward to catching a glimpse of my first Member of Parliament," said Mary, "in the flesh rather than as a talking head on the box."

She had already listened to divergent views as well as that of her husband. 'A real gentleman – not like those awful Labourites you get in the Commons these days . . .' That from Louisa Channing. Not having heard the expression before Mary thought it made the Opposition sound like an undesirable biblical tribe – perhaps the lot who had prowled and prowled around.

According to Primrose Sutton, Stephen Durward-Cooke was a prude and a baby-food burglar, taking bread from the mouths of deserving single mothers. Judging by the reports of some of his speeches in the Press, Mary thought she might have a point.

The students themselves simply referred to him as "just another Tory bastard" and called his attitude to the Germans "blimpish", a word Mary had not heard before but guessed was no compliment.

She arrived at the College of Further Education just before twelve o'clock. The town had been unmoved by the prospect of any eminent visitor, going about its business as usual in street and market, but inside the college gates there was an air of suppressed excitement. The young persons milling around were for once unfettered by books or bulging sports bags and that freedom to skip about and wave their arms kept the scene in constant motion and made it difficult for the staff to give any impression of control. Those supposed to be vaguely in charge hovered round the edges like border collies uncertain of their sheep.

Mr Bradshaw had kept a seat for her, and ushered her into it with some ceremony. It was an offer her natural kindliness had made it impossible to refuse.

After a few minutes' wait, it became apparent that Mr Durward-Cooke had been smuggled in by a side entrance since he arrived all in one piece in a nice grey suit, along with the Head of College and a covey of hangers-on.

Mary had to admit that the Member for Welchester West had presence, being broadly built, tall and handsome of feature, although his face tended towards the porcine rather than the aristocratic, which disappointed Mary since she expected that in England persons of quality should look the part. Certainly Durward-Cooke had the assurance of his kind as he strode ahead of his companions with the easy walk of someone who keeps fit despite a natural heaviness and a thickening waistline. His manner was affable towards the small welcoming group with just enough condescension to keep them in their place.

He pulled the cord amid some forced laughter, the blue velvet curtains parted, he read the notice without actually moving his lips and made sure it contained nothing subversive. He then spoke a few well-seasoned words on the need for libraries, the glories of the written word, and the amount of money his government was spending on higher education. Nothing he said could have raised a hair on the nape of even the most Marxist head. His muted praise for Newtown Council and its education committee was warm enough to produce smiles on

43

the faces of their assembled representatives, at the same time being just short of insolent.

You're a smart operator, thought Mary, as she watched him from her seat by the wall where she had been effectively pinned down by Mr Bradshaw who seemed to regard her as some kind of prize pet. He had engaged her in conversation as soon as they sat down and when the little ceremony was over was reluctant to let her go. Not that Mary minded. Stanley Bradshaw's subject was English literature of the nineteenth century and his particular enthusiasm the lives and works of Mrs Gaskell and the Brontës.

"Being from the North, myself . . ." he would say to his students. Mary Kemp, who had but vague geographical knowledge of her adopted country, was left with an impression of Stanley adrift on an inhospitable moor watched over by a group of noble dames. Being honest when it suited her, she related this image to Mr Bradshaw who was very taken with her phrase but said it referred to another lot of ladies and belonged more properly to Thomas Hardy.

This lively discussion would have been delightfully prolonged had it not been for a loud crashing noise coming from the cafeteria into which the honourable visitor had recently been ushered, presumably for some refreshment after his arduous duties.

"Something's going on," said Mr Bradshaw as he and Mary made their way in the same direction. "The students, I expect," He sighed, resigned to the phenomenon. He pushed open the glass doors but did not stand back as was his custom when with a female. "Best if I go first, Mrs Kemp."

There was a further crash of china, and some object whizzed through the air and hit the wall beside them with a dispirited splosh. At the far end of the room where a few tables had been laid for coffee and biscuits the official party appeared to be trapped between the service counter and the emergency exit. Retreat that way was impossible for the door itself had been slung back on its hooks to accommodate some ten or twenty students piling in on top of each other.

Their ringleaders already held the floor. Fruit and vegetables had veen dispensed without benefit of crockery, and they were now looking to the second echelon for succour and support.

"How the hell did that lot get into the garden?" Mr Bradshaw asked of no one in particular. "It was supposed to be out of bounds today."

They climbed over the bloody wall; Mary didn't answer him aloud but felt it should have been obvious to this man of the hills.

He did surprise her, however, by immediately taking the initiative and striding forward into the mêlée with the clear intention of bringing order out of chaos.

"Come on," he said to the leading men. "You, Josh Larkin, and you, Billy Semple . . . you've had your bit of fun. Time for the reckoning. And you lot can clear off the way you came in. Get a move on."

He lumbered over towards the exit door, shepherding students before him. Stanley was a large man with impressive shoulders, to stand in his way was to risk being mown down like grass before the scythe.

"That's enough now, lads and lassies, the less you do the less trouble you'll be in. Get back the way you come." His accent broadened as he advanced on another group and swept them before him.

Amazingly, it worked.

The leaders, a sulky Larkin, a speechless Semple and a bearded youth in a bobble hat who seemed to have difficulty with language, had their hands empty by this time with nothing left to throw, but more importantly they were at a loss for words. In Mary Kemp's not inconsiderable experience of riots this last deficiency usually led either to blows being struck or the whole affair to fizzle out.

In this particular encounter there had never been any real danger that it would come to fisticuffs. Besides, the numbers on the student side were by now so reduced as to make it foolhardy to try anything other than escape. There was a lot of muttered swearing and half-hearted jeering but eventually even the recalcitrant bobble hat was shuffled off by his fellows and pushed out through the narrow door.

Stanley replaced the locking bar, and tossed the key back

to the girl behind the glass counter who was hanging her head
and a ripple of long pale hair low over a tray of buns. As well
she might; it would have been she who, at some pre-arranged
signal, let in the Golden Horde. Mr Bradshaw knew it, and she
knew he did. What interested Mary Kemp was the fact that the
girl was Blanche Quigley.

"The tumult and the shouting dies . . ." the senior lecturer
in English was saying as he crossed the room back to Mary.
She was absolutely delighted with him, and didn't know what
to admire more: his ability to deal with students or his skill at
producing an on-the-spot quotation. She also appreciated the
fact that he took not a blind bit of notice of the official party
huddled in their corner, dusting themselves down in an agony
of embarrassment.

Just before Mary allowed herself to be gently ushered out
by Stanley Bradshaw – now breathing hard through his nose
– she saw the head of college offer the Honourable Member
for Welchester West a splay of paper napkins as if asking him
to pick a card. His reward was a look which spat nails.

"Does this kind of thing happen often?" she asked as she and
Stanley emerged from the front of the building where only a
few students were hanging about. Those who glanced in their
direction did so with an air of nervous apprehension. The news
had travelled fast.

"All the time," said Mr Bradshaw, cheerfully. "From ages
past, students and city apprentices, ever on the boil. No
country's any good without 'em."

Mary thought it an enlightened point of view and said so
before they parted at the college gates. She had been interested
to learn that, although names had either been taken or at least
memorised by members of the staff, little action would follow
– at least, Stanley hoped not.

"I'm not a great believer in those sorts of record," he told
her. "Many an eminent statesman would have been doomed
to obscurity had their student activities counted for much."

"Surely not our guest of today?" Mary queried, mischie-
vously.

Mr Bradshaw had snorted. "Him? He wouldn't know an
alternative idea if it came up and bit him. A goody-goody

all the way through, our Stephen, and stamped Conservative from birth like a stick of rock."

Beyond that comment the English tutor would not be taken. The subject was obviously of far less interest than the books which he then recommended to Mary.

They parted the best of friends, and as Mary walked back through the town to Albert Crescent she realised that she had found the events of the day so far quite exhilarating. She was also intrigued by the presence of Blanche Quigley at the brief skirmish in the cafeteria. She knew the girl had various jobs. She was, as she said, 'marking time' before taking up a career; though what that career would be nobody, including Blanche herself, seemed to know. There had been talk of fashion modelling, interior design, perhaps something in cosmetics – it was all very vague when it was talked about at Miss Weston's, and Primrose Sutton tended to be sceptical.

"It was that posh school she went to," said Prim, "gives them airs and graces instead of A levels. Now she's at a private crammer . . . bet that's expensive." She curled her lip. "Much good may it do her – she and brother Jasper haven't a brain between them."

They were not twins, though they looked it and liked to refer to themselves as such. Jasper was the older by some ten months, but they had the same blond hair and pale skin, and a certain awkwardness of body as if never quite sure where they stood. This unsureness lent both the Quigleys the artless appearance of some medieval portraits where the subjects had been caught between the rock of faith and the spring of enlightenment. Blanche tended, in her choice of clothes, to underline a maidenly aspect which was why she seemed to Prim to be on the dim side. Mary Kemp took a different view; she reckoned Blanche Quigley was sharper than she looked, and well able to take care of herself. It was rumoured that she should have gone to finishing school in Switzerland to prepare her for a life more elevated than to be found in Newtown, but her father had had heavy losses at Lloyds, and so she would remain, for the time being, unfinished. Blanche seemed to have taken the reverse in family fortunes fairly well; perhaps she'd never wanted Swiss polish in the first place and preferred her present free and easy non-occupation.

Whatever the circumstances, perhaps it wasn't so strange that she should be found behind the counter of the college cafeteria, maybe she planned to get in by the back door. Mary was amused by the idea.

She had the opportunity that evening of talking over the affair of the students with Primrose, who had asked her to baby-sit. Since the death of the middle-flat tenant Prim had to fall back on her second line of helpers, and on this particular evening Mary agreed willingly. They could have a good gossip when Prim returned from having her hair permed.

"Can't spare the time during the day, what with Auntie Gwen, and Liza-Jane, but my friend does it cheap if I go after hours."

The end product didn't look cheap to Mary, it looked stylishly expensive. She knew better than to comment.

Primrose was surprised to hear that Blanche Quigley was working in the college cafeteria, surprised and displeased.

"Are you sure it was her?"

"Of course I am. That hair of hers. She could model shampoo."

"She did for a time. But they found her too gawky."

"I think gauche is a nicer word."

"Same thing," said Prim, absently. "Did Blanche have anything to do with the student demo this morning?"

"Not when I saw her," said Mary, "but she may well have helped in getting them in the door."

It was that aspect which was annoying Prim, as if Blanche had stolen her thunder. "Perhaps she met one or two of them when she was in the pub with me, but I shouldn't have thought she was their type."

Mary was amused. Primrose Sutton had always considered herself the leader of her little set, and even in the brief time she'd been at the college she'd made a bit of a name for herself as a turbulent spirit and one deserving respect in the small ebullient world of student politics. But, as in wider spheres, reputations have to be constantly replenished if they are to keep their shine, and in this Primrose had fallen behind. She was now obviously chagrined to find another, if not precisely taking her place, but nevertheless on the fringe. What made it worse was that the other should be a friend, one she had introduced, and one moreover whom she considered well below deserving status.

She was shaking her head.

"Josh and the others, they'd never take to Blanche. I mean they'd see through her right away. Too posh for them. Middle class, and a niminy-piminy into the bargain. What on earth was she doing anyway serving in the canteen?"

"Perhaps the Job Centre sent her," said Mary, laughing at the way the words came out. But Prim wasn't laughing; she was fretting in a way out of all proportion to the incident.

"Why does it bother you so much, Prim, that Blanche should be there? After all, you've said she takes all manner of jobs just to fill in her time."

But Prim was closing up in that abrupt way of hers. "I just find it odd, that's all. Maybe I'll ask her about it when I see her."

Apparently that would be soon, for both Quigleys were coming in tomorrow to view the middle flat. Now it was Mary's turn to be surprised.

"I didn't think it was big enough. Anyway, don't Jasper and Blanche still live with their parents?" She had heard them talk of a large place on the edge of town.

"Got to be sold, hasn't it? Mr Quigley took a right toss over Lloyds." Prim didn't sound too unhappy about the downturn in the fortunes of the elder Quigleys. "Not that they've been left without a roof to their mouths when they've got that villa in Spain and a cottage in Devon. But there's to be what Jasper calls 'retrenchment' so he and Blanche could do with some temporary accommodation. Of course it's all being arranged through Uncle Simon, he owns the Acme Company and as likely as not he's putting them in as caretakers pro tem till another tenant shows up. Business is a bit slack in the property market right now."

It was the first time Mary had heard of any actual Quigley connection with what she still looked on as Miss Weston's house, so she enquired further, and learned either all that

Primrose Sutton knew on the subject, or as much as she was willing to tell.

Simon Quigley had always been in the property business, having inherited an established family firm of auctioneers and surveyors which he had expanded along with Newtown itself. He was now head of a nice little empire of property companies of which Acme was but a small part.

Primrose didn't like him. It was not clear to Mary whether this was for personal reasons or because he was the very model for the successful Thatcherite businessmen who, according to Prim, blocked the sunlight from the lives of lesser souls. Mary was not sure that Prim had even met the man.

Reverting to the subject of the flat itself, Primrose said there was a box-room which Miss Juniper had used only to store books in. "It'll do for Jasper. He'll be up with Gregory half the time anyway." She gave something between a snort and a giggle. "Oh, no, not that . . . they're just good mates."

"I didn't think otherwise," said Mary, who had drawn her own conclusion, "but how come they went to the same school? I thought the Venns didn't have any money whereas the Quigleys obviously had."

"Greg got what's called an assisted place . . ." Prim was always eager to instruct Mary in the finer points of the English education system which, to her mind, underpinned the whole social structure of the country, ". . . the bright boy from the working class gets a leg up, see? Gets to join the privileged at a minor public school. And he's got the chip on his shoulder to prove it," she finished, darkly.

It was something about Gregory that Mary had herself noticed, but she did not comment. Once Prim got started on the class system she was apt to go on a long time, so Mary said she must be going and she went into Miss Weston's bedroom to say goodnight to the old lady.

It was a pleasant room, one of the largest on the ground floor and tastefully furnished with what was presumably Miss Weston's own furniture. Primrose kept it spotlessly tidy, and would have had a portable television for the invalid but, as she said, Aunt Gwen refused. So long as her eyesight held out, she would read, so between them Prim and Mary kept her in a constant supply of Catherine Cooksons and Danielle Steeles. Nothing too racy, and they must all end happily, Prim had said once Mary was enlisted on the weekly library run, but Mary had brought *Far from the Madding Crowd* and received a nod of smiling approval when Miss Weston had finished the book.

"Well, leave it at that," Lennox Kemp had remarked on being told of this venture. "Just don't get her on to *Jude the Obscure*. I read it in my carefree youth and was suicidal for a week. Fortunately my team won on the Saturday and Jude went back into obscurity."

"One of the things I like about Hardy is his choice of names," said Mary. "Sue Bridehead, Thomasin Yeobright, Eustacia . . . they sound like flowers or stars. I wonder if the Venn parents were thinking of Diggory when they called him Gregory?"

"H'm . . . I don't see him as a rural character, he's a very urban type. And, by the way, I hear he's just been given his articles by old Roberts, and he's halfway through his law degree course at night school; so whatever Primrose may think of his education, it seems to have paid off."

"Oh, I think she was only making a political point. She does the same when she talks about Simon Quigley. All Prim's judgements are parti-coloured!"

"Simon Quigley's all right. Seems straight enough in any dealings I've had with him, and he's done a lot for the town one way or another. He's been Chairman of the Council for the last two years and I don't suppose his relationship with the Durward-Cookes has harmed him either. Simon's not above a bit of back-scratching if it means money."

"Tell me more. Prim never mentioned that side."

"I'm surprised she didn't. She must know of it through the Quigleys, and it would have suited her book – local businessman gives a big hand to brother Tory. Or the other way round, of course."

"H'm. Is it a close kinship, then, this connection?" asked Mary.

Kemp broke into song: "There lived two sisters down in the Dell. They were wealthy young women whose parents were dead . . ."

"Oh, do go on," said Mary.

"I can't keep up the poetry," said Kemp. "Anyway, Colonel Perceval Cooke married Olga Durward and took on the family name along with the money – hence their son, Stephen's, present name. Simon Quigley's Uncle Daniel married the younger, Dorinda, didn't bother with the name and probably got less."

"Very wise. Durward-Quigley would be a bit of a tongue-twister. So they all lived happily ever after?"

"Ah, as to that, I can't say. I only know what I've told you because Archibald Gillorn was the Durward family solicitor and I saw some of their papers when I worked with the old man up in Chancery Lane – but that's a long time ago."

Mary knew that Lennox missed the old gentleman – the one they called 'Old Archie' – who had died some years ago. It was he who had pulled Kemp out of the wilderness when he'd been struck off by the Law Society and was living on the edge. However, neither she nor her husband cared to dwell too much on their pasts. She had an interest now in someone else's.

"Is that place still there? The Dell, as you called it?"

"It's called Deloraine Court, and it's now on the outskirts of the town, which has crept up to its very doors. Much of the land went for housing years ago – and council housing, at that. But I think the house and gardens remain. It's not that long since Stephen Durward-Cooke's mother died, and that's where she lived and he was brought up; although I don't suppose he was there very often because he would have the usual boarding school education from the age of seven – that initiation into leadership you must have come across in your sociology studies." Kemp liked to tease his wife about the subjects she had chosen for her late self-education – subjects about which he pleaded ignorance. But this time she was not rising to the bait.

"Who lives in the house now?" she asked.

"No one. It's been empty since Mrs Durward-Cooke died – and that's a few years ago. I believe it's on the market, but there's been no takers. I wouldn't know about that: Roberts are their solicitors, and I think Simon Quigley has a finger in that pie too."

"Dear me, what a lot of connectedness there is about. Well, poor old Stephen didn't get much of a welcome in his home town the other day. I guess the Quigley girl must be some kind of relation. Would he know that?"

"I doubt it. This is another generation, remember. It was Simon's uncle who married Dorinda Durward, so you can work out the relationship yourself. It's Simon Quigley's brother John who's the father of those you call the twins."

"I suppose it's because they're Simon's niece and nephew they get the flat at a low rent to tide them over Daddy's losses at Lloyds – at least that's what Prim says. According to her Simon Quigley's a millionaire."

"In Newtown gossip, that goes for everyone whose bank balance is in credit. It may well be true, of course. He's never married, and he inherited a prosperous business which he has expanded. Perhaps he'll take on young Jasper."

"I doubt he's got the head for it." Mary contemplated Blanche's brother for a moment. There was something lacking in the boy – but the same could be said about the girl as well. It was only when the two of them were together they seemed to be whole.

"Going back to the other sister, the one with the pretty name, didn't she have any children?"

"No. She was still living at Deloraine Court at the end of the war. She would have been getting on a bit when Daniel Quigley came and whisked her off abroad."

"So both sisters married travelling men."

"I'm sure they wouldn't have put it like that. Colonel Percival was regular Army, and Daniel Quigley served his country in one or other of our far-flung colonies."

"The white man's burden, I've heard of that. And the fair Dorinda, she would share the burden. Did it eventually kill them?"

"I understand they both enjoyed a peaceful retirement in, I think, Kenya. Dorinda died some time ago, and Daniel only last year."

"Not killed by revolting natives, then?" Mary sounded disappointed.

Kemp was amused. "Did you get all your English history from the cinema?" he asked. "When Kenya became independent," he explained, "some of our people stayed on.

They had made their lives out there, and presumably found it suited them. Contrary to popular opinion, many actually got on well with the natives."

"So Dorinda never came back to Deloraine Court?"

"They might have come on leave from time to time. But of course it was no longer her home. Olga and Perceval went on living there even after he retired from the Army. I don't think Olga had ever left."

"You mean she never did the dutiful army wife bit – following the flag with the teasmaid?"

"I understand from an elderly client who knew her slightly that Mrs Durward-Cooke was – er – delicate."

"Too delicate to go abroad? I thought it was the other way round. Hot climate dries the skin and causes wrinkles, and, my dear, you just can't get the cream . . ."

"She was said to suffer from neurasthenia . . ."

"And that covers a multitude of evils." Mary tended to be sceptical of layman's language when it came to the nervous system. "Poor Olga. Seems a shame the sisters had to be separated."

"Well, they were at Deloraine Court a long time together. I understand that Dorinda was always the stronger of the two and looked after Olga. There's even a tale, according to my friend, that she saved her sister's life when Olga went into labour and all the roads out to Deloraine Court were blocked by snow."

"On the Feast of Stephen?"

"Near enough."

Mary was quiet as she cleared away the dishes. Kemp followed her into the kitchen and watched her face as she methodically stacked plates. She was completely absorbed in her own thoughts but he wasn't altogether surprised when she suddenly turned, and burst out:

"Oh, how I would love to see that place, that Deloraine Court. Do you think I could visit it?"

Kemp knew he would have to humour her once she had an *idée fixee*.

"And you shall visit it, but not before you've sorted out those books from Miss Juniper's. I stub my toe on that great box every time I go into the study."

54

Seven

P rim Sutton had looked the books over with the eye of a market trader, and scoffed: "Nothing in this lot would fetch a decent price." She trailed a casual finger along a nice set of Nelsons' classics. "All that old stuff we had at school . . ."

"Well, I didn't," said Mary. Books in the home of her girlhood had generally been stolen; the younger Smiths, her half-brothers and sisters, thieved out of pure devilment from an early age, and books from libraries and schools were easy pickings before the girls got on to nicking cosmetics and the boys to the more manly sport of the unauthorised appropriation of automobiles.

It was through tales like these that Mary, the older woman, had gained the respect of Primrose, whose views on juvenile crime tended towards the romantic. "Manchester was deadly dull," she complained. "Wish I'd been brought up in the States."

"You wouldn't if you'd lived real poor in Vineland, Pennsylvania," Mary said, drily. "Besides, you had the Mersey beat to brighten your childhood."

"You don't think my folks would let me listen to any of that!" Prim sounded genuinely horrified. "They were solid Chapel – even dancing was a sin."

"What a very deprived upbringing you had, Prim."

At this point in the conversation, Prim had begun to wonder if her new friend was taking the mickey. "That was why I ran away," she told Mary, even now taking pride in the exploit.

However, when questioned about where she'd run to, at what age and with what consequences, she had been evasive. Prim didn't like specifics, she was a great one for the universal catchword, the panoramic vision, a kind of blanket she drew over those aspects of her life she preferred to keep hidden.

Mary recognised the great differences between them without letting them spoil a burgeoning friendship. It amused her to see Prim Sutton as a gaily coloured balloon bobbing about on the surface of things and only loosely attached to the here-and-now; whereas she, Mary, had always kept herself firmly anchored in the present, her past a map she knew but did not want to return to, her future a blank waiting to be filled in as events unrolled. She knew she lacked imagination. She suspected that Prim possessed an active one and that although she was quite capable of sorting out fact from fiction, she sometimes didn't bother to try.

She put Prim out of her mind, and concentrated on the books. She found them easy to arrange because Grace Juniper had kept them in orderly sets, and the sister had simply taken them out shelf by shelf to fill the boxes.

By lunchtime the tall bookcase in Lennox's study, which had up till now only contained a few dog-eared old law books – their modern counterparts had to be accessible to all his staff in the office library – began to look more cheerful as its purpose became fulfilled. Mary sat back on her heels to admire the ranks.

Only a few were left at the bottom of the last box, and these seemed to be of a dull, educational nature: textbooks on remedial teaching, speech therapy and phonetics, an atlas of the British Isles (which Mary put on one side to study later, since her knowledge of her adopted country was woefully inadequate and one of her fellow students had laughed at her for thinking Wessex was an English county) and a couple of books on archaeology. Mary was interested in none of them, but it didn't seem right somehow to throw them out so soon after Grace's death so she put them away at the foot of a cupboard. She had been folding up the boxes as she went along, but this last one kept sticking because of a large flat book wedged in a corner. I suppose this is what is known as a coffee-table book, thought Mary; all it needs is four legs. She glanced at the picture on the cover as it was eventually extricated before putting it away with the other uninteresting stuff. A soft painting in faint blues and rose colours. '*A Garden in Summer*' it said, and then in smaller writing below the title: 'by Olga Durward-Cooke'.

Well, perhaps not so uninteresting after all . . . Mary took the book over to an armchair and opened it. Apparently it had been privately printed. In a foreword Mrs Durward-Cooke dedicated 'this small offering' to her family, in the hope that they had appreciated and loved the garden of Deloraine Court as she did.

Mary turned to the blank page at the front of the book, and saw that the fly-leaf bore a handwritten inscription: 'To my very dear Gwendolyne, from Olga' and dated a Christmas four years back.

Mary skimmed through the pages. The book had a nice feel to it, and the photographs, some black and white, some coloured, were good although possibly not professional. The written contents came in rather thin paragraphs and were charming rather than inspired. There were lots of lists of shrubs and plants, and one or two pictures of the house itself, which looked mid-Victorian with twentieth-century additions. The lawns were impressive and there was an air of secluded privacy as if the whole place was open to the sun's eye but no other.

In the course of her nursing career Mary had been in grander homes set in more extensive grounds in Long Island or upstate New York, but the views she now held in her hand of Deloraine Court gave her a little shiver of curiosity. Though it could of course just be that inscription to Miss Weston. How had she come to be Mrs Durward-Cooke's 'very dear Gwendolyne'?

The chance to find out came a week later when Primrose made one of her forays into Oxford Street, 'to buy clothes for Liza-Jane', she said, although the toddler's face had fallen at the prospect and only lifted at the promise of the cinema afterwards. The child seemed to Mary to have her priorities right at an early age; she manipulated her parent as Prim in her turn manipulated others.

"Miss Weston does so enjoy your visits." Prim was wheedling, and Mary was well aware of it. "If you wouldn't mind popping in about teatime . . ."

Mary took a cake she'd baked. She was no match for Prim when it came to cookery, but the old lady smiled with her eyes when she'd finished a slice of it. "Good," she managed to say after some effort. She was better when there was only the two of them; she would concentrate hard on what she wanted to say and keep to a simple word.

After tea, Mary produced the book on the Deloraine Court garden, and brought it to the old lady. "I think this belongs to you. I found it among Grace's books. You must have lent it to her at some time."

But Miss Weston shook her head vigorously. She made a movement of her good hand, holding it outward, palm upturned.

"Oh, I see," said Mary, understanding the gesture. "You gave it to her. Well, it should come back to you now. Was the lady who wrote it your friend?"

She put the book in Miss Weston's lap, the page open at a photograph of the writer, a thin, once-pretty, middle-aged face. The old lady traced the outline of the features with her fingers, her eyes lowered, a suspicion of moisture in the corners.

"She died, didn't she?" said Mary, gently. "That must have been a sad day for you . . ."

Miss Weston nodded again. She was turning the pages, looking for something, then she pointed. It was at a picture of the house taken from the lawn, and her finger was on the glass veranda which extended from the front down one side where it opened out into a large conservatory which lightened the whole aspect of the premises as a gaily coloured awning might transform a dull wall.

This conservatory was mentioned several times in the text which Mary had read. Mrs Durward-Cooke's husband, the Army man, had travelled widely and because of her love of plants he had apparently brought back many exotic species which required a warmer climate than the garden could provide. For these plants the conservatory had been built some time after the war, and in it they flourished. The writer described how, as she grew older, the happiest of her winter hours were spent within its ambience.

Miss Weston was trying to say something, pushing the book towards Mary, her finger still on the page.

". . . Da . . . Dad . . ." she got out, at last.

Mary was delighted to understand. "Your father?" She asked. "It was your father who built that conservatory? Well, and isn't it the fine piece of building? That side of the house would be bare without it. The family must have been very pleased."

Miss Weston was all nods and smiles, but when Mary said again that she must have the book back she warded it off with her hand. Looking Mary straight in the eye, she said: "You . . . for you . . ."

"Why, thank you," said Mary, leaning forward to kiss the withered cheek. "I shall be glad to keep it."

She could see how it was with Miss Weston. Possessions were becoming a problem for her, just things to be kept tidy by someone else, small burdens she could not deal with herself. That was why she preferred library books, which could not become permanent features in her room; it would be the reason she had given the book on the Deloraine garden to Grace Juniper. Some old people liked to have the feel of tactile remembrances round them, taking comfort in collections of photographs, old diaries and such souvenirs of their lives as they could cram into their remaining space, living in rooms where silver-framed faces of the dead had to be dusted daily along with the china shepherdesses and tiny useless ornaments, each one a reminder of happier times when they had been bought, or given by friend, husband, lover or child long gone elsewhere.

But there were others, more tidy-minded, who preferred to unclutter their surroundings, sticking only to what was necessary, clearing the decks, as it were, so as to leave no trouble for those who must come after them. Mary recognised Gwendolyne Weston as one of these, and sympathised because she too liked to keep things simple, and had never been acquisitive.

As she cleared the old lady's cup and plate she noticed

Miss Weston's normally expressive face looked blank, the mouth pulled down at one corner, the eyes inward and far away. It was the look she had when conversation tired her, and Mary instinctively put an arm around her shoulders. "You would like to rest, wouldn't you? I'll take you to your room to lie down.

But Miss Weston shook her head, frowning now. Mary realised her expression – the stillness of her body, the unfocused eyes – meant she was concentrating hard, trying to grasp at some thought, some memory which kept eluding the search for it. With a sudden impatient movement of her good hand she reached again for the book which was still lying on the table. Mary placed it where the hand could turn the pages, and once again Miss Weston stopped at the pictured house, and tapped the conservatory with her forefinger.

"You're trying to tell me something, Gwen?" But Miss Weston seemed too deep in her own thoughts to hear her. When she did look up, Mary saw that behind the eyes a struggle was going on, an immense effort was being made to bring something to mind.

Strokes affected memory and Mary knew that Miss Weston's had been a massive one, but knowing so little of the medical history she could not tell whether there had been some recovery or the hope of it. She smoothed the page on which Miss Weston's finger was still beating a faint tattoo, and said, gently: "Is it about the conservatory your father built for them?"

But whatever memory was desperately trying to surface, the effort to retrieve it had been too much. The invalid pushed the book away, and let her hand fall limply to her lap. She closed her eyes, the frown of frustration deepening between her brows. Mary brought the wheelchair, took her into the bathroom where she bathed her hands and face, talking softly all the time about the ordinary things, the sweet smell of the soap, the little bottles of aromatherapy oils – one of Prim's minor indulgences – the plastic ducks which Liza-Jane lined up along the bath. Mary went on talking till the lines on Miss Weston's face softened and at last she relaxed and smiled, herself again.

It is not right, Mary thought, to awaken memories when they cannot be expressed; the old lady had enough disability to contend with, better to let the fields of mind and memory lie fallow if that is nature's way.

"But of course you want to know," said her husband that evening. "You're dying to find out what the connection is between Miss Weston and Deloraine Court."

"Well, yes." Mary had to admit. "I just don't get it. This 'very dear Gwendolyne' stuff. I mean, they were of a different class . . ."

"Whoops! How very English you're becoming. You're even starting to think like them. But in this case you're quite wrong."

"I am?"

"The people at Deloraine Court had never been real gentry, not like the Courtenays out at Ember for instance. No, the Durward-Cookes made their money in commerce like everybody else around Newtown, including the Westons. George Weston would have been a highly respected figure before the war. He was a master-builder, which meant a great deal more than it does now when any enterprising plumber or joiner can set up as such. The Weston family would be in good circumstances, your Gwendolyne probably went to the girls' high school rather than the local elementary and her father would pay fees for her. As a matter of fact," Kemp went on as Mary poured more coffee and saw that he was prepared to chat, "I took an elderly client to lunch the other day and because of your interest in this house next door I led him on to talk of the Westons."

"You're as bad as me. Curiosity Kemp, the ears and eyes of Walthamstow . . ." There was nothing Mary liked better than to hark back to her husband's lean years when he'd worked for McCready's Detective Agency in what she still thought of as a sleazy downtown suburb. She hadn't known him then but the image persisted of a man out of luck, out of a job, chucked out of his profession, but never out of resource. That kind of man might have appealed to her more than the present well-to-do respectable lawyer, but she let the thought slide by.

"So, there's no reason why Miss Weston and Mrs Durward-Cooke should not be friends, they might even have gone to school together," Kemp went on. "It was only after the war that George Weston's business went downhill – and that surprised everyone. Although business would be slack in the duration he wasn't in the forces because of his age, and he was in the position to pick up any that was going. And he'd be the only one in Newtown to take advantage of the post-war building boom, but it seems he didn't. It looks as if he couldn't handle money. Drink and gambling did for him, according to my elderly friend, and eventually the firm went into liquidation – not voluntarily at that."

"Primrose says that if he'd let his daughter do the books he'd never have gone broke."

"Perhaps by the time she came back into the business it was too late. My friend remembers Gwen Weston being in the uniform of one of the women's services."

"That figures. There's an air of tidiness about her. You get it in women who've been in training together, like nurses. Maybe she took up the bookkeeping as a clerk in one of the forces."

"Well, it wasn't enough to save her father's business – though it may have prevented his personal bankruptcy. George Weston seems to have done a deal with his creditors. Interestingly enough, it was another connection of the Durward-Cooke family who benefited most by getting hold of a lot of properties going cheap."

"Don't tell me. The Acme Property Company, and good old Uncle Simon . . ."

"At that time it would have been 'Quigleys, Auctioneers and Land Agent' – but yes, Simon did well out of the winding-up of Westons."

"Perhaps he has a conscience about it and that's why he lets Miss Weston go on living in the house next door even though he owns it."

"I've met few businessmen with a conscience," said her husband, drily, "but perhaps Simon Quigley is an exception. I wonder if it's really he who's paying Prim Sutton to look after the old lady."

"Someone does," said Mary, decisively, "and there's no

doubt everyone keeps an eye on her as if she were some kind of treasured object. Now, Lennox, you haven't forgotten your promise that I could visit the ancient dwelling of the Durward-Cookes?"

Eight

There was no reason, Mary found, why she should not visit Deloraine Court. The only question was: should it be a clandestine trip or one properly authorised? She, of course, given her nature and upbringing, favoured creeping up on the place alone and without credentials. Lennox soon laughed that one out of court.

"Don't be silly," he said, "you want to see the house then do it correctly. I'll tell Simon Quigley you're looking at the place on behalf of a client and you are a friend of the wife. Considering how long it's been on the market he'll jump at the chance of a likely purchaser."

"I'd prefer no one to know," said Mary, vaguely, unsure herself why she felt that way. "I only want into the grounds . . ."

"Trespassing isn't a crime so long as no wilful damage is done, but it's not an activity I'd recommend to a practising lawyer's good lady. Let me get the particulars of sale from Acme Properties and at least get you off on the right footing."

"'A fine late-Victorian country house . . .' That's stretching it a bit," Kemp commented a few days later as he studied the brochure. "There's council estates right up to its walls."

"It's just like the picture in Miss Weston's book," said Mary, looking at the photographs, "and they're all taken in the summertime, too, with the roses in bloom."

"H'm, and some years ago," said Kemp. "Good agents' practice. They're hardly likely to give you a view of the dustbins at the back. And they're asking far too much. Five hundred thousand. For that you'd expect to get real countryside and a lot more land. I'm surprised Durward-Cooke hasn't come down a bit if he really does want the place off his hands."

"Maybe he's not keen on letting it go. Maybe he's thinking of his mother and how she loved her garden . . ."

"Not a chance. Stephen Durward-Cooke hasn't a sentimental bone in his body. He's got a big house in his own constituency to keep up, two boys at public school and an extravagant wife – he needs the money."

When Mary told Gwendolyne Weston that she was going out to see Deloraine Court the old lady's eyes lit up and her cheeks flushed pink. "I shall look particularly at that conservatory your father built." Mary took up the invalid's good hand and felt an answering squeeze from the thin waxy fingers. "And when I come again I'll tell you what I think of it."

"You're really not thinking of buying that place?" Blanche Quigley had been in the room that morning while Prim was out shopping.

"Oh, it's not for us," Mary reassured her, "it's a friend who's interested. But as you're here you can tell me the way to get there. You must know the house pretty well."

"I know where it is. You go out the Ember Road and turn right at the crossroads where it says Thornton Lea. The entrance to Deloraine Court's about half a mile on from there. But you're mistaken about me knowing the house itself. I've never been, neither's Jasper. That side of the family were always a bit stand-offish with us."

"Any reason for that?" Mary made the enquiry sound sympathetic.

Blanche shrugged. It was a pretty habit of hers as it sent a ripple of light across the waterfall of her hair. Mary could never be sure whether Blanche Quigley was aware of those little tricks she played with her appearance. There was something about both the twins that looked innocent yet had a studied air.

"Our side was always in trade," she said, "even if surveying and auctioneering was at the upper end."

"While the Durward-Cookes . . . ?" Mary prompted.

"Were serving their country." There was scarcely an inflexion in the girl's voice even to hint at mockery.

"As Stephen the MP is doing now?" Mary couldn't resist the comment but realised she might have gone too far as Blanche gave her a cool stare and no reply. "Anyway," Mary added, hastily, "it's not your family I'm interested in, just the house."

As she drove out from Newtown she thought of the Durward daughters and their marriages; one little piggy had gone far afield, the other little piggy had stayed home. Which had had the more rewarding life? Ah, well, they were both dead now. The bricks and mortar of their girlhood home had lasted longer than their mortal flesh.

The house was easier to find than she had expected. The brochure had mentioned seclusion but the Thornton Council Estate was just across the road from the gates of Deloraine Court, the inevitable local art splattering the stone entrance posts up to the height an average ten-year-old could reach. There was a prominent 'For Sale' notice, and two wooden placards saying 'Keep Out' which had also received the attentions of the juvenile arts brigade. There was a padlock on the chains which secured the gates but Lennox had obtained a key.

"Not to the house itself, mind," he told her, "for that would mean a rep from the agents to show you round. You didn't want that so I emphasised my client was at this stage only interested in the location and the size of the grounds."

Mary put her car in the council car park, where it would be inconspicuous. Even so, she felt self-conscious as she crossed the road and unlocked the chain holding the gates. These places do cut people down to size, she thought, as they swung open. The words 'Deloraine Court' were deeply incised on the stone pillars on either side, and the gates themselves were of intricate ironwork intended to impress. She closed them, padlocking the chain back in place, then turned to face the drive which swept grandly round a clump of silver birches before disappearing behind thick screens of rhododendrons. The width of the driveway and its smooth surface of ochre-coloured chippings continued and complemented the splendour of the entrance. Mary found it intimidating.

That's because I'm on foot, she thought. I should be on a horse or in a fine motor car. Only the gardeners and the maids would have walked . . .

As she walked, however, she saw that tufts of grass and weed were growing up through the tiny stones, and even before she glimpsed the house, the unkempt bushes crowding in on either hand had reduced the driveway to a mere tunnel arched by wildly overgrown branches.

Lennox had warned her: "Take care," he'd said. "Deloraine Court's been empty a long time, you may have to fight your way through the brambles. Nature has a way of getting her own back when a place has been neglected. You're a city girl, you might fall into a thorn bush – 'Annihilating all that's made, To a green thought in a green shade . . .'"

Her husband tended to use quotations to deflect her purpose. He had not succeeded, but she could see what he had meant. The greenery intensified as the driveway narrowed, in threat now to the long tentacles of undergrowth through which she had to tread warily.

Although she had seen the photographs in the book and studied the agents' brochure, the house itself when it appeared was something of a disappointment. It was of more modest dimensions than the grand entrance had seemed to warrant. It crouched hesitantly against a vast arboreal background. Perhaps those trees had grown taller since the photographs had been taken. The grass of the front lawn certainly had as Mary left the drive and made her way through it feeling as if she were being photographed on safari.

As she neared the house she regained her confidence, for the warm brick and the cream facings, the wide lower windows and even the little hooded ones under the eaves had a friendly look. Why don't the local council take it over, she thought, being of a practical rather than romantic mind, and use it for play-groups, a nursery school or a youth club – amenities she understood were lacking in the surrounding estates. Remembering the price being asked soon knocked that idea on the head. Demolish the house, then, and use the grounds as a building site? But no new council houses had been built in Newtown for over a decade. Perhaps none were needed. More likely the price was still too high for an impoverished authority, and entrepreneurial private developers had been thin on the ground while recession lasted, biding their time till the boom years returned.

Obviously it would be the latter kind of enterprise that would be welcomed by both Acme Properties and Durward-Cooke himself and that would be the reason for the high asking price. Of course the house itself would have to come down, but there was enough acreage to provide for a fine array of so-called 'town houses' with private gardens and sufficient open space to give them a rural look. Keep as many trees as possible, put a guardroom at the imposing entrance and little watch-towers at every corner and you have a very attractive project – country properties within commuter distance of the capital, with a 'green' outlook but security guaranteed.

Mary was feeling quite carried away by this cynical speculation as she reached the shallow steps leading up to the front door. There was a wide stone ledge to one side. She cleared it of the fallen red and gold leaves from the creeper above, and sat down. Although it was September, the previous month had been wet so that the trees still held on to their green, tinged here and there with bronze, and although the flowers in what had been formal beds were wild and leggy, they nevertheless flaunted their colours like summer fashions gone too far.

Thinking, as she had been, of the future of Deloraine Court she felt suddenly sentimental. She patted the rosy brick of the little wall. "Its a pity, sure, about you," she told it, "but they'll decide you've had your day. And that'll go for old Mr Weston's conservatory as well, so I'd better take a look at it before it bites the dust."

As a structure it had stood up well to its years. In her book Olga Durward-Cooke had said that the glasshouse, as she called it, was built in the early fifties to house the many exotic plants her husband, the Colonel, brought back from countries to which his military service took him. Despite post-war shortages, the local firm who did the work (she did not name them) were to be congratulated on its appearance and its subsequent use. She had been delighted with it, she wrote in her rather breathy, girlish prose, and it had become her 'playroom'.

Certainly it was large and, to Mary's eye, more like something seen in public gardens rather than the kind of conservatory it was now fashionable to attach to any suburban dwelling. Although it was modern, care had been taken to keep it in the

Victorian tradition, right up to the curlicued topknots at either end of the serrated metal crest along the roof. The bargeboards matched those on the house, and although the paintwork was no longer white and there were panes of glass cracked or missing, the building was still a fine piece of architecture. Miss Weston's father had gone to a lot of trouble. Perhaps business had been slack at the time. Perhaps he valued the Durward-Cookes' good opinion.

Mary walked along the side of the conservatory and tried to look in the windows but she was hampered by the mass of overgrown shrubs which spread themselves up against the low brick wall which served as footing for the glass. At one point, however, they gave way to some shallow steps leading to what appeared to be a door, although this was effectively screened by a rampant rhododendron. She pushed the dark shining leaves aside. It was a door, and although closed it hung loosely from a broken hinge.

Mary found the temptation difficult to resist. She went up the short steps, and very gently pushed. If it doesn't give way, she thought, I'll go back. I'll have done no harm . . .

But the door swung open. It creaked alarmingly but the offer it seemed to be making of a look at the interior was too good to refuse. Mary stepped over the threshold. It was dark because wide-leaved plants were crowded at the windows, searching vigorously for light while others stretched out feelers across the narrow space between raised beds. Some effort had been made to keep nature at bay but it looked as though the vegetation would win in the end, in here as well as outside in the gardens.

As she walked down the centre aisle she found the answer to that hybrid name, glasshouse or conservatory. The end at which she had entered was an entirely functional greenhouse, the room she was now approaching had wood-block flooring and there had been some attempt at furnishing. The wickerwork settee and chairs with gaily striped cushions looked like a good try by the agents. There were a couple of glass-topped tables on which some copies of *Country Life* were spread casually. Lifting one, Mary saw it was dated eighteen months ago. Under it was a brochure like the one Kemp had obtained, and under it a set of drawings with what looked like a plan of the greenhouse addition.

And in the hand of George Weston himself I've no doubt, thought Mary, carrying the papers over to a window where there was more light. Now I wonder if Miss Weston would like to have these? I could always ask Acme Properties for copies . . .

Something moved outside the window, too sharply to be merely the soft afternoon breeze stirring the leaves. Startled, she pushed the papers deep into the pocket of her black anorak, and retreated through the space between the plants towards the door. There she stopped and listened, but heard nothing. Perhaps it had only been the shadow of a broken branch swinging in the wind. Nevertheless, she took care to move the door quietly to let her slip out on to the step where she turned to close it . . .

Afterwards, all she could remember was something upswept – an arm, a weapon? – glimpsed out of the corner of her eye as she was knocked off balance . . . then a blank void . . .

When she came to – and she had no idea how long the void had lasted – she was staring up at the sky through a canopy of dark leaves. She felt content to lie there a moment, for something told her that if she moved her head it would hurt. But the sleeve of her jacket was being mauled by some savage beast, and the only way to escape was first to get on her knees and then stand up. When she'd accomplished that, she found herself staring into the furious face of Stephen Durward-Cooke – a very angry animal indeed.

"What the devil are you doing here?" he demanded. No solicitude for her well-being, no kindly arm about her shoulders; in fact, just the opposite. He was hauling her to her feet just as roughly as he must have pushed her down.

"I was attacked . . ." She felt the back of her head. "You hit me . . ."

"So that's going to be the story, is it?" Durward-Cooke's eyes bulged like a bull terrier's. "Not content with trespass, breaking in, and damage to property, you think you'll get away with it by trumping up charges. Of all the lying . . ." Words of sufficient venom had begun to fail him even before Mary had regained breath and her own anger.

"I was hit," she repeated, "and pushed."

"You were hit by this when you did the damage." He stooped and picked up something from among the leaves. Mary looked at it, and at her surroundings. She had fallen – or been pushed – into the great bush which grew up beside the steps up to the greenhouse door. It came back to her that she had turned to close that door. She saw that what Durward-Cooke held in his hand was the ornamental piece of wood from the apex above the door. She had noticed it when she had first seen the building, thinking it fanciful but in keeping with the lacy work on the bargeboards.

She decided it was about time she had her say but any attempt at explanation was drowned in another torrent of words from Durward-Cooke, whose ire seemed only to be refuelled by any speech from her. Perhaps that's why they don't mind hecklers, she thought wearily, they just bring up a fresh head of steam.

"I'm fed up with you council estate scum breaking in here and tramping all over the grounds. You've no respect for other people's property and you bring up your brats the same way. But when it gets to stealing from the house itself . . ."

"I've stolen nothing." Childhood memories of similar accusations flooded Mary's mind. "Look, you can see for yourself." She turned out the pockets of her anorak, leaving the drawings lying snug against the lining, and showing only the little wallet she carried with her driver's licence, keys and money. It was not her habit to carry a handbag unless dressed for it, and this had been no such occasion. "And I have keys to get in here because I'm looking over the grounds for a prospective purchaser. You can check with the agents."

But she might as well have been talking in a foreign language; the Honourable Member for Welchester West had cloth ears when he wished. He belonged moreover to the tribe of those who are never in the wrong – and when they are they put up the screens and blast all comers with high velocity rhetoric.

"A likely tale," he sneered, for all the world like a character

71

in melodrama. "I bet you stole those keys. I've a mind to take you straight to the police station but I haven't got the time. Just get out of here before I change my mind."

"You are mistaken," Mary protested, trying out one of her upper-class accents.

It was no use. Tory ministers do not make mistakes and, although Stephen Durward-Cooke was only a junior, he had nevertheless the proper Conservative attitude to his own infallibility; it was God-given and absolute.

"It's you who are mistaken," he roared as if he were on a platform and Mary lost somewhere in the back of the hall, "mistaken, and been found out. Now, get out! Go back where you came from on that lousy council estate, and you can tell your mates that the next time I catch any of you in these grounds I'll prosecute."

As he turned sharply on his heel, Mary heard him mutter: "Bloody layabouts . . ." before he strode off, presumably towards some urgent engagement upon which the future of the world depended.

As she came round to the front of the house, however, he was standing in the open doorway, watching her. She had no option but to return the way she had come, down the drive between the whispering laurels.

"Oh, talk among yourselves . . ." she told them savagely as she went past. She felt more than anger; she had been brought low, humiliated and rendered wordless by a hectoring bully-boy – for, whatever his position and class, she had sensed under the man's outward behaviour that surge of almost sensual pleasure all bullies feel when a victim has strayed within the orbit of their power. What lower-class louts did with fists, Durward-Cooke and his like did with words.

She saw that his car had been parked at the front door of the house. That must have been the movement she had glimpsed for a second when she was in the conservatory, perhaps the sun glinting on the windscreen and reflected back from the glass. There would just have been enough time for him to get out of the car, walk round to the greenhouse and attack her as she shut the door. He was a powerful man, and tall, tall enough to reach up for the wooden strut he'd used as a weapon. But surely, even for an enraged property-owner intercepting a burglar, wasn't his action a bit forceful, a bit extreme to be used against a woman?

So Mary made her protest that evening to her husband.

Lennox Kemp just looked at her. "Were you wearing that anorak thing of yours, the one with the big hood at the back?"

"Yes. I thought it might rain in the afternoon, and, anyway I wasn't dressed for going into town."

Kemp considered the facts. "Well," he said, "I hate to say this but looked at from the rear you could easily be mistaken for a lad, given what you're wearing. Did you have your wellies on?"

"Gum boots? Of course. You warned it could be rough underfoot."

"And he saw you at the door of that greenhouse thing. You could have been breaking in. You said the door was off the hinge . . ."

"No." Mary was trying to be accurate. "The hinge was broken but the door itself was intact in its frame. You're not trying to tell me his action was justified?"

"Not quite. But what he may have seen is someone breaking into his property. The place has been empty so long there's bound to have been vandalism and this time he thought he'd caught a villain in the act."

"He could have explained . . . Spoken first and acted afterwards." Mary's fury revived. "The man's an insensitive boor, he just wouldn't listen to me."

"Ah, that's the politics leading the man. His lot aren't taught to listen: they might hear something to make them think and thinking hurts." He looked down at the drawings Mary had spread out on the table. "Let's see what you've got here."

One was an old plan of the house, the rooms marked and designated: drawing-room, dining-room, morning-room, parlour, bedrooms, one bathroom, kitchens, sculleries and outbuildings, including the small glassed-in area on the south side. The other plan was of the conservatory-greenhouse which had replaced it. In one corner of this sketch were the words: 'Geo. Weston & Co., Bldrs, Newtown'.

"These will have to go back," said Kemp, "they're stolen property."

Mary looked offended. "I only wanted Miss Weston to see them."

"I know, but in the circumstances I think I should return them to Mr Quigley and say you picked them up by mistake. It's just to forestall any complaint Stephen Durward-Cooke might make." Seeing her pained expression, he added: "I'll have them copied in my office first, of course. Then you'll have something to show Miss Weston. Now, to get back to whether you were deliberately felled or not, tell me more about this ornament thing. Where was it when you saw it first?"

"On the point of the glass roof above the door. A tall man could easily reach up and twist it off. The wood was rotten but it was heavy, rounded like a chair leg."

"Its called a finial. It should have been secure enough unless you shook the door-frame when you went out."

"I was so careful closing the door, I'm sure nothing I did could have dislodged that ornament. Maybe you're right. Durward-Cooke thought I was one of the local louts – as he would call them – and when he discovered he'd knocked down a woman he covered up his mistake by a furious show of temper."

"Or it could have been someone else . . ."

"No way." Mary was emphatic. "I'd have known."

Kemp shrugged. "Sounds as if it was open house out there. Perhaps there were other prowlers . . ."

But he did not pursue it. Intuition told him that Mary had been hurt in mind more than body. At thirty-six she may have considered herself immune to the kind of slights suffered in girlhood. When poverty-stricken in Vineland, she had struggled to bring up her errant siblings. The odd one out in a tribe of no-gooders, she had by guile and good fortune broken free but early memories can rankle when a nerve is touched.

"That man made me feel like one of those people on the council estate," she said now, as if following his line of thought, "and they sure have my sympathy. All very well for the likes of him, being well born and having that command of language his private education gives him. But he could just have done it with words, he didn't have to knock me down as well. That time I saw him at the college I was hoping one of those tomatoes would hit him. Now I know he'd probably have thrown it back . . ." She stopped when she saw that her husband was smiling.

"And you can stop grinning," she said. "It's no laughing matter."

"That's what they said when Gladstone made a joke in the House," said Kemp, hoping by the diversion to take her mind from the subject of Durward-Cooke to the more immediate one of what they were going to have for dinner. Lennox was beginning to feel that the obnoxious member for Welchester West had invaded their kitchen.

It was bad enough that Kemp would now have to compose a wretchedly tactful letter to Simon Quigley and return the drawings. Inadvertent appropriation rather than petty pilfering.

Nine

G ood fortune, however, intervened and there was no need for the apology; instead the drawings were simply referred to in the postscript to another letter altogether from Gillorns, solicitors to Simon Quigley of Acme Properties. 'Our representative happened to pick up some drawings of Deloraine Court while inspecting the property. In view of the above we shall hand them over to our client – with your permission, of course'. A bit cheeky perhaps but Kemp was feeling jubilant; a buyer had been found for the whole Deloraine estate.

Alan Brinscombe had made a lot of money in the building boom of the early eighties when he and his brother Dennis ran a successful builders' business in Newtown, catching its development at just the right time.

The building trade has its shady back alleys as well as superior façades. Dennis Brinscombe had strayed into one of these in pursuit of not altogether legitimate profits and it was Lennox Kemp who had extricated him, and saved the firm from collapsing in the resultant mess. Both brothers had been grateful. Dennis, having learned his lesson, kept the business ticking over through the depression while Alan, the elder, had retired to his Spanish villa to enjoy a well-earned rest.

But it was Alan who was back, sitting now in Kemp's office, looking tanned and healthy but by no means relaxed.

"Boring," he said, "that was what we found it. Golf, sunshine and too many oranges . . . boring. Brenda got fed up making marmalade. I got fed-up talking to ex-pats. Neither she nor I spoke Spanish so I couldn't even go down to the local. I've worked all my life, Lennox, I just can't stop. I've got plenty of money but idleness don't suit me."

"How did you hear about Deloraine Court?"

"Dennis gave me a buzz. I knew it was up for sale a couple of years ago, thought it must have long gone. Then he tells me it's still on the market. Well, as things stand with the business of course it was out of the question. But, if I came back in, I've got the capital and he's still got most of the work force."

"And you're dying to get cracking." Kemp laughed. "You want back in the game."

Alan Brinscombe looked somewhat shame-faced. "Most people would envy me and Bren," he said. "Enough money for the easy life, no need to work. But it don't suit us, being rich. We've never had kids. What's the point of us with all that capital invested? You know I've damn nearly doubled it since I left the firm?" he added, slyly.

"Good money buys good financial advisers," remarked Kemp, "and you yourself were always a canny investor. Why are you so keen on acquiring the Deloraine estate?"

"Because it's there," replied Alan, simply, "and by this time the vendor must be desperate and ready to do a deal. That's the kind I like."

"He's not lowered the selling price."

"Can't understand why not," said Alan, "the place'll be derelict by now. Anyway, it's the land I'm after. I gather from Dennis that there's planning permission for fifty units. Well, I wouldn't try to squeeze in more. High-class development, that's what I've got in mind. There's money in the City of London these days, and them that's making it need homes they can commute to. I'll give them town houses with a bit of style, a lot of meadow grass, clap on a few tree preservation orders and they'll think they're saving the countryside. Those high-paid yobs, they're not looking for a semi in Walthamstow . . ."

"Don't knock Walthamstow," said Kemp, absently. "Some of my best work was done down there."

"That's right. That detective agency you were in before you came out here and went legit." Alan grinned. "Me and my lot, we were just along the road in Hackney Wick. I learned it all under the railway arches in me dad's building yard. If I made enough for the brass I screwed off them old gas cookers, I could get to the pictures of a Saturday . . ."

It was because they had reciprocal knowledge of each other's

background that the two men had always got on so well
together. Now they could laugh in reminiscent mood about
past times which for neither of them had been pleasant.

Kemp, struck off by the Law Society for embezzlement
of trust funds which he had used to pay off his first wife's
gambling debts and eking out a living on the darker side
of the profession which had rejected him; Alan Brinscombe
struggling to climb out of the criminal class to which his
father, albeit unsuccessfully, had belonged; they could both
look back now with some measure of complacency, but neither
could entirely forget nor wish to expunge from the tablets of
their memory certain impressions of another life.

However, as if the two of them realised at the same time a
more realistic aspect of their present meeting, they looked at
the clock in Kemp's office.

"You'll be charging me for this," said Alan, getting to his
feet. "That's one thing didn't bother us in Spain: time. I tell
you, mate – there was too damn much of it."

"Bring Brenda round for dinner one evening," Kemp told
him at the door, "I think our wives will like each other. In
the meantime I'll get on with the paperwork. Are you going
to haggle the price?"

"I don't haggle," said Alan Brinscombe, seriously. "I'll just
tell them what I'm prepared to pay, they can take it or leave
it. But I know they'll take it. My accountant's done his sums,
what I'm offering's a fair price."

"How well do you know Deloraine Court itself?"

"The house you mean? Not at all. I'm not interested.
When we had that contract for the council estates those
Durward-Cookes tried to block every planning application
that went in, but they couldn't stop the development. That
would have been the rising young MP and his mother, the
Lady Deloraine herself . . ."

"She wasn't titled, Alan."

"Acted like she were. Anyway, it's what the men on the
site called her. She'd be floating around these great gardens
of hers like she was Queen of the May."

"Ah, that reminds me. I've got some plans of the house . . ."
Kemp turned back to his desk.

"Don't bother," shouted Brinscombe from the corridor. "I'm not interested in the house. First thing we do when we get in there is pull the place down."

Mary didn't tell Gwendolyne Weston that when she spread out the drawings on the old lady's little side table. "I've had a look at your father's handiwork," she said, "and what a fine piece it is . . ."

She described what she had seen, concentrating on the plants still growing in the greenhouse. Though she had had only a brief glimpse of them before catastrophe struck, she had taken the trouble to look up their probable names in Olga's book.

"There were some with pink and white petals," she said, remembering how the blooms had been crushed up against the glass as if desperate for a glimmer of sun. "They'd be camellias, I'm thinking. And creamy white with real dark fleshy leaves, would that be a gardenia? I've never seen them grow like that." She didn't add that those plants still alive were out of control, and under them there must have been many others that had died long ago.

But Miss Weston knew how things would be. Her face was sad as the wax-white fingers of her good hand played on the lines her father had drawn, then they pointed down at his signature.

"He would be his own draughtsman, then?" Mary inquired.

A fierce nod, with pride.

"Would you be wanting to keep these?" said Mary. "They're only copies, but you're welcome to them."

There was no response. That blankness with which Mary was becoming familiar had settled over the old lady's features and her brow was furrowed; some inner struggle was going on in a mind half-crippled. Had it been only a broken limb, thought Mary sadly, it could have been splinted, mended, exercised and made whole, but as it was the brain the original influx of blood must have done irreparable damage.

Yet there was something there. Miss Weston's eyes were looking inward but they were not vacant; it was as if they scanned a screen covered in hieroglyphics they could not read. Her forefinger was pressing so hard on the sketch the paper was beginning to crease. Over and over again she traced the lines of the greenhouse.

"You're trying to tell me something?" Mary had suddenly caught a look, a spark in the faded blue eyes. "It's about the conservatory your father built?"

"Now don't you be getting her in a tizz." It was Prim Sutton's hard little voice behind Mary. "Just look what you've done."

With a movement that was so abrupt as to be rude she elbowed Mary aside, and put an arm round the old lady. "Can't you see all she wants is the bathroom? Come on, Auntie Gwen, I know what you need."

She hustled Miss Weston into the invalid chair, and marched off with her to the bathroom where she banged the door hard as if to show she would have no more interference with her duties.

Mary stood for a moment, then she gathered up the drawings, thoughtfully, folded them and put them back in her pocket.

It was always the same in this house, there seemed to be always someone about, someone watching. The old lady had been alone when she came in; she assumed Prim was out to fetch Liza-Jane from playschool. Presumably she had returned by the back door . . . Or had she been there all the time?

She heard the front door slam, and the little girl came running in, still in her cap and coat. "Look what I draw'd, Auntie Mary . . ." Mary laughed at the onion-shape and tuft of black hair.

"I hope that's not your mum, and her kind enough to collect you today . . ."

Liza-Jane's face took on the expression infants adopt when they decide grown-ups are all idiots. "I come with Amy's mum." She giggled and raced off towards the bathroom door where she collided with the invalid chair coming out. "For goodness' sake, child, why can't you look where you're going? And stop tearing about like that. If you've wet your pants again . . ."

It was obviously not going to be one of Prim's better days, so Mary prudently retreated to the quieter atmosphere of her own home.

There she took out the drawings and looked at them again but they told her nothing new. The one of the house itself was a mere sketch, drawn to show where the new glasshouse would replace the Victorian structure – a mere glassed-in lean-to extending only a short distance out from the south wall. Beyond it there had been a rosebed and presumably this had had to be sacrificed for the new conservatory. As Mary had seen from her brief visit to the gardens there were in any case plenty of other rosebeds scattered about.

George Weston had been as painstaking with his drawing of the building as he had been with its construction. Exact dimensions were given, and there was a note to say he had 'cast metal cresting, traditional finials' (not also of metal, Mary noticed, or she might well have ended up in hospital) and 'some ornamental panels, from glasshouses recently demolished at Seldon Park'. Obviously Mr Weston had been a man of resource. And he would have needed to be, Lennox had told her, because at the time he was doing the building for the Durward-Cookes his trade would still be hindered by post-war shortages.

Nowadays, thought Mary, if you wanted a conservatory you just went out and bought one. Pity the whole thing would now have to come down to make way for Brinscombe Bros.' dream houses . . . but she wasn't going to brood on that. She was not sentimental, and her only visit to the house had ended unpleasantly. All the same she felt a slight pang of wistful regret for the lost beauty of the gardens; the roses shedding their petals year by year, the trees turning to gold, that lusty growth under the glass still thrusting upwards.

As she put the drawings back between the pages of *A Garden in Summer* she glanced again at the photograph of the writer. 'Lady Deloraine' the building workers had called her, half-mocking. There had been no love lost between the owners of Deloraine Court and the up-and-coming developers spreading out from Newtown into the surrounding countryside. Perhaps it had been wise of Stephen to go for a constituency far from the house where he had been born. Mary knew little of how the British parliamentary machine worked – though it did

seem a lot simpler than the one it had spawned in the States
– but she was learning fast.

The midday mail brought a letter from Grace Juniper's
sister. They had kept up a desultory correspondence since
Mrs Prentice's return to Yorkshire, and Mary had sent her the
letters of condolence which came in from schools where Grace
had taught and been remembered. Primrose Sutton passed them
on to Mary: "Well, you know the sister . . . I wouldn't know
what to say. The whole thing was so embarrassing."

It seemed a mild word, and inappropriate to a death, but
Mary had found that Prim could be, if not exactly callous,
at least insensitive to other people's feelings. Moreover, it
was as if she wished to keep Grace Juniper firmly where she
belonged – in the past. Prim did not want to discuss her or the
accident. Of course, being Prim, she was ready to rationalise
this attitude. "Best for all concerned," she said, "specially the
old lady and the child, if it's not talked about. Least said,
soonest mended." She had a way of making clichés sound
newly minted.

In deference to her wishes – after all, it was practically
Prim's house – Mary spoke of Grace only when she and Miss
Weston were alone and – as she had noticed in recent weeks –
that was seldom. The interdict appeared to have been handed
on to both the Quigleys and Gregory Venn; an attempt by Mary
to raise the subject in conversation had been brushed-off – in
marked contrast to the days immediately following the event
when Gregory seemed bent on needling Primrose about the
circumstances.

'How is the elderly lady next door?' Shirley Prentice had
written. 'Our Grace took a great interest in her for she'd done
speech therapy at a stroke clinic. I wonder if she ever solved
that problem about the dig? I know Eric sent her some books
– it's a hobby of his since he retired. He doesn't want them
back – he's got quite enough already . . .'

Mary wondered what Shirely Prentice meant by 'the dig'
and remembered the books on archaeology put away at the
foot of the cupboard in the study. She looked them out, and
sure enough on each of the fly-leaves: 'Eric Prentice'. Well,
archaeology wasn't on her present course of study – which she

had been neglecting lately with this diversion – so she would put it on one side for now.

All the same, she vowed, one of these days I'll have a proper word with Gwen Weston alone. All it needs is time and patience.

Ten

"I'm running out of time and Mr Brinscombe's running out of patience." Charles Copeland was exasperated. He seated himself on the edge of a chair in Lennox Kemp's room and tossed the Deloraine Court property file on to the desk.

Kemp picked it up. "What's the trouble? I thought it was all going smoothly. Alan agreed the price with Quigleys, spot-on, and I had Cedric Roberts on the blower in no time. He's acting for Durward-Cooke. I thought the rest was plain sailing."

Charles was Gillorns' conveyancing clerk and he had dealt with Brinscombe Bros.' acquisitions competently enough in the past.

"It's nothing to do with Roberts," he said. "As the vendor's solicitors they've been as anxious as we are to see the sale goes through quickly. We should have been exchanging contracts by now, the bulk of the work's done – and then there's this hitch."

"What hitch?"

"It's the agents. They're stalling."

"But that's ridiculous!" It was an agent's business to find a proper purchaser at a reasonable price then bow out until it was time to collect their commission – in this case it would be a fat one. "How do you mean, the agents are stalling?"

Charles sat back more comfortably. "I get along fine with young David Roberts who's in charge their end. We have the odd pint together. We don't usually talk business but I was so fed up after over a month's delay that I asked him outright. He said, 'Don't blame us, mate – it's Simon Quigley who's thrown a spanner in the works.'"

"How?"

Charles shrugged. "I think Roberts are as much in the dark

84

as we are. All young David could tell me was that Simon
Quigley had said hold the exchange. I got a right earful from
Mr Brinscombe when I told him. It means he can't get on the
land to clear it, and there he is with his demolition gang at the
ready, and all his extra equipment hired. It's a condition of the
contract that he gets access on exchange."

"Yes, Alan's always worked like that – and it's in the
vendor's interest, too. Means the developer will hardly pull
out when he's spent money on the site, and both parties get
an early completion."

"Mr Brinscombe's threatening to withdraw altogether if they
don't get on with it. And it's no skin off his nose that I can see.
He can always take his money back to Spain."

"H'm . . . I'm surprised that Roberts don't advise their client
to ignore Simon Quigley. Durward-Cooke's never going to get
a better offer for the place than this one of Brinscombes'. I
wonder what on earth Quigley's up to . . . Leave the file with
me, Charlie, and I'll have a look at it."

"If you find anything amiss in there, Mr Kemp, I'll eat the
paper it's written on." Charles prided himself on his work,
and was indeed meticulous to a fault in his investigation
of title, perusal of the often badly smudged print on local
searches, and interpretation of sometimes ambiguous planning
conditions. Now he stumped from the room in a huff.

After an hour – and as he expected – Kemp could find
nothing wrong, nothing missed and nothing mishandled in
the purchase file. Roberts had obviously held the deeds to
the property for a long time and knew them backwards, old
planning consents had been regularly renewed and enquiries
updated, plans of the boundaries were accurate, and all the
conditions on the contract were reasonable and nothing was
too onerous for the purchaser. Kemp noticed that some of the
less important work at Roberts, solicitors for the vendor, had
been done by Gregory Venn. Apparently the young articled
clerk had been given something to cut his teeth on. Interesting
that, the connection between young Venn and the Quigleys . . .
But, so far as Kemp was aware, neither Jasper nor Blanche
was connected with the business of Acme Properties although
Simon would be their uncle. Their own father was 'something

in the City' – although, like not a few others, recently affected by shortfalls at Lloyds.

Kemp pushed the file to one side. There was nothing in it which would account for the delay in exchanging contracts, and he could see from recent letters the frustration being felt by Charles Copeland.

He reached for the phone, and asked the switchboard to get him Cedric Roberts.

After the usual pleasantries, Kemp said he was phoning about the Deloraine Court property; why the delay?

"I'm sure it's not our doing . . . David's handling it."

"I know that, but I'm asking you, Cedric. Stephen Durward-Cooke's your client, and you know Simon Quigley. If there's been a falling-out between these two, then you're the one who'd know . . ."

"What do you mean, a falling-out? Who told you that?" Cedric Roberts' speech was a little slurred; Kemp knew that he liked a drink at lunchtime and a nap in the office afterwards. He seemed to have caught the old man just as he was waking up; but Kemp decided to press on.

"Nobody's told me anything except that the agents seem to have stepped in just when contracts are about to be exchanged, and no reason given. Now, you've got the vendor's interests at heart so I'm letting you know that Brinscombe is prepared to pull out altogether if things don't get moving – fast."

"No need to take that attitude. I'll have a word with David . . . I'm not quite – er – *au fait* with the matter myself . . ."

Kemp knew that Cedric Roberts was rarely *au fait* with anything that went on in his offices after three in the afternoon, and it was now nearly four o'clock. He had no wish to rile the old boy who, in Kemp's opinion, ought to be considering strategic retirement.

"Why not have a quiet word yourself with Mr Durward-Cooke," he suggested, diplomatically, "and find out what the hold-up is about? You might also tell him that Alan Brinscombe isn't bluffing about a possible withdrawal from the deal. Strictly off the record, Cedric, he has the capital to buy the Deloraine property twice over. He's looking at the development as something to stave off old age

. . . a challenge, if you like to keep his brain from going soft." Kemp thought this approach might appeal to Cedric since he was himself coming up to seventy and possibly regarded attendance at his office every day in the same light.

Cedric grunted. "You make him sound a proper Don Quixote," he snorted.

"Well, Alan Brinscombe has been in Spain a few years – perhaps he didn't find enough windmills left there." Both men laughed at their opposite ends of the phone, but it was Kemp who added on a harder note: "Just make sure your client understands the position – he may not get another chance. And if you've got a line to Quigleys you might find out what their problem is." Kemp tried to keep his voice non-committal although everyone who did business in Newtown was well aware that Quigleys and Roberts were in each other's pockets and had been for years.

"Well – er – I do see Simon from time to time . . ." Cedric seemed to hesitate in going further, but then something occurred to him. "As a matter of fact I did him a favour not long ago."

"Yes?" Kemp prompted.

"A young protégé of his . . . wanted articles . . . I took him on. He's doing all right, actually but, yes, maybe Simon owes me one . . ."

"I'll leave it with you, then. Don't want any upsets over this, do we? Stakes are too high, eh?"

As Kemp put the phone down he told himself he was getting as cynical as everybody else. Well, money talks when you want anything done, he admonished his better instincts.

Kemp had other instincts, too. They led him into thinking it was time he had a look for himself at this piece of valuable property.

"Get on to Quigleys," he told his secretary, "and tell them I want to check up on some measurements on the contract plan, and would be grateful for access. Say I'll pick up the keys to the gates on my way."

"No need to stop for those keys," she told him as he was leaving the office, "Quigleys have got someone out there already this afternoon. They'll get him on his mobile and he'll let you in."

On an impulse Kemp went home first.

He found Mary with G.M. Trevelyan, trying to come to terms with English social history, but she was not averse to leaving it for a frolic out in the late autumn sunshine.

"I don't get it," she said as they drove off. "How could all those Victorians have had such optimism. It's pathetic."

"They wouldn't have thought so. It's only because we've lived in the aftermath . . ."

"When everything went crash, bang, wallop?"

"You could call it that." Kemp thought his wife might have a point in her view of the twentieth century.

"Where are we off to?" she asked when they were out on the ring road.

"Deloraine Court. As you're so interested in the place I thought you'd like a second look – from a more privileged position this time."

"Thank you, sir," she said, primly. "You know I'm beginning to understand where people like the Durward-Cookes get their high and mighty airs from. They take their stance on privilege as if it was a right. You'd think that for them it was built into the constitution."

"We haven't got a constitution."

"Maybe that lot wouldn't have got so cocky if you had."

"Don't be too sure of that. It's probably them would draft the thing. You'd be better talking this thing over with your social studies mentor. When it comes to politics, I'm just a cynic. Well, well," as they reached the turning into Deloraine Court, "looks like we're expected, the gates are open."

"I do feel more equal arriving in style," Mary observed as they drove up to the front of the house. "Good heavens, it's young Jasper."

It was indeed Jasper Quigley who was standing on the front steps. He looked rather uneasy as they approached. "Hullo," he said, "I came out with Uncle Simon."

As it was only Jasper, Mary felt she could take the initiative.

"That's some car," she remarked, nodding at the vehicle

standing in the driveway. It looked to her like something left over from a Gulf War battlefield. In civilian space it was the type of machine driven by those who liked to look down on their fellow motorists.

"Great, isn't it?" said Jasper, patting the high bonnet. "Uncle lets me take the wheel sometimes when we're out on a job."

"I didn't know you actually worked for your uncle," said Mary. "I thought you were with the Acme." She was being deliberately mischievous and knew it.

Jasper blushed – like his sister's his skin had that tendency. Before he could reply, Kemp said, smartly: "They're the same thing, Mary. Don't tease."

Then he turned to the man who had emerged from the shadow of the porch. "Ah, Mr Quigley."

Simon Quigley was much more like Mary's idea of an English Member of Parliament than his cousin. Whereas Stephen was inclined to puffiness, this man of property had a long, lean look, and the high-boned features of a true aristocrat.

Kemp and he shook hands. "Haven't seen you since that Amwell planning inquiry. Hear you got married." The accent, the nasal bray were the same as his cousin's. Upper class, cutting as a crystal edge, the voice must make an impression on clients but would be built-in and not intentionally patronising.

Kemp introduced Mary. "Oh, so you're the one. Stephen told me about that little episode . . ." He turned away and spoke to Kemp as if further explanation would be wasted on a mere woman. "Says he's sorry . . . genuine mistake . . . Now if you'll just show me where you want to take those measurements, Kemp, then I'll be glad to come with you before the light fails."

Kemp was having none of that. "My client's business, Mr Quigley. Distances between trees and houses. Brinscombes putting in for preservation orders, wouldn't do to get it wrong, eh? Don't worry about us, my wife and I will be here for some time."

"I could lend you young Jasper . . ."

"Wouldn't dream of it. I'm sure you've got other things to

attend to elsewhere. Lock up the house, of course, we've no interest in it." By now Kemp had produced measuring tape and a notebook and pen which he handed to Mary. "Let's get on with it before it gets dark. If you'll let me have the key to the gate, Mr Quigley, we'll secure it when we leave. By the way, you might tell your cousin that if the deal with my client doesn't go through, I don't see any other developer being interested. Do you?"

Lennox Kemp may have measured up to the estate agent neither in height nor high-handed manner, but when required the terrier in Kemp could bite. Simon Quigley looked too stunned for words, then in silence while Kemp waited, he detached the large key from the bunch he carried, and handed it over. There was a giggle from Jasper which was instantly smothered. Mary grinned at him, making him more self-conscious than ever so that he moved into the shadow of the big Land-rover for protective cover.

"Better make some show of taking those measurements," muttered Kemp as they walked across the lawn in the direction of a clump of elms, but he need not have worried. Behind them they heard the front door slam, and a moment later the car roared down the drive, spurting gravel from its tyres. Jasper was at the wheel, his uncle stony-faced at his side.

"Let's go look at that conservatory," said Mary.

"What do you hope to find?"

"I haven't a notion, but those drawings that I found in there are now sticking out of Mr Quigley's top pocket."

"Is that so? Well, well. His office made a great fuss about getting them back; I can't imagine why. Anyway, I returned them."

"But not before you'd made copies," said Mary, producing them. "They're getting a bit dog-eared with me carrying them about but I'm thinking they meant a lot to the old lady. It was almost as if she was trying to tell me something about the actual building."

They rounded the corner of the house as the lowering sun was starting to cast long shadows across its walls.

"Somebody's been having a right go at it," exclaimed Mary,

"that door's hanging off its hinge, and there's a lot more glass smashed. It wasn't like that when I saw it."

She followed Kemp as he walked gingerly up the steps, and ducked in the door. "And all the plants have gone," she cried as she stepped over broken pots, wrecked shelving and heaps of soil.

"I think Mr Quigley and young Jasper have been clearing up in here."

"Clearing up! They've made a right mess of it. And the conservatory's ruined." All the wicker furniture had disappeared, and the floor was stripped bare.

"Probably in the back of the Land-rover," said Kemp, "and some of the plants too. The rest are just thrown outside." There was a lot of dark foliage lying on the ground beyond the broken glass of the windows.

The patio doors that led from the conservatory into the house were securely locked. One could only look darkly through at a large, bare, unfurnished drawing-room, which in turn stared back as if the glazed doors were no protection.

"They were open when I was here," said Mary, "and I had the thought at the time that I could have gone in. I do like looking in other people's houses."

Kemp shuddered. "That's what the burglar told the judge, Mary. It's a tendency you must curb." He looked round at the devastation. "Well, I don't see anything here that need detain us."

"Sadly, no . . . but then I don't know what I'm looking for. Why should Mr Quigley want to destroy this place? Because that's what he's been doing. There's a couple of pickaxes lying outside, and he had soil on his nice pinstripe. What on earth were he and Jasper up to, trying to knock this place down?"

Kemp shrugged. "He'd probably say it was because it's a dangerous structure, young trespassers might get hurt by falling glass."

"You can't be serious?"

"Neither would Quigley, but it would be a good enough excuse."

"Yes, but why?" Mary persisted. "You said yourself that

Brinscombes would demolish the whole house as soon as they got on the land."

"So why are one man and a boy out here doing the job for them? I agree it's a puzzle. Come on, let me have a look at those sketches again in a better light."

They sat on a garden seat against an ivied wall that caught the last rays of the dying sun, and Mary spread out the drawings.

"What did it say in the book," Kemp asked her, "about how the conservatory came to be built?"

Mary thought back carefully. The fact that she had so recently come to studying made her brain retentive of words. "Colonel Percival was still in the Army. He wanted to give his wife a present of a conservatory for her beloved plants, and he did it real cute. Took her out with him to Singapore on his next posting – she did not usually go with him due to her frail health – and when they were away he had the conservatory put up by a local builder. This happened in the early fifties. Her book simply says how delighted she was with it, and that the builder had a real feeling for the Victorian. I can't remember anything else except that, in the end, Olga Durward-Cooke thought it was worth losing the other rose bed which had been there too long anyway."

"I can see from the plan where the original bed was, just beyond the lean-to with the glass roof tacked on to the side of the house – that's all the first conservatory would have been. It was only after some Dutchman worked out how to build with sloping glass that they became all the rage. The rose bed would have been laid out when Deloraine Court was built – probably in the 1870s."

"There are mentions of gardeners in the book, but only one of them by name. Samuels, she called him, with that kind of distant affection the English gentry seem to keep for their butlers and pet dogs. He'd be dead by now; she wrote about him as if he was already old."

"H'm . . . I wonder if Barry Samuels who runs that big garden centre on the ring road is any connection. Perhaps horticulture stayed in the family. Come on, Mary, it's getting cold out here and it'll soon be dark."

They went back to the car but before she got in Mary turned

for another look at the house. "Deloraine Court," she said, "must have been the fine place when it was alive. Now it's to be razed to the ground. There's an expression my mother used when she talked of the great houses gone in the Troubles . . . bare earth, neither stick nor stone to show they'd ever been . . ."

"Well, there'll be a tidy sum out of it for Stephen Durward-Cooke," said Kemp, briskly. "And no troubles that I can see – unless it's of Quigley's making. I still can't figure out why he was so disturbed at us being there. He couldn't think up an excuse fast enough or he'd have stopped us going round on our own."

"It's that conservatory." Mary was certain. "If only poor Miss Weston could talk, I'm sure she'd tell us . . ."

"Tell us what? That the body's buried in the rose bed?"

Mary stared at him, startled, until he burst out laughing.

"Only a joke," he said. "It's what they say in crime stories when they're all gathered in the library asking each other whatever happened to Uncle Silas. And, talking of uncles, I heard you twit that lad about him working for Acme Properties. I thought Jasper was in the City?"

"He was, but Primrose murmured something about his firm cutting back; maybe he was one of the twigs they pruned. She said his uncle was helping out. Like most of what Prim says it's a bit vague." Mary had lost interest in Jasper Quigley. "Don't you think it's time we had some shrubs to fill those gaps in our garden," she said, casually. "That garden place might be worth a visit."

Her husband said nothing. He knew that when Mary got a bee in her bonnet it would go on buzzing till it was let out.

Eleven

"And I'll be back later for some paving stones – but that's more in my husband's line . . ." Samuels' Garden Centre provided a handy wheelbarrow which Mary had brought to the cash desk. Her visit was not entirely inquisitorial; it was the season to buy fresh bulbs for the patch of grass where the back garden of 2 Albert Crescent met the sluggish trickle of the River Lea. Had it not been for that remark of Lennox's she might well have bought them in the town. As it was, her order for bulbs and new shrubs was a substantial one, so that when she enquired of the boy carrying her purchases to the car if Mr Barry Samuels was available, the owner himself popped out of his office as soon as he was told. It was a quiet weekday morning, Barry was fed up checking his VAT returns and glad of the break. Besides, his assistant hinted that Mrs Kemp had already placed a large order.

"If I could just take another look at those flagstones," she murmured, "to get some idea of the colour."

"Sure. We've a wide selection." Mr Samuels, a middle-aged man with an out-of-doors complexion, led the way through the store and out of the back into the sunshine. He liked to chat with customers when he had the time and this small unassuming woman had a pleasant manner. When they had dealt satisfactorily with the Kemps' need for new pathways and possible renewal of a patio, he invited Mary to sit for a while on a fine bench – perhaps hoping she would find it comfortable enough to merit a place in her own garden. By now Mary had learned much of the Samuels' family history, and knew she had struck gold.

"So, your late father was a head gardener?"

"In the London parks he'd been, before coming to Newtown.

That was back in the thirties. Come the war, he was too old for calling-up and he was glad of the job out at Deloraine Court."

"And I am sure they must have been equally glad to have him. The Durward-Cookes, I mean."

"Oh, you know the place, Mrs Kemp?"

"I am afraid not as it was in those days. I've only been there recently but I can see what beautiful gardens they must have been, and of course Mrs Durward-Cooke mentions your father in a book someone has shown me."

"Oh, that." Barry Samuels gave a grin. "She might have given him a bit more credit. He worked all hours to fit in with her wishes but it didn't do him much good in the long run; he was given the chop when it suited them. And there was no redundancy money in those days . . ."

"It sounds a mite ungrateful," said Mary, just to show whose side she was on.

Barry took a chance on her lack of accent, and a quick assessment of the clothes she was wearing, to air views that might have remained hidden with some other customers.

"Typical of that lot," he said, "thought they owned us in those days. My dad took it bad being given the sack the way he was – and all because of a damned greenhouse. But I tell you this, Mrs Kemp, it was a lesson to me. Made me swear I'd be my own boss when I came out of the Army. I'd never go hat in hand to any employer . . ."

"And you've proved yourself the better man for it," said Mary, glancing round the prosperous-looking premises. She gave pause enough to show her appreciation before enquiring, innocently: "The greenhouse? How did the greenhouse come into it?"

"Dug up his prize roses to build it, didn't they?" Barry Samuels caught himself re-living an old bitterness, the sense of injustice which had clouded his father's latter years so that when Barry had come home the house reeked of it. "I'm sorry," he said, lamely. "It was a long time ago, and you'd not be interested."

"Oh, but I am." Mary assured him, gently. "Would that be the greenhouse George Weston built?"

Barry nodded. "Mr Weston and my father had a right

95

falling-out over it. Not that they'd ever been cronies – George Weston thought himself too high and mighty for that. 'The Colonel's orders'," Barry aped the strangulated vowels, "'the Colonel's orders must be obeyed', old Weston kept saying as if he was his batman. So the rose bed had to go. Well, there wasn't much my dad could do about it except dig it up as ordered. But, oh, no, that wasn't good enough for Mr Weston, he'd do any digging that had to be done to his precious foundations. He said Dad wasn't fit, that he was to keep off the ground, mebbe do a bit of grass-cutting and the like, but not go near where Weston was putting up the greenhouse. Dad swore afterwards that those roses got took up and died, for all that George Weston said he'd re-plant them. So, by the time the gentry came home from their Army posting, Dad was in a right bolshie frame of mind, I'd say. Anyways, it wasn't long before they gave him the push."

"I think they were very unfair," said Mary, "and I don't like the sound of Mr George Weston at all. All those roses . . ."

But Barry Samuels was thinking that perhaps he had gone too far, and he returned to the philosophic view which was more normal for him to take in his everyday dealings. "Two old men quarreling . . . I guess it makes no difference now . . ."

For the purpose of continuing goodwill, Mary went along with that. "I guess not," she said, and abandoned for the moment the discord between builder and gardener, which seemed an echo of the traditional difference between those who till the land and those who put up homesteads. "I live next door to Miss Gwendolyne Weston and it was her gave me the book."

"Good Lord, is she still alive? Worth ten of her old man, my mother always said. Yes, Miss Weston was in with the nobs up at Deloraine Court, and I think Mrs Durward-Cooke was grateful for her company after the Colonel died, for she took it bad and never went out much from what I hear. Is she in good health? I don't think she ever married . . ."

Mary explained Miss Weston's circumstances and in return was given a little more of her earlier history, as seen through the eyes of Barry's mother. As a girl, Gwen had been considered 'clever' (not meant as a compliment) and because she had been sent to private schools she was rather above the common lot. She had been made an officer in the ATS (as it then was) which gave her status on her return to civilian life and, in Barry's opinion, she should have been allowed to run the business if old Weston had had the sense to see it.

"But by that time the firm was going rapidly down hill," Barry finished off – not without a certain relish in his tone as if perhaps George's failure compensated for the other wrong done to Barry's father.

"What was the problem?" asked Mary.

"I dunno. Got too big for his boots, I reckon – that and the drink. Too much money and he couldn't handle it, so folks said . . ."

"How did he come into money? When was this?" Mary was really interested.

"Must have been in the fifties . . ."

"About the time the Durward-Cookes had the greenhouse built?"

"Probably about then." Fortunately Barry Samuels had not taken her interest as anything out of the ordinary; he told a story well and this one had the added spice of his own father's involvement. "It's often the way with small builders like George Weston," he went on, sagely, "they have a bit of luck and they begin to think they're the sons of Wimpey. They branch out in all the wrong directions and end up like he did in Queer Street. I heard there was hardly a penny left when the firm went bust. I'm glad to hear that Miss Weston's at least got a roof over her head. It was no fault of hers."

Mary thought it was time she left the shop.

"I have enjoyed our chat," she told Barry Samuels as he accompanied her to the door. He was equally delighted with the large order now lying snug in the boot of her car, and the promise of another one when Mr Kemp had decided on the type of paving stone he wanted.

"Give my regards to Miss Weston," he said, diffidently, "if she'll remember me as a lad doing gardening with my father. That is if she's not upset by it reminding her of that old quarrel."

"That's a kind thought, Mr Samuels. I'll just say you were

asking after her. What a fuss to make about an old rose bed! You'd be thinking George Weston had found a gold mine in it . . ."

"That's what folks said at the time." Barry laughed. "Or that he'd struck oil on the land and needed to keep it secret!"

"What do you mean, paving stones?" said Kemp that evening. "I didn't know we had a path to pave."

"Just that broken bit at the foot of the garden by the stream," said Mary, "but it can wait. I'll not be going back to Samuels till I've spoken to Miss Weston about that rose bed."

This was easier said than done. To Mary's surprise and frustration, she found it difficult to get the old lady alone. It was not only that Mary's tie to Primrose Sutton had somehow loosened lately, but Miss Weston herself had become almost inaccessible. Excuses were made, explanations were volunteered – Aunt Gwen wasn't well, it was inconvenient, there were other arrangements – but Mary was finally left with the feeling that she was no longer welcome as a visitor to the house next door.

It was not in her nature to resent this change of attitude on Prim's part. Mary had lived long enough in the company of women to know that there are shifts in friendships, small breaks occur and widen, that people like Prim are as volatile in their relationships as in their style of living, and can change allegiances as casually as their clothes. Now that Blanche and Jasper Quigley were settled in the flat upstairs, possibly Prim felt she had plenty of sitters on hand to be with the invalid when required. Mary would have accepted this state of affairs and simply curtailed her visits, had it not been that she genuinely liked Miss Weston and thought her feeling reciprocated.

Moreover, even on the few brief occasions she had been back to the big untidy sitting-room, she was sure she had seen in the elderly lady's eyes a kind of appeal, as if she too wanted to speak; and almost instantly there seemed to have been a closing of ranks of the others present to prevent it. It was an odd piece of by-play she might well have ignored had it not occurred more than once.

Meeting Blanche Quigley by chance one day gave Mary

the opportunity to test the water. Blanche was a softer target than Prim.

They met in the Cabbage White, a pub much frequented by students, where Mary had gone for a drink and a sandwich between classes. Mary was, somewhat inappropriately, in the company of Josh Larkin and Billy Semple, two of the ringleaders of the fracas at the opening of the new library; so it was no wonder Blanche stared when she came in the door. Mr Larkin was at present studying the Mafia with more zeal than his modern history course prescribed and he had heard – probably through Primrose Sutton – that this frumpy-looking mature student, Mrs Kemp, had had sinister gangster connections back in the States.

"Those blokes you knew from Las Vegas," he was asking, "did they really wear sharp suits and look like gentlemen?"

"Depends on your idea of a gentleman," replied Mary. They had not been especially gentle with her, but she had earned their respect for her devious and lying ways, and she had at least survived to tell the tale. Seeing Blanche hovering in the doorway, however, she put off any further revelations. "I'll see you again later, Josh," she told the boys, "In the meantime I want to have a word with Blanche. Do you mind?"

Despite the softest of voices, when Mary took a firm line most people found themselves obeying. The young men rose and went over to the bar as Mary beckoned the Quigley girl to her table. "Can I get you a drink, Blanche?" she said, quickly. "Come and sit with me."

Blanche hesitated. Larkin and Semple had passed her with a casual 'hiya' and no offer of company. She sat down with Mary.

"That's nice of you, Mrs Kemp," she said. "I'll have a gin and tonic."

When Mary set the drinks down she gave the girl one of her rare broad smiles. "I'm so glad to see you," she said, pleasantly. "Now that I'm not so often in Prim's house I really miss you young people."

"I'd noticed you'd not been in . . . thought it was because you were only a friend of Grace Juniper."

Mary looked shocked. "Of course not. I'm a friend of Prim's

99

as well, but she seems to have gone off me lately." No sense in being other than direct.

Blanche shrugged her pretty hair from her shoulders, and laughed. "That's Prim all over. Here today, gone tomorrow . . ." She sipped her drink slowly, looking obliquely at Mary over the glass.

"And are you still at the studying, Blanche?" Mary did not want the girl to think she was being interrogated about the situation at Miss Weston's, although that was in fact the whole purpose of the conversation.

"Got to get two A levels, haven't I?" Mary noticed Blanche had picked up the inevitable interrogatory tone used by most of the students; it went oddly with her upper-class accent. "I'm doing Eng. Lit. and trying to upgrade my French. I speak the bloody language better than our tutor, but the grammar's a bugger." Blanche was chancing her arm but Mary looked anything but shocked.

"You'll get by," she said. "Are you still up in the flat?"

"Got nowhere else. Anyway, Uncle Simon wants us to keep an eye on the place till he gets new tenants."

"I met your uncle the other day," said Mary, and added with a touch of mischief, "and I've also encountered his cousin, the MP. He must be kin to you also."

Blanche shrugged. "I wouldn't know."

This girl is set to shrug her life away, thought Mary, suddenly rather sorry for Blanche. She would drift into college and out again, just as she would drift into a series of fashionable little jobs unworthy of her latent intelligence, and into relationships that would be as pointless. She seemed, for all her youth, already to have been drained of the will to make anything of her life. Perhaps her very nature was as frail as her looks, and incapable of nurturing so crude a quality as ambition. But she was obviously not devoid of curiosity for she suddenly said: "Do you know why you've got on the wrong side of Prim, Mrs Kemp?"

"No, I do not. And it's Mary to you, even if it's over the hill you think I am."

"Sorry. It's just that it's different away from the house."

"And your mother brought you up to respect your elders?"

100

Blanche laughed at this piece of inspired guesswork. "Well, yes . . . Mary. Anyway, you never seem old to me."

"And I consort with the likes of Josh Larkin. Tell me, Blanche, why am I no longer in Prim's good books?"

"Oh, it's all to do with Miss Weston." Blanche hurried to get over the gaffe she'd made about Mary's age. "Primrose fusses over her like an old hen, and gets jealous if anyone else gets in on the act."

"She does look after the old lady very well . . ."

"She doesn't have to be so damn protective about it." Blanche was obviously having a go at Prim, which made Mary wonder if there had been a falling-out.

"It was the same with Miss Juniper," the girl went on, "only this time she's worse. Never lets any of us talk properly to Aunt Gwen any more. She's like a jealous cow with a pet calf . . ."

"What do you mean it was the same with Miss Juniper?"

"All that stuff about trying to improve her speech. Grace was good at it, and the old lady was responding. Prim was furious. They'd tried all that years ago at the clinic, she said. It only upsets 'my charge' as she called her, and then Prim's left to calm her down."

"But she still asked Grace to sit with Miss Weston . . ."

"Ah, that was only at night after Aunt Gwen had been put to bed. Prim reckoned she was tired by then and didn't even want to talk."

"You get on well with the old lady," said Mary, thinking a little flattery would help to keep the conversation going. The girl was more animated than she had ever seen her. "You have a deal more patience than Prim."

"I've got more time." Blanche could be down to earth when she chose. "But it's her makes the rules. Don't encourage Miss Weston to talk, she says, it upsets her mind and she might have another stroke. Prim says these are the doctor's orders."

"Well, I know that Dr Parks calls from time to time and keeps an eye on things, so perhaps it is what he says."

"Don't you believe it. I asked him once if it hurt to try to help with her speech and he said, not at all, anything that stimulates her mind is good for her. What I'm trying to tell you, Mary," the girl wound up, "is you should take no notice of Prim because I think Miss Weston wants to talk to you."

This was so much in accord with her own line of thought that Mary was for the moment startled. "How can you know that, Blanche?"

"That book she gave Grace Juniper, the one about the Deloraine Court gardens, well, every time she sees me now Miss Weston keeps trying to say the name, 'Olga . . .'. Of course that's my great aunt, the one who wrote the book. Then she managed to get out another word or two, 'Mary', she said, and 'book . . .'. I think she wants to talk to you about it."

"Is that right, now?" Mary was struck by a sudden thought. "Miss Weston does know who you are, then? If so, then you would be the obvious person she'd want to talk to about that family."

"The Durward-Cookes?" Blanche showed signs of impatience. "I've told you before, I never knew them. I think we were taken out there once when we were kids. I don't remember Uncle Percy being there so perhaps he'd died but I do remember her, Great Aunt Olga. She was weird, not quite with it, all floating chiffon and gum boots . . ." Blanche began to laugh. "Yes, I do remember the gum boots. She had tea served in the conservatory, great gloomy place with plants everywhere. Jasper and I got the giggles, said there were earwigs, so we got thrown out into the garden. Mum wasn't bothered – she couldn't stand that family anyway. Thought the old girl was bats and ought to be in a home."

"What about the other sister, the one with the outlandish name?"

"Dorinda? I don't think I ever saw her because she and Uncle Daniel were out in Kenya, but my parents thought she had more guts than the rest of them. Of course, being Quigleys they were closer to us and they used to send Jasper and me birthday and Christmas presents. I must have been about ten when she died and I remember there was talk about someone going out for the funeral, but in the end no one went."

"And your great uncle, did he come home then?"

"No, he stayed on. I've heard my mother say he was a very lonely old man but well looked after out there. I think the parents would've liked to send Jasper to Kenya when he left school – that was the old idea; if you didn't know what to do with the boy, send him to the colonies."

"From my reading," said Mary, "it was the Grand Tour of Europe . . ."

"There's nothing grand about the things my family gets up to. Anyway, Uncle Dan didn't encourage the idea of being visited so the trip fell through. He seems to have been a very decent sort. We've just found out that he's left a bit of money to Jasper and me – which has made Dad feel guilty because nobody went out when they buried him. It was left to his native servants to pack up the bungalow and the stuff keeps arriving at our house or Uncle Simon's. Pretty tatty it is too, as if termites have been at it, and of no value whatsoever unless you think ebony elephants are the in thing. And, you know what? Jasper and me, we don't get that money till we're twenty-five! The Will was made back in the dark ages when they'd never heard of a majority of twenty-one, never mind eighteen."

"He'd be the decent man, then, leaving you anything at all," said Mary, and meant it, "seeing as he'd never even met you."

"It's not a lot," said Blanche, hurriedly, as if that made up for what looked like the family's casual attitude to the death of their relative.

Mary had to look at her watch. "I'll be in the bad books of Mr Bradshaw if I don't get a move on," she said, getting to her feet. "Nice to talk to you, Blanche, and thanks for the tip about Primrose. I see Josh looking over at you – I think they'd like you to join them now you've finished with this old person."

Twelve

M ary had much to think about, but she tried to put it aside so that she could concentrate on Mr Bradshaw's notes on the reading of *Shirley* – a book she found impenetrable. The name, however, called someone else to mind and that evening she rang Grace Juniper's sister in Yorkshire.

"It's your husband I want to bother," she said when she and Shirley Prentice had exchanged greetings. "Something you mentioned about a dig?"

"Wait, I'll get him. I know he did wonder if anything came of it . . ."

Came of what? Mary had been unable to find anything in the book on archaeology which might point to why Grace had raised an enquiry with her brother-in-law, so when he came to the phone she asked him direct.

"Well, Grace for once was rather vague," he said. "I'm afraid I don't have her letter any more, the one where she asked the question, but all she wanted to know was what would happen if a builder in the course of his work turned up something of an archaeological nature. She asked what procedure would follow."

"Did she say what the find was?"

"Oh, I don't think it had got as far as that. She stressed that her question was a purely hypothetical one. In my reply I set out the steps that are normally taken. After all, this kind of thing does happen occasionally to builders, particularly when they're clearing a large area of open land. Experts would have to be called in. If there were coins or significant pieces of pottery, the local museum would have an interest; and of course the council would have to be informed if the site looked as if it might be important, and then the builder could get a licence.

I gave Grace all this information in my letter to her . . ."
Eric Prentice paused, "but of course she would only have
got that not long before the accident. Shirley tidied her desk
and brought her personal papers back here." Mary heard him
call, "Shirley?" and waited.

After a few moments he came back to the phone. "My wife
says my letter wasn't among the recent ones she took from
Grace's desk to see if they needed answering, so perhaps she
had simply handed it on to whoever asked the question in the
first place. Now that you have brought up the matter again,
Mrs Kemp, can I take it there have been developments?"

Those dark dales in the North breed astute people, thought
Mary but she was unsure of her ground. Besides, she felt that
it was hardly fair on the Prentices to involve them further.

"It's nothing but my own curiosity," she explained. "I think,
like you say, it was just a hypothetical question. Grace liked to
discuss all manner of things and she was a stickler for proper
procedures. If a subject came up she would want to be accurate
and get it right before she spoke up. She taught me a lot about
that, Mr Prentice, for I've not the methodical mind myself. I
still miss her."

"Aye, Grace was a grand person. Nice to hear you talk of
her that way . . ."

When she put the phone down Mary glanced at the clock.
It would be another hour before Lennox was home, and their
meal was safe in the oven. If she slipped in next door now
there might be an opportunity to speak with Miss Weston.

The big sitting-room looked more untidy than usual. Perhaps
it was because Liza-Jane's toys were scattered everywhere and
the child herself looked as if she was on the verge of a tantrum,
averted only by Mary's entrance. Prim had shown her in,
just a shade reluctantly, but by going over immediately to
the little girl and putting into her hand a miniature fluffy
teddy-bear, Mary seemed to have stopped tears that were
about to flow. "I found him all by himself on a stall in the
market," she whispered, "and I thought you'd be giving him
a good home . . ."

Most of that was true. Mary tended to pick up discarded bits
and pieces left by children on the assumption that to new eyes

they still had novelty. As a child herself, she had never known a toy fresh-minted from a shop. This woe-begone bear had the kind of lopsided grin that was irresistable.

"He's sweet," said Liza-Jane. "He can join my gang."

When she had taken the new recruit away to be introduced, Mary got up off her knees and gave her attention to the other occupants of the room.

There they all were, as usual: Gregory Venn and Jasper lounging on cushions in front of the television, Blanche hanging her pretty hair over the arm of the sofa as she tried to gather together the child's tea set strewn on the carpet at her feet, while Primrose was not really doing anything but standing by the kitchen door as if ready to defend her territory.

"Long time, no see," drawled Jasper over his shoulder.

"Hello there," said Gregory. But he got up and joined Blanche on the sofa where he sat closer to her than was necessary. "We haven't seen you for a while, Mrs Kemp. How are the studies going?"

The young man was being more polite and friendly than he'd been in the past, so Mary sat down in an armchair beside him and Blanche and soon was engaged in conversation.

It was not long, however, before Primrose came over to them. Something was displeasing her and Mary did not think it was entirely her own presence. Even at the front door, although Prim had started off with a gruff: "Oh, it's you, Mary," which in anyone other than Prim might have sounded rude, yet there had been almost relief in her voice as she had gone on: "Well, come on in, then. Aunt Gwen's gone to bed early, but everyone else is here . . ."

And so they were, but in no wise as one big happy family. Liza-Jane wasn't alone in appearing ready to snap. Threads of tension stretched tight across the room; conversation was going on only for the sake of outward amicability; the deeper reality flowed under and was turbulent.

Jasper had looked put out by Gregory's move to the sofa area, and Mary thought his ears seemed almost pinned-back along the line of his pale blond hair as he strained them to hear what was going on. The television screen might as well have been blank.

Primrose, meanwhile, was hovering over and above the couple on the sofa for all the world like – and Blanche's words came immediately to Mary's mind – a jealous cow. It was not difficult now to see the cause of her displeasure. When not exactly addressing Mary herself, the couple on the sofa were totally absorbed in each other and it was as if Mary was being given one end of the invisible string that was jerking each individual and giving rise to the atmosphere she had noticed on first entering the room.

Gradually she realised that Gregory Venn was a changed man; it was not only that his manners were better, but something more basic. Since she had seen him last he had grown up. Gone – at least for the present – were the frisky, puppyish ways of his youth, and in their place he had the more serious, thoughtful, if slightly priggish, mannerisms of the man he would become. It was not hard to see one of the reasons for this transformation, and possibly the most important, in his attention to Blanche. As Mary watched the pair of them she was amused to discover that not only was Gregory Venn in love, but he was head-over-heels in love; and it looked like first love, worship-the-ground-she-walks-on kind of love, a love that couldn't be hidden, a blush-and-stammer love that showed itself in every gesture, every glance at the girl beside him who sat with slim legs primly crossed, and that waterfall of hair which could drown a man.

All the time the three of them talked of this and that, of college tutors, and student complaints, Mary's head was reeling from this untoward discovery she had just made, and she trusted her amusement didn't show.

She could no longer miss the reason for Prim's displeasure; it was obvious in every look she gave the youngsters that she strongly disapproved of their pairing off. Now she tried, almost physically, to separate them on the pretence of collecting Liza-Jane's toys from under the sofa cushions.

"Move over, Greg – can't you see I'm trying to tidy the place up?"

He did move, but quite ostentatiously nearer to Blanche who giggled, and shot a glance at Mary as if to say: 'I told you so . . .'

To distract Prim, whose face was red with suppressed anger, Mary remarked, quietly: "Miss Weston is early to her bed tonight. Is she not well?"

Prim pulled out a piece of doll's furniture with an air of triumph. "There, I knew it was down the back of the sofa . . . Auntie Gwen? I'm afraid she's poorly." She glared down at Blanche who had just removed Gregory's hand from her knee, but had not relinquished it. To his obvious delight, she raised it to her face. "You've been at Jasper's soap again," she murmured. "I like the smell of it better than your old coal tar."

It looked like a deliberate attempt to incense Prim further. She stood before them like a small thundercloud waiting to burst. It was clear to Mary that Blanche had annexed young Venn in whom Prim had an almost proprietory interest; she regarded him as part of her property, one of her entourage, a member of her little court, a subject for an exchange of banter, a sparring partner, whatever; but certainly not one to be taken over right under Prim's nose by a slip of a girl like Blanche.

Whether there was more to it than that, Mary could only surmise; but, despite the difference in their years (and Prim was always at her most vague when it came to her age) there had been an element of flirtation in the interplay between Prim and the young clerk.

It was on Blanche's defenceless head that Prim poured out the force of her fury.

"It's all your fault that poor Auntie's not well. You had her up to high doh last night with all your silly talk. When I got back I thought she'd have a heart attack. For all your airs and graces you haven't got the sense of a two-year-old. You'd no right to go worrying the old lady with all those questions. I'm not letting you go near her again . . ." Prim had to stop her tirade to get breath back.

Blanche flushed, her fair skin colouring right up into her scalp. Mary thought it unlikely that the girl had ever had to endure such a bad-tempered attack as this, for her look of frailty would deflect most people's anger, even if she merited it.

Here, however, she had a champion on hand.

Gregory jumped to his feet. "That's no way to talk to

Blanche. You asked her to baby-sit last night when you were out at the Castle, and the old lady *did* want to talk."

"Huh. You an expert on paraplegics now, are you?" Prim was not going to have the wind taken out of her sails by any act of knight errantry. "You've never raised a finger to help Aunt Gwen in the past. What's your interest now?"

Gregory stuck to his guns. "I called in here last night before I went to my evening class, and she was tapping away on the table like she does when she wants attention. When I went to her she kept pointing her good hand at Blanche who was in the kitchen, and then putting her fingers to her mouth. We all know that means she wants to talk to a particular person . . ."

"She'd want the bathroom, that's all." Prim raised her voice so that she was almost shouting. "If I'd been here it would have been me she'd want. And when I did come in, what a state she'd got herself into – thanks to Blanche. You were bloody glad to see me, I can tell you. You couldn't have coped if she'd had another stroke . . . nursing training hasn't been one of your options, has it?"

The girl dropped her eyes. "I did get her into bed," she muttered. "I was worried . . . she was trying so hard to get words out . . ."

"Just what Dr Parks says she mustn't do." Prim took a more level tone as if she had won her point. "She must not be allowed to get frustrated because that way the blood will surge in her head and there'll be a haemorrhage. That's what I keep telling you: Auntie Gwen must not be upset, and I'll remind you that it's me who's in charge of her."

Miss Weston not being her patient, Mary could not be sure that Dr Parks' instructions were being properly interpreted by Prim; it might be that the old lady could be more upset by being actively discouraged from trying to communicate – particularly if she had something she deemed important to say. Also, to one of Mary's nursing experience, Prim's explanation of the danger of possible stroke sounded crude, but it was obviously enough to cow the young people who had by now wilted into an embarrassed silence.

Mary was not going to be allowed to escape easily for Primrose now turned to her as a prospective ally. "Isn't

109

it true, Mary, that a second stroke could be really dangerous?"

"Of course it is," said Mary, tartly, for she had no wish to be drawn in on Prim's side, "but from what I've seen of Miss Weston I think she is more robust than you make out. Letting her communicate with people at her own speed might well have a calming effect on her."

"Well, I've got my orders," said Prim, stubbornly.

"I must be going," said Mary, rising. "May I see her just to say good night?"

"No." Prim was curt. "She's asleep."

Blanche looked up at her in disbelief, but at that moment Liza-Jane came running over to Mary. "I've called him Little Ted," she said, "'cos he's so tiny. Thank you, Auntie Mary for bringing him."

The child's politeness showed up what in the mother could only be pettiness. Denied the support she had hoped for in Mary, Prim had taken a small revenge which was obvious to everyone.

Mary went to the door. "I'll see myself out," she said. "Bye, all."

As she left the house she was heavily conscious that her visit had not exactly shed any sweetness and light into its highly charged atmosphere.

"They're all brimful of emotions but so tight-lipped about it that it hurts to watch them," she said to Lennox after dinner. "Prim's been sharpening her claws. She's a great stirrer, but she likes to be the one with the spurtle – now it's got out of her control. She's jealous of Gregory Venn for falling in love with Blanche – and oh, boy, is he in love! I think brother Jasper is just the teeniest bit jealous because his best mate and his sister have only got eyes for each other. As for Blanche, well, any girl would be flattered to be the object of such infatuation as young Venn's, even if he is only a skinny youth. I don't think Blanche has ever really liked Prim and that casual camaraderie she had with the boys, which Blanche couldn't quite manage on her own with the students. And in Prim's dislike of her there's always been that hint of envy, the private school, the privileges. Maybe there's something of the north-south divide about it . . ."

". . . fickle is the South, And dark and true and tender is the North," said Kemp. She stared at him till he said: "Not me. Tennyson."

"I don't believe a word of it," she said, flatly. "Anyway, it was the class divide I had in mind."

Thirteen

For many years Lennox Kemp had avoided Law Society conferences on the premise that for a man to get the full benefit from such diversions he needed a wife. Now that he had one he had rather enjoyed last year's event – as had Mary, who attended it in the same adventurous spirit she brought to all of her new experience in England, as if she were an intrepid voyager in a strange land, fully open to the experience. What had surprised – and delighted – him was not just her childlike wonderment that such junketings existed in such a sober profession, nor her evident enjoyment of them once she was there, but the fact that she herself was a great success. Dowdy and inconspicuous she might be, but she had a ready tongue, no inhibitions about using it, and a devastating smile when she chose to shine it.

"It's because I'm not in competition," she told him placidly as she scanned the other wives as if they were horses in the paddock. "They are, and they can't help it. Their mothers were comparing them with their peers since the day they were born. It's there in the great English education: you have to keep up with Emily, have better teeth than Caroline, and prettier hair than poor old Vicky. And they have to marry so well: Gerald has to have a better position in the City than Raymond whose father went to Eton, Cecil have titled connections though Peter's house in the south of France is several points up, and Andrew's shooting lodge in Scotland scoops the pool. You should hear them in the powder room, and over the little tables while you men are collecting our drinks at the bar – it's all the great game of who's doing well, and who's losing out. And when they've reached an irreproachable plateau themselves, then it's time to start on the next generation. Talk about totem poles and shell necklaces among the natives; these ladies could give them tips on how to wear their trophies. I listen to them talk, and take a look at them, they're waiting feverishly to get a word in all the while someone's speaking, counting up the points they're going to make, and watch their score. It's fascinating, like being at the races, and watching the bookies instead of the horses . . ."

"You did the same in America," her husband remarked, mildly. "It's just as competitive a society."

"Well, not my part of it. All I got was the taste for listening. There it was dollars and cents; here it's class, you've got it or you haven't. Don't look at me like that, I'm not complaining. I just love your English ways . . ."

They were in the hotel bar waiting for Kemp's friends with whom they were to dine, and they were early because Mary's idea of dressing for dinner was to take a quick shower and slip into something easy to wear. This time the soft rose colour of her dress warmed the pale grey of her eyes, and the dark brown of her hair simply shone after a brisk brushing. Kemp had to admit she looked like a daisy, fresh and button-bright.

"And what do these awe-inspiring dames think of you?" he asked.

"Oh, they stub their smart little toes on the likes of me. They're well drilled in spotting accents, but I make sure that mine defeats them. Americans are such a mixed lot, my dear! So I give them all the voices of America just to confuse the issue. For they do desire to know most earnestly where you're coming from, who were your people and what did they do, and as I'm not having any of that, I keep changing the record. Might be how the lingo's talked in the Windy City, or way down in the ole cotton-pickin' South. I keep them guessing as to what I could have been over there. Maybe a writer from Boston – she spoke like her mouth was stuffed with sugar-plums, I used to practise it in front of one of her gilded mirrors when I nursed her husband. Or I talk like they do in New York, with that Yankee snarl that would lift you off the sidewalk. Then I have a rich papa and drawl like the belle of Memphis, Tennessee."

"You're just gifted, that's what's the matter with you.

You're a right little impersonator. It's as well you don't let on how admired you were by the Mafia . . . Anyway, I prefer your Irish accent."

"Which is the most unreal, to my great sorrow, for there was no one else to take it from when my mother died. But let's not get sentimental. Are we not here to enjoy ourselves?"

"That's part of the object of the exercise. The other is to exchange legal chat – gossip to you – and of course, you're absolutely right, Mary, it is competitive. Who's up, who's down . . ."

For gossip was not confined to ladies' powder rooms; he himself had encountered an old friend from the College of Law in the washroom, and had inquired about a fellow student: "What happened to Soutar? He was a brilliant student, got all those prizes."

"Oh, he came to nothing. Married his typist and ended up in the provinces."

Kemp had long given up wondering about their opinion of himself. His downfall was twenty years behind him, his career re-established, his future certain. There had been a lot of clucking when Archie Gillorn had rescued him from Walthamstow; there might still be fellows at this conference who would purse their lips knowingly at the mention of his name. It was good to be with Mary. They suited one another, cared little for the opinion of others, and she gave him a view of life as idiosyncratic as his own.

They stayed on till the Sunday evening as their journey back from the resort was not a long one. Lennox was saying goodbye to colleagues while Mary lingered in the lounge among the debris of Sunday supplements and discarded teacups. The hotel was winding down after its efforts.

She sat on the edge of an armchair as a nearby television was showing the news: '. . . and we are now going over to Newtown where the body of the girl was found . . .' A picture came up on the screen, a man standing among trees, behind him an enclosure marked off by coloured tape. '. . . this is the bridle path beside which the body was discovered yesterday morning by a man walking his dog in what is called Emberton Wood. The body has since been identified as that of Blanche Quigley, aged eighteen. Miss Quigley was a niece of Mr Stephen Durward-Cooke, the Member of Parliament for Welchester West, and the Quigleys are a well known family in Newtown. All the police will say at this juncture is that death was caused by strangulation. It is understood that a young local man is helping with inquiries at Newtown Police Station where an incident room has been set up. I am now returning you to the studio . . .'

Mary steadied herself, but when she came up to her husband she was still white and shaking.

"What is it?" Her appearance gave him immediate concern.

"Blanche Quigley," she said, tersely, "she's been killed . . ."

"My God . . . Not an accident, you mean?"

"Strangled, they said . . . her body was found yesterday in Emberton Wood." Mary could scarcely get the words out, they fell heavy as lead.

Kemp stopped only to collect his coat and their cases before hurrying Mary out to the car, and they were well on the road home before either of them spoke.

"That reporter said a young local man is helping with inquiries," Mary said, dully. "I wonder . . ."

"Come, no speculation. I'll phone John Upshire the minute we get in. You've had a shock, my dear; these people are close to you."

"First, Grace Juniper, and now Blanche . . ."

"We'll talk about it only when we know more. It's distressing for you but we must keep our minds open."

He was hurt for her. He had not known the girl but he knew that Mary was suffering all through the drive back to Newtown. "And we never even looked at the Sunday papers," she said at one point. "We were too busy chattering."

When they arrived he went straight to the telephone. As he had anticipated, Detective Inspector John Upshire was the senior investigating officer. The incident room at Newtown Police Station was already taking calls. But John Upshire was not there.

"He's gone home, Mr Kemp. Its been a hectic thirty-six hours." Fortunately Kemp knew the officer in charge and did not have to explain the reason for his call.

Mary had unpacked, and was in the kitchen making supper, though neither of them felt like eating. She had more sense than even to try to listen in on Kemp's telephone conversation.

When he came in to the kitchen he glanced at the clock. "John's at home," he said. "He'll be having his supper. I'll give him a ring before he puts the cat out."

Inspector Upshire was a friend of them both, and they knew his solitary domestic habits.

"If he's gone home," said Mary, slowly, "what does that mean? I thought investigating officers didn't get much sleep when there's been a murder on their patch – as they call it."

"It's meant to look that way, but they're only human – they have to eat and sleep like the rest of us. In this case . . ." He hesitated. "I have to say that it doesn't look good for the young man they've got at the station."

"He's been arrested?"

"He's 'helping us' was all the officer would tell me but from the way he said it and the fact that John himself has gone home – well, you can put two and two together."

"They think they've got their man?"

"I'm afraid so."

"And his name?"

"Ah, that of course he would not tell me. But John might well do so . . ."

Mary's eyes darkened. "I guess you're right . . . I've gotten myself too close to those young people next door . . ."

Two Americanisms in one sentence; she was certainly anxious. They spoke no more about it whilst they had supper since any discussion would be dispiriting and lead nowhere.

Mary was washing up when Kemp went back to the study, and he was there for a considerable time. He had only just put the phone down when she came in with the coffee. "We'll have a couple of brandies," he told her, "then I'll give you the thing verbatim."

After Kemp had given the Inspector an outline of Mary's connection with the dead girl and with the others next door, John Upshire had told him they were holding Gregory Venn on suspicion of murder. He had been unable to give them any convincing explanation as to why he had not committed the crime; he had been on the spot where Blanche Quigley had been strangled. He said he had been with her earlier, that there had been a quarrel – a slight tiff, he'd called it, Upshire reported with only a hint of scorn in his level voice – and she had been alive when he left her. He could not account for his movements in the next few hours until he got back to 4 Albert Crescent about one o'clock in the morning when Primrose Sutton, according to her statement, had heard him go up to his flat.

"From what John tells me," Kemp ended, "the whole operation went like clockwork. He sounds very pleased with himself – as well he might. It's textbook stuff, a credit to the system. The body found at eight on Saturday morning, the girl's handbag beside her which gave her name and address. The Quigley parents are on holiday in Spain . . ." he paused as he saw Mary wince, ". . . but they will know by now. It was Jasper who made the formal identification, and at the same time told the officers that Blanche had gone out with Gregory Venn on Friday evening and had not returned. When the police car brought Jasper from the morgue the officers went straight up to Venn's flat. He already looked as if he hadn't slept, and when they told him Blanche was dead he collapsed. They took him down to the station about six on Saturday evening, and he's been there ever since. I've told you this twice – once as an accurate record of what passed between John and I on the phone, and now in my own words. Any questions?"

"They haven't charged him yet? What are they waiting for?"

"They took samples of blood, hair, saliva, and semen. There had been sexual intercourse not long before death. He admits it."

"So, what are they waiting for?"

"The report from the lab showing a match." Kemp sighed. "But it sounds as if there's enough evidence without that. Blanche and he drove to that spot in his car, she was found lying on his rug with an empty bottle of wine and two glasses beside her, and his fingerprints are everywhere."

"An open and shut case, that's what you said John called it?"

"And he's not the man to make a mistake. In the past I've found him over-cautious, if anything. Of course, our conversation tonight is completely off the record. The Press won't get any of it until young Venn is charged, but . . ." he ended, grimly, ". . . they won't have long to wait . . ."

Mary lay a long time awake that night. Her thoughts were uneasy and this uneasiness tended towards irritability which further stretched the boundaries of sleeplessness. Over and over again she told herself that the tragedy of her young neighbours – whatever form it took – was beyond her reach; she could help none of them. The older Quigleys she'd never met, they had lost a daughter and her heart went out to them; Jasper had lost a sister and, having seen them as a pair, she knew it must be for him like losing a limb. Remembering the look on Gregory Venn's face as he sat with Blanche on the sofa only a few nights ago, she was jolted. There had been so much love in his look, calf-love maybe, but all the more sincere because it lacked the footholds of experience. Surely a love like that could never kill?

Mary turned and turned these things over in her mind, surprised at the intensity of her feelings. She thought she had reached an age and a situation in life where nothing short of her husband's illness or death – for Mary was one of those who take nothing for granted – could shake her out of the serene contentment marriage had brought.

In any case, it was unusual for her to be moved by worrysome thoughts. She'd always lived for the day, and was not given to contemplation or introspection, her psychical self never having had much time given it.

As a child she'd lived the hand-to-mouth existence of the very poor; there might be supper or there might be a slap round the ear, the breakfast bagels brought by a charity-minded neighbour had to be grabbed and guzzled before the stepfather stirred from his sweaty, drunken stupor. It was up to Mary, the eldest (and none of his kin) to share out the food, first to the invalid mother, then the baby – from whose birth she would not recover – and the toddlers, lastly a few crumbs for herself, till she was of an age to go foraging, to the bakers for day-old bread, to the deli for ends of ham and rinds of cheese.

So she had grown up without thought for a past or a future, only the daily battle of the hours, caring for the sick, the interminable cleaning-up, the relentless search for food to sustain the family, and the getting of whatever cash was going in the hands or pockets of the layabout, Smith, profligate when in work, tight-fisted when out of it.

School for Mary had been simply a few hours off, the bliss of sitting still. She heard nothing and saw nothing, just revelled in the respite from toil. If she had had feelings, emotions, sympathies, they were concentrated on only one person – the sweet, ailing, Irish mother. For the rest of the Smith tribe, Mary would dutifully do her best and no more.

In the end, of course, her work for them had come to nothing. They had followed their father's ways, lazy and improvident, the boys drifting into petty crime, the girls settling for hopeless marriages. Even after the mother's death, Mary had continued to stand up for them in court, argued their cases with social workers and police, and given up her own hard-earned nurse's wages to keep a roof over their feckless heads. She had been over thirty when the chance came to make a life for herself, and when she reached for that chance with both hands, she abandoned the young Smiths without so much as a backward glance.

Deep in her mind it must have lain these past few years. Mary turned restlessly, careful not to disturb Lennox who was sleeping the sleep of the just appropriate to any decent lawyer. Four-in-the-morning thoughts are the pits. How many times had Mary counselled her patients on that when they complained of their insomnia? Relax, she'd tell them, turn off that thinking tap, and no drips from it . . . let your mind go blank . . . Her voice would take on a hypnotic note as she smoothed their pillows, the sleepless, the troubled ones, the elderly.

But it wasn't working for Mary herself tonight as her thoughts refused to be submerged, and her anxieties for the young people next door rose up like real not imagined evils. The past and the present clashed in her mind, a mind unprepared for such a conflict. Was it possible, it suddenly came to her, that her attachment to these youngsters, her interest in their lives and now her intense compassion for them, sprang

119

from a feeling of past guilt, her abandonment of the Smith tribe in far-off Pennsylvania?

It brought her sharply wide awake. Always practicable, she slipped on shoes and a dressing gown and made for the kitchen, and the inevitable cup of tea. Ten minutes later her husband found her leaning on the draining board and gazing into space.

"I didn't mean to wake you."

"Is there any more tea in that pot? Come on, Mary, this is what marriage is all about. What are you doing awake at this hour?"

"I feel so silly . . ."

"I have always favoured silly women, particularly at four o'clock in the morning but they never came to me for advice in that state. By the time they got to my office they were all dressed up and ready to lie their little heads off." He sat her down in a chair, put his arm round her shoulders and pulled her close. "Tell me," he said.

Fourteen

The next morning just after Lennox had left for the office there was a knock on the Kemps' back door. This was rare since even tradesmen used the front rather than fight their way through the thickness of bushes in the side passage.

When Mary opened the door Primrose Sutton almost fell into her arms, ashen-faced, her hair uncombed, the hood of her anorak pulled roughly over it. Without a word, Mary hugged her for a moment, then eased her out of the garment, and took her gently through to the sitting-room and on to a sofa.

"Put your feet up," she said. "You look all in, and you could do with a drink. This calls for more than tea."

Prim gulped. "Oh, Mary, how right you are. It's those bastards out front . . . they're camped there, just waiting. When I took Liza-Jane to play-school there was only the local man. I know him and I got past by shouting at him but when I got back they were all there . . . I could hardly get in my own door."

Mary poured a brandy and ginger ale which Prim took eagerly.

"Is Miss Weston all right?"

Prim took a good sip of her drink, let out a great breath, and nodded. "It's a wonder she is, what with the police and now that lot . . ."

"Has Gregory come home?" Mary knew the question was a hopeless one, but she had to ask it.

"No . . . and I don't think he's going to . . ." Prim's voice broke on the words as the tears began, running like rain down her cheeks.

Mary knelt by the sofa and took her in her arms. "There, there . . . cry your heart out. Let it go, Prim dear, just let it go . . ."

It was half an hour before Primrose ceased to sob, wiped the last of her tears, and sat up.

"I'm sorry, Mary . . . but I didn't know where else to come, who to talk to . . ."

"You've come to the right place. Now you go and tidy yourself up while I make some coffee, then we'll decide what's to be done."

Soothed by Mary's calm acceptance of the situation and by that offer of practical help, Prim went meekly to wash her face.

When she came eventually into the kitchen, Mary was at the back door. "I've put up the old side gate," she said. "It was lying back in the hedge. It'll stop any of the mob if they try to sneak in. You and I can use the rear doors. Can Liza-Jane stay with someone?"

"I've already thought of that. I saw Melody Trafford's mum at the school, and Liza-Jane's to go there till I fetch her. I did say it might be a day or two. Mrs Trafford, she looked at me at bit odd like – she's probably heard something – but she agreed to have Liza. Melody's been a playmate for ages."

"Good," said Mary, handing over a cup of coffee. "Now you sit there and we'll work out something for Miss Weston. Does she know?"

"The bloody telly . . ." Prim stuffed her knuckles in her mouth; she had thought she was done with crying.

"Of course . . . she'd see it on the box. How has she taken it?"

Answering specific questions was good for Prim; it steadied her mind.

"Aunt Gwen's strange at times, but the elderly are like that, aren't they? Things we know are serious, they skate over. Of course, she doesn't know about Greg . . ."

"None of us knows," said Mary briskly, as the mere mention of his name seemed about to re-open the floodgates. Prim concentrated on trying to answer the question. "Like I said, she was upset but not as much as you'd expect. You know what you said once, there's only room for one thing in her mind at the one time?"

"Something like that."

"Well, that's what she's been like since she heard it on the news. She's not even tried to speak, just drops her head the way she does when she doesn't want anyone to talk to her. Makes it easier for me . . . She's stayed in her room most of the time . . . She's not even wanted the telly. It's as if she's not interested . . ."

"It's probably too much to take in. I think, in a way, victims of stroke – if they're sensible – limit their intake to just what they can cope with. Miss Weston was always a sensible woman. Things like that don't change even through whatever trauma originally caused the stroke. To be practical, Prim, you and I must see that she has company, doesn't brood, and is kept occupied. Now, you haven't the time but I have. OK?"

Prim nodded. She looked miserably lost. Gone was all the perky confidence which had been her charm, the lone woman against the world attitude which had seen her through so far in her loosely held existence, a feminist stance against the dominance of males, the intransigence of a minority view, all the ethos of the modern young lady on the make. It had been shattered like glass against a stone. Primrose had been hit where she had not expected it and the shock had crumpled her defences, laying bare her vulnerability.

Mary suspected it was more than the plight of Gregory Venn which was draining the bold spiritedness from Prim. The edginess she had shown in the last few weeks had hardened into an acute state of anxiety. She could not keep still, her eyes had a tendency to turn inward, she would begin to speak then stop while Mary waited, looking at her with raised brows. It was obvious that there was something on her mind.

Nevertheless, at the end of an hour's talk Mary had imposed some order and a programme to deal with immediate arrangements. She would be with Miss Weston for the remainder of the day and see to her wants, allowing Primrose time to get a good rest, and, if she liked, to get in the household shopping as usual.

"Just be polite but firm, and say you don't know anything," she advised when Prim protested that people would be bound to stop her in the street. "The more you're seen going about in an ordinary way, the less they'll have for

123

gossip – and it'll be good practice for you to tell them zilch."

"I'd like to tell them to eff off," said Prim, glumly, with a hint of her old sparkle, "and that goes for the reporters as well."

"Best keep it clean," said Mary as she locked the back door behind them, and crossed the passage way between the two houses. "And if they do come knocking, let me deal with them."

It was strangely quiet in the big sitting-room, usually the scene of so much movement and chatter. On hearing that Mary had come, Gwendolyne Weston indicated that she would prefer to leave her bedroom and sit with her guest, so Prim made up the fire while Mary helped the old lady get ready to be wheeled through.

When Miss Weston was in the bathroom Mary tried to shoo Prim away to lie down. "You don't look as if you've slept for nights," she told her, knowing this was probably true; a couple of nights had passed since the discovery of the body, and what of the early hours of Saturday morning when Gregory had been heard to return – had Prim been awake then too?

Still Prim hesitated. She was hovering, doing unnecessary things, moving cushions, pulling at curtains, brushing imaginary specks from the polished table top, all the time Mary had been busy with the old lady. Now she caught at Mary's sleeve urgently. "You'll not upset her . . ." she said, the words coming jerkily. "She mustn't be upset . . ."

"Of course I'll not be upsetting her. That's why I'm here, to reassure her that things will go on normally. I can read to her, or play that two-handed patience she's so fond of. It'll be up to her as to how she'd be wanting to pass the time. What on earth are you so bothered for, Prim?" she added, for she could see the girl was still reluctant to leave.

Prim didn't answer. She was frowning as she tended to do when thwarted, and her colour had risen showing temper just beneath the surface.

"Sure it's only right that Aunt Gwen should have company," said Mary, soothingly, "she'll be grieving for Blanche in her own way."

"She got too close . . . she upset her . . ." Prim burst out, "She talked too much . . . They said for it not to happen . . . She wasn't to be allowed to get upset trying to remember . . . It'd be bad for her . . . like as not bring on another stroke . . ." Prim was almost shouting now, the words barely intelligible while her hands pummelled the back of the sofa. "Nobody told me what they were doing here. I was only doing my job . . ."

Mary decided to sort out the pronouns later in her own mind, for they were none too clear. "Hush now," she said, "don't take on so . . ." She saw the need for a sterner tone. "You'll do more harm to the old lady if she hears you in the state you're in. Come and lie down in your room and try and get some sleep. Perhaps you could do with a sedative." She knew that Primrose was against any but herbal medicine, and would only allow her invalid charge the minimum of sleeping tablets prescribed by Dr Parks. It was a policy with which Mary was in full agreement; she had noticed that Miss Weston was in any case a sound sleeper.

"I don't want any bloody pills." It was with relief that Mary watched Prim stump off into her room and slam the door behind her. The imputation that she might need the aid of drugs had had the desired effect.

It was true what Prim had said, Miss Weston was in a strange mood that day. She was, however, calm and it seemed to Mary a great deal more in control of herself and able to communicate better than previously. She ate a good lunch, had a short rest and then continued to enjoy Mary's company until Prim woke up at about five o'clock. Prim herself looked rested, and agreed to go out to do the shopping when Mary said she could stay for another hour.

Looking back that night on the time she had spent with Miss Weston, Mary tried hard to put all that had been said, indicated, or simply inferred, into some kind of perspective. This was for the benefit of Lennox Kemp who now had his own reasons to be interested in the inhabitants of the house next door.

On arriving at his office that Monday morning he had been told there was an urgent telephone call from Cedric Roberts.

"Lennox? Thank God you're there. Heard about young Venn?"

"Ye-es . . ." Kemp ventured cautiously.

"He's being held on a charge of murder. Hell of a thing for us . . ." There was a silence while Kemp digested this thought for today from the senior partner of the firm in which Gregory Venn was articled. "Well, of course, we had Nick Stoddart down there with him right away . . ."

"Of course," Kemp murmured; it would be the obvious move, Stoddart being Roberts' criminal lawyer.

"Fact is, Nick can't do it."

"Why not? I should have thought it was right up his street." Kemp knew how Nick loved to cut a dash in the Magistrates' Court and would relish even a walk-on part on the stage of the Old Bailey. "Why can't he take on Gregory Venn?"

"Because that young fool won't have him."

I can't say I blame him, Kemp thought but had to acknowledge that he was prejudiced. He and Stoddart were old adversaries. He had found Nick to be an untrustworthy colleague and, despite considerable skill as an advocate, the braggart in him tended to overshadow his duty to clients. Perhaps young Venn had sensed this.

Cedric was going on: ". . . Nick's just back from the station now. Venn has dismissed him as his solicitor. He wants you."

The words took Kemp's breath away.

"Says he lives next door to you, and you know him."

"The first is true enough, but the second most certainly is not. I don't know Gregory Venn. I have only met him on one occasion. Anyway, he's your clerk, Cedric."

There was the sound of a heartfelt sigh. The senior partner had reached the age when all he wanted was a quiet life, and no shocks to the firm whose future income would fuel a comfortable retirement. "I know . . . I know . . . it's a bugger . . ." He sighed again. "But that's what Venn has told Nick. He wants Lennox Kemp to represent him. Do you hear me?"

"Yes, I hear you. Hang on a minute." Kemp gathered his thoughts: there was professional etiquette to be observed; there was the question of Mary's involvement with the group in the next house which included Gregory Venn; there was that telephone conversation he had had with John Upshire – but there was a young man charged with murder whose desperate need had to prevail . . .

First, as to the ethics of the situation. "All right, Cedric, I'll see Mr Venn but I make no promises to take him on. Before that I must have a conference with Nick Stoddart. Tell him I'll be down at eleven."

"I'll tell him. He's been hopping around like a bullfrog fit to burst since he came in. Er . . . thanks, Lennox, I know you'll do your best for young Venn. Mightn't be a bad thing for it to be dealt with outside our firm, eh?" Cedric Roberts, that wily old Welshman had brightened up considerably now there was the chance to shift the load of trouble from his doorstep. "And of course we'll back any application for legal aid for the unfortunate young man. Oh, and when it comes to choosing Counsel, I'll be glad to put my word in."

"Yes, yes," said Kemp tersely, anxious to get the old buffer off the line. "Just make sure Nick's in his office when I get there."

Stoddart was in fact striding up and down the room venting his anger on the carpet, but his mood had passed from the manic to the coldly contemptuous. "I'm glad to be shot of him," he said to Kemp who came in and shut the door. "Snivelling young brat . . . Never did like him."

"For goodness' sake, sit down, Nick, and give me the background on Gregory Venn. It'll save time if I have to see him."

"What d'you mean, 'if'? He's asked for you – God knows why . . ."

Stoddart threw himself into his chair, and twirled his desk calendar; at least the pent-up rage was starting to seep out through his fingers.

"I haven't yet taken the case, Nick, and it would certainly have looked better for this young man if his legal support was coming from the place where he worked,"

"Well, he won't have it, damn it. He's stupid for getting into this mess in the first place, and now he's turning down the best legal help he's going to get."

This was no time to clash antlers as to who was the local king of the courts. Kemp had found that the only way to deal with Nick Stoddart was to cut through the egotistical bluster and get to the perfectly competent lawyer underneath. "When were you called in, and who by?" he asked.

"Late on Saturday night when they had young Venn at the station, and he'd told them where he worked. I suppose he did ask then for someone from the firm, or the police just assumed it . . ."

"And you were with him when he was being interviewed from then on?"

"Yes. All the time. There wasn't much I could do when I realised what they'd got on him, and most of it he wasn't denying . . ."

"When was he actually charged?"

"Nine thirty this morning. I'd got there about an hour before. It was Inspector Upshire told me they'd got enough to charge him. I wasn't surprised."

"What was Venn's demeanour this morning?"

"Different from the previous day." Stoddart took time to think. "Yes, I'd say, quite different . . ."

Kemp waited. He knew that in their line of work one learned to be observant, quick to notice those little giveaway signs and movements which indicate unease or indecision under questioning. Nick Stoddart was good at this; he watched witnesses like a hawk and pounced at the merest flicker of doubt.

He told Kemp that Gregory Venn had been uncommunicative during all the previous sessions of questioning. "Moved like a zombie, and responded – if you can call it that – in the same way . . . as if he'd been stunned. Took ages to answer questions as if he wasn't taking them in properly. Then he just mumbled."

"Drink or drugs?"

"Oh, nothing like that. He was simply being unresponsive. I left in the early hours when Inspector Upshire thought we'd all be better for some sleep. Venn had broken down several times, said he was too tired to talk. Well, he'd admitted he'd had little sleep the night before. But that was all he did admit . . ."

128

Stoddart reported well on the interview so that Kemp had the full facts which did not differ from those already gleaned from John Upshire during that telephone call.

"Who did the questioning?" he asked.

"Upshire had his whole team on to it. They were of course hoping for a confession when he broke down, but they didn't get it, despite them going for the hard and soft the way they do. You know the form, Lennox. John Upshire acting the big chum and leaving the tough part to that sidekick of his, Detective Sergeant Martin. Give them their due, they're good at their job, and they're fair. They need to be. I was there and they know me. Anything out of order and I'll make sure the tape catches it for later."

Stoddart's reputation for nitpicking was well known but Kemp didn't want it enlarged upon at the moment. "You said that Venn's attitude had changed this morning when he was charged. In what way changed?"

Nick shrugged. "He seemed to have got himself together . . . come out of whatever dream he'd been in yesterday, and the night before."

"Perhaps he had needed sleep. Did they go on with the questioning all yesterday?"

"There was no need for it to be so rigorous . . . I think they'd got what they wanted, short of full confession. They were only marking time till they got the lab reports."

"And there must have been enough evidence from those to charge him?"

"I guess so. But, believe me, Lennox, his whole story's so full of holes . . ."

"I'll come to that in a minute when we go over the notes you made on first interview. Just tell me how he came to dismiss you. This happened after he was charged?"

"As I said, he seemed to have got his head more together by this morning, except of course for this ridiculous notion of having you . . . Sorry, Lennox . . . Anyway, he'd listened quite calmly to the charge being read, then he repeated what he'd been saying all the time – 'I didn't do it . . .' It was at that moment he turned round and told me he didn't want me to represent him any more – he wanted Lennox Kemp. After all

I'd done for him, the ungrateful young brat tells me to get out. He was bloody rude about it, too. You just ask DS Martin."

Kemp would do no such thing; there could be a number of reasons why Venn wanted a change of solicitor, the first that came to mind being that he couldn't stand Nick Stoddart. As this was not a thought to be voiced, Kemp steered Nick away from any further outburst of personal resentment by asking for details of the articled clerk's background. He also asked for the written notes taken by Stoddart at the police station on Saturday night.

Fifteen

When Kemp returned to his own office an hour or so later he told his secretary that he did not wish to be disturbed, and then he carefully considered all there was to be known about Gregory Venn.

He was an only child. His parents were middle-aged when he was born and they were both now dead. His father had served as a non-commissioned officer in what had been the local county regiment, and when Gregory had emerged as star pupil of his primary school an application for an assisted place at Welcombe Park – a public school which favoured boys from a military background – was successful. He had left there with a good clutch of A levels, and had begun a law course at college when he got the job at Roberts'. Since then he had been taken as an articled clerk by the senior partner in the firm, and enrolled with the Law Society in order to take the Solicitors' Examinations. There was no doubt the young man had had a bright future before him if he'd kept his head down and not got into trouble. Now it looked like goodbye to all that.

Nick Stoddart had been right; the story told by Venn about that Friday night was as full of holes as Gruyere cheese, and the manner of its telling – judging by the notes made by Nick – so disjointed that it lacked all credibility. It was almost as if Venn himself didn't believe it.

He said he had known the deceased for some time, having been at school with her brother Jasper, but there was a vagueness about how long he had been going out with her. Last Friday night had differed from other evenings because instead of going into town for a drink or the cinema, they had arranged a late picnic in the woods, driving there in Venn's

131

Vauxhall. In his note Nick put an exclamation mark against this choice of an outing in October, but in fact the weather in the past week had been unseasonably warm. Questioned as to who suggested such an excursion in the first place Venn said the idea had come from Blanche who was 'fed up with stuffy old pubs'.

They had reached a suitable glade, off the beaten track in Emberton Wood some time about nine. Yes, Gregory knew the spot; he and Blanche had been there before. However, after saying how he had taken the rug from the car and fetched the picnic basket which Blanche had prepared, Venn's recital of facts seemed to have trailed off.

"It was like pulling teeth," Nick had explained, "getting anything out of him that was relevant. Blanche went to look at some foxgloves, she hadn't liked the pizza he'd brought as his contribution to the meal. He'd opened one of the bottles of wine, and they both drank. I said it must have been quite dark by then. He said he hadn't noticed. Oh, there was a lot of wine drunk – the police found empty bottles. Venn said he'd bought the wine from Jasper Quigley who always had some in stock. That young man must be quite a connoisseur, it was a rather fine claret – a bit expensive for someone like Venn, but one of the things he did mutter was that it was supposed to be a special occasion . . ."

"Not surprising his story getting blurred," Kemp had commented drily at that point, "if he and Blanche were drunk on love and wine."

"The contents of her stomach will tell a tale, no doubt, and I don't know about the love." Nick had apologised for the scrappy state of his notes but repeated that Venn was pretty incoherent. He had admitted that sexual intercourse had taken place between himself and Blanche but he'd no idea of the timing of that, nor anything else. Nor would he say what had caused the row between them.

Going through the notes again Kemp was trying to make out a possible series of events. There had certainly been a quarrel, and it was because of that quarrel that Gregory Venn said he left the scene of the picnic and walked off into the wood. He'd said he wanted to clear his head. He had no idea how long he'd walked, where exactly he'd been, nor what time his walk had taken, could have been a few minutes, half an hour, an hour, even longer. He said that when he did return, 'She was just lying there, dead'.

Stoddart had asked him how he knew she was dead, and he had stared blankly for a moment and then said: "I had to turn her over, didn't I, to see her face? She was dead."

"I lost all patience with him, Lennox," Stoddart had sounded angry even in telling it. "I asked him what the hell he thought he was doing leaving a young girl in a dark wood, in the middle of the night, possibly in a state of inebriation. He'd no answer to that, either for me or the police."

After reading the notes once more, Kemp had to admit that Stoddart seemed to have done all he could; Gregory Venn's story was thin as corn silk and could be torn apart as easily. He sighed, gave instructions, and drove down to the police station where the accused young man was being held.

Kemp found little to like about Gregory Venn. After half an hour with him on the opposite side of a badly stained and scarred table which wobbled on an uneven floor – Newtown Police Station had been built in the penurious fifties and only rarely, and equally meanly, refurbished since – Kemp felt a deal of sympathy for Nick Stoddart. The first part of Gregory's story certainly tallied with what he'd told Nick and the police. It was straightforward, and simple to the point of idiocy. Even when Kemp pressed for more details of why he and Blanche had gone to the woods, Venn would not elaborate further beyond saying she had suggested it; but something had moved behind the shifting eyes, suggesting emotion, and emotion of any kind had been lacking so far.

Kemp did not like the word 'shifty', with its connotations of duplicity and wrong-doing, but unfortunately it described Gregory Venn as no other word could. He had been aware of it on his meeting with the young man the night after Grace Juniper's death but had dismissed it as just a trick of the mind, an association with his impression of a Dickensian clerk – thin, pale and peaked of face – and the shiftiness which tended to stick to such a character. There was no doubt Venn did not possess the frank, open countenance a lawyer might hope for

133

in a client and one that would appeal to a jury. But one must make do with the material on hand, and perhaps the word shifty had come to mind only because of certain aspects of Venn's physiognomy. It might have nothing to do with his true nature.

Kemp concentrated on the essential facts, known and admitted, and tried to link them with Venn's inadequate replies, seeking any shred of possible innocent explanation for behaviour which reeked of guilt, and hoping that something would emerge to throw doubt on the police case already so neatly parcelled up and ready for the prosecution.

"Why did you leave the scene of the picnic?" He was getting tired of asking the same question over and over again.

"I don't remember."

"You and Blanche had been drinking a lot of wine, isn't that so?"

A nod.

"How many times had you filled her glass, or did she fill it herself?"

"I don't know."

"You bought the wine from Jasper. Did it cost a lot?"

This time the nod was more emphatic.

"So it was for a special occasion?"

Again there was a movement behind the eyes. Venn didn't answer so Kemp waited, and then let the moment pass. "Was it special to you, Gregory?" he asked, eventually. The young man attempted to swallow as if something stuck in his throat. "Yes."

"And you'd had sex before, you and Blanche, so it wasn't that . . ." Kemp's tone was ruminative as if thinking aloud. Venn made an impatient gesture as if he found the topic either distasteful or irrelevant.

"Then it was something else . . ." Kemp took it slowly, "something more important?" He noticed that for the first time Gregory Venn's eyes were focussed directly on him. "It meant a lot to you," Kemp continued, gently, fearful of losing the thread.

"Yes . . ." It came on an outgoing breath, like a sigh.

"You wanted her to make some kind of commitment?"

134

A shifting look, sideways, as if Venn dared himself to come to the truth. Kemp sat back and let a moment go by before he put the next question.

"And Blanche wasn't sure?"

He knew instinctively that he had got to the nub of it, it was hanging there in the space between them, but he was totally unprepared for the rush of tears that burst suddenly from Venn's eyes, and ran, uncontrolled, down his cheeks.

Later, Mary said: "He asked her to marry him, and she wouldn't say yes or no. That would be like Blanche . . ."

Kemp had asked her for her view, feeling that do so was not only quite ethical but also imperative. She would know more about the relationship between Blanche and young Venn than he could ever hope to, for one was dead and the other in jeopardy.

Kemp had left the police station in a disturbed state of mind. He had agreed to defend the accused not just because it seemed a hopeless case and he liked a challenge, but also because in those last moments of the interview he had felt a sudden sympathy for the unlikeable youth who had so helplessly broken down in front of him. Not that the breakdown had thrown any light on his story, and it had certainly not led to the confession so eagerly awaited by the officers in the CID room who had been alerted to that possibility by Kemp's call for an end to the interview, and a cup of tea for the accused. Of course it would make their case so much easier if the collapse and the weeping meant that Venn was ready to get it all off his chest, and admit guilt. But, despite his obvious misery and loss of control, he still muttered through sobs that he hadn't done it, that he didn't know what had happened to Blanche after he had left her, and, no, he didn't need medical help – he was all right now that Mr Kemp was taking his case . . .

Which may be fine for him, thought Kemp as he left the station, but how are the efforts of a provincial solicitor going to help him?

It was Mary who now reminded him of his task. "And you'll not be telling me whether it's guilty or innocent you think he is?"

135

"No, I'll not be doing that, and none of your quaint Irishisms will make me."

"But isn't it right that you'd not be defending someone if you were absolutely certain of their guilt?" She went on, without so much as a blush.

"I would advise them on their plea," replied Kemp, amused at her persistence but not giving way, "but the rest would be up to judge and jury."

Mary seemed satisfied, and changed the subject – but not by much.

"I've said to Prim not to talk about it, just be thankful the Press will now leave her alone."

Kemp agreed that it would certainly be a relief to the neighbourhood when the news came that Gregory Venn had been charged. The whole matter could, for the time being, be dropped down the oubliette marked '*sub judice*'.

"I am being a comfort to Miss Weston," said Mary, piously, "and I think she likes having me around now that Primrose hasn't so much to say for herself."

The note of smugness – unusual in her – and the slap at her friend, both in one sentence, made Kemp stare at his wife with some suspicion. He couldn't help wondering what she was up to. He had decided it might be better not to ask, but her next words jolted him.

"The old lady was so upset by being told by Blanche that Deloraine Court is to be sold . . ."

"When did that happen?"

"Must have been before the end of last week. Let me see . . . Prim was out waitressing Wednesday night, so Blanche was sitting with Miss Weston when it seems she had what Prim calls 'a bit of a turn'. Blanche calmed her down – she was better at that than Prim gave her credit for – but the next morning Prim found she hadn't slept well and was so agitated that she called the doctor. Nothing was found to be wrong, but today when I was talking to her Gwen wanted that garden book. When I brought it she thumped it with her fingers as if trying to say something. I got a pad and a biro – that's frowned on by Prim because it's quite a struggle for her to write with her left hand – and after a bit she managed to put down the word 'sell'. I told her that it was to be an estate of smart houses with plenty of green grass which I thought would please her."

"And did it?" Kemp found himself caught up in the narrative.

"It did not. Her face closed up the way it does when she's annoyed. I asked her how she had known about the sale and she pointed to the flat upstairs. I said, 'Blanche?' and she nodded. But then I think it came back to her what had happened. It wasn't right to go further so I diverted her into watching television. When she has to struggle so with thoughts it doesn't seem fair to press her. Bad enough when you have to voice thoughts that disturb, but for them to remain unspoken must hurt . . ."

"I wonder why Blanche should tell her about the place being sold."

"Oh, I think Miss Weston likes to show people that book – she's proud of the inscription from Olga, and wouldn't that be Blanche's great aunt?"

"And Blanche would quite casually mention the sale? H'm, you may be right . . . And that reminds me – I must have a word with Charles tomorrow to find out whether contracts have been exchanged yet, otherwise I'll have Dennis Brinscombe down on my head like a load of his own bricks."

For life must go on; there was other work to be done at Gillorns, besides collecting all the information that would be necessary before preparing the brief to Counsel to act in the defence of Gregory Venn. And when it comes to that, thought Kemp, I'll take old Cedric up on that offer of his, and get the best.

Sixteen

C hief Detective Inspector John Upshire was not pleased. "Changing solicitors at this stage – more bloody paper-work," he grumbled. "And it stinks of desperation."

"Thanks," said Kemp, drily. "I may have come out second best, but I don't see myself as a totally broken reed."

"You know I didn't mean that." The Inspector was testy, uncomfortable for once even in his own home and out of working hours. "I'm not sure you should be here at all," he went on, muttering something unintelligible about ethics.

"You wouldn't know an ethic if it came up and bit you," said Kemp. "Are you going to throw me out?" Upshire was unwinding himself from the depths of his armchair.

"For God's sake, Lennox. I'm just getting us a couple more jars from the fridge . . ."

Kemp grinned. Their friendship had weathered rougher patches than this. "Quite like old times," he said, as John Upshire refilled their glasses.

"Well, at least this time you can't pull any of your Perry Mason stuff over the case. You'd find the CPS a harder nut to crack than we used to be."

"Ah, happy days . . ." Kemp smacked his lips over the good ale as much as over the memories. "We'd be defending your villains one week, and helping you put them away the next."

Upshire nodded. He had still been with the Met when Lennox Kemp had been a young solicitor in Leatown with a law firm which handled much of the legal work for the local police force. Since coming to Newtown some ten years ago Upshire had learned to appreciate how that early training had made Kemp an assiduous searcher after truth – and, sometimes, a damned nuisance.

"The system had to change with the times," said Upshire, grudgingly, "there were a lot of flaws. I'm not saying the CPS is perfect – they're nitpickers to a man . . . or woman . . . there's plenty of them about these days."

"I like them," said Kemp, amiably, "you should get yourself one."

"H'm." John Upshire's bland blue eyes turned to the ceiling. "There's the widow of a colleague I used to know in the Met. She's in her forties. I've been seeing her . . ." His face took on a complacent look.

"You old fox! Mary did remark the last time you came to supper that you seemed happier."

"Well, enough of that." The Inspector made the abrupt change in tone which might startle a subject under interrogation. "Doesn't Mary's involvement with that lot next door bother you in your professional capacity?"

"No," said Kemp, and left it at that.

He and John Upshire went on to talk of other things with the companionable ease of old friends as if the fate of Gregory Venn no longer concerned them. Nothing could be further from the truth. While the Inspector and the CPS built up their case, brick upon brick, against the accused, Kemp went to see him in the Lea Prison where he had been transferred after a brief appearance in the Magistrates Court and his plea of 'Not Guilty' was entered.

The Lea Prison was neither the Fleet nor the Marshalsea although its name held echoes of both as it sprawled like a great horned toad on the wetlands where once the River Lea had tried to figure out a way into the Thames estuary. The buildings, however, were post-war and some attempt had been made in those enlightened years to render them not altogether inhospitable. Gregory Venn in fact did not seem quite out of place there, as if he had been washed up on a shore he recognised.

He was still uncommunicative about what Kemp saw as essential gaps in his story but at least he no longer gave way to weeping. He simply lapsed into sullen silence which was both unproductive and irritating. On other irrelevant matters he was given to sudden bursts of candour – none of which helped his putative defence.

139

"That Stoddart," he told Kemp, "he's a prat. And as for old man Cedric, he couldn't convey a semi-detached in the suburbs. All he's good at is buttering up old ladies whose trusts he's got his paws into. As for David, he's got a brain the size of a pea. Did you know he failed his finals four times? It's only because he's family that he's in there at all."

"Nick's a good lawyer, and it was Cedric Roberts who gave you your articles." Kemp was beginning to agree with Stoddart that Venn was an ungrateful brat. There was a real bitterness in this attack on the firm which had employed the young man, and the only reason for it was that Kemp had taken Cedric's advice and decided to brief Quenton Spence as Counsel for the defence. Venn would have none of it.

"Spence is from the set of chambers Stoddart always uses. I've been up there with him, and they all get very jolly together like old boys on the spree. I don't reckon Quenton Spence is any good. I'd rather have someone of your choice . . ." He looked at Kemp slyly. "Don't you know any good women barristers?"

Kemp didn't know whether to be amused or shocked. Now that the young man before him had stopped being the politely spoken clerk possibly on the make but still a recognisable type, he seemed to have metamorphised into a form of alien life.

"I know several," he replied, "but none, as yet, better than Quenton Spence." And you would be wise to take what's offered and be thankful, he muttered to himself. Cedric Roberts had hinted his firm would pay additional costs where Legal Aid fell short but, as a former client (one on a mitigation-or-nothing course) had remarked: 'When you're going to be banged up for fifteen years you're not bothered who's paying the bill.'

Perhaps Gregory Venn also saw his case as hopeless and was just as reckless as to where the chips may fall. No matter how Kemp turned the conversation there were grievances now being voiced which had been suppressed, presumably for the sake of appearances and career. Even trying to elicit good points on behalf of his client from early strict upbringing, school and academic success all Kemp was getting in return was a torrent of resentment. Gregory saw himself and his parents as patronised but for ever underlings and

140

used by all political parties as pawns in the great educational game.

Finally, Kemp broke into the tirade: "And did you see Blanche Quigley as part of this scheme to keep the working classes in their place?"

Venn stopped, and stared blankly ahead. "My relationship with Blanche is . . . was . . . a private matter," he said, stiffly. "We had a mutual respect. We gave each other space . . ." His voice trailed off, leaving an echo of what could have been lines from any television interview with a pop star on his or her love-life.

Kemp ignored the words, but pressed on.

"You were deeply in love with her? Is that not so?"

Gregory brought his fist up to his mouth. His eyes lost the sparkle they had had when he was making metaphorical hay out of the iniquities of the class system. They became still pools of abject misery.

Kemp felt there was nothing further to be gained from the interview. After dealing with a few practical matters concerning his next visit and what he would expect from it, he left the young man to his thoughts and fears. He may not have much liked Gregory Venn but he felt enormous, helpless pity for him.

Something of this feeling went home with him so that after supper Mary remarked:

"I'll not speak of the case because I can see it's heavy on your mind, but I'll try and divert you from it. Come to think of it that's what I've been doing all day – trying to divert poor Miss Weston from brooding."

"And did you succeed?"

"I don't know. It's not a cheerful household to be in. Prim's worried sick. I suppose it's over Gregory, though I never thought her feelings for him went that deep. But he was one of her little band, and so was Blanche, so I can't blame her for acting like one bereft . . ."

"Bereaved?" Kemp sometimes had trouble following his wife's turn of phrase.

"No, bereft . . . she's lost something. Prim's the kind who makes props out of other people. They hold up her life, now

141

two of them are gone and her world's wobbling. And there will be other changes."

"In what way?"

"Dr Parks came this morning. The old lady's blood pressure is up – which isn't surprising in view of all that's gone on – and there's talk of hospital."

"So Prim might find herself out of a job?"

"It's possible but I don't think it's in the immediate future. Anyway, I know what's putting up Miss Weston's blood pressure."

"I hope you know what you're doing, Mary. If Dr Parks is anxious about the old lady . . ."

Mary took a peach from the fruit bowl and cut it precisely to the stone.

"Miss Weston's blood pressure is raised," she said, "because she's excited. Something which was simmering in her mind has come to the surface. You remember Miss Juniper's book on archaeology and the query she asked her brother-in-law? Well, I have a theory about that so today I took both books in next door, the Deloraine Gardens one and the one on archaeology."

"And what startling revelation followed?"

Mary carefully wiped up the juice which was running down her chin. "Not so fast. Dr Parks had advised rest so she was in bed. I sent Primrose off to the shops and said I would be sitting with Aunt Gwen. She was sleepy but when I put the two books down on her bedside table she sat up and put her good hand on them, thumping it up and down. I said: 'Miss Juniper studied archaeology?' She shook her head. 'Just one point,' I said, and she nodded vigorously. Her eyes were so bright, and her mouth worked as if words were on the tip of her tongue . . ."

Unlike her usual style of coming straight to the point, Mary was spinning out her tale as if venturing on an uncertain course. "She caught at my arm and gestured towards the little desk she has in the corner of her room. Now I've always been very careful never to intrude upon Miss Weston's private business – that's strictly between herself and Primrose . . ."

"You mean money matters?"

142

"Yes. I'll say this for Prim, although she can be pretty casual about her own affairs, she's meticulous when dealing with Miss Weston's. She'll bring in her mail, open it and put it in her lap, and only if the old lady needs any help will Prim read them to her. I've been there when it happens, and I keep my ears open. Prim is very, very careful."

"A wise precaution for someone in her position. She doesn't want anyone saying she takes advantage."

"It's almost as if she's being watched . . . Prim herself, I mean, not only the old lady . . ." For the moment Mary had strayed from her story. Now she took it up again. "Today it was obvious that Miss Weston wanted something from the desk but could not get it for herself and she wanted me to do it for her. I asked her if that was so, and she nodded, yes, so I went over and opened the desk. Inside was as neat as a new pin. I gestured with my hands, right or left? Left, she answered with hers. She was quite enjoying the game. The only papers in the pigeonhole to the left were bank statements and there's little enough on them for I've heard Prim read them out to check the items with Miss Weston. Anyway, I asked her if it was those she wanted and, to my surprise, she nodded, so I took them over and gave them to her. And it was then I lost her . . ."

"How was that?"

"I just could not make out what she wanted from them. She held the small bunch in her good hand and began tapping them on the books, harder and harder. And because I simply could not understand, or because she could not make me understand, she began to get upset and angry. She threw the slips of paper up in the air so that they scattered all over the bed . . . I knew I mustn't go on with that . . . I soothed her, talked to her of other things, I acted like nothing had happened. I took her into the bathroom for a wash, then I gathered up the bits of paper and re-made the bed, and by the time Prim came back Miss Weston was sleeping peacefully . . ."

"And of course you just happened to bring back one of these slips . . ."

"Two, as a matter of fact." Mary fished them out of a pocket. "But they don't tell me anything."

143

"I suppose you shouldn't have taken them but as you have, well, let's have a look."

At the beginning of each month an amount was paid in, a modest sum. "That's her annuity," said Mary, "that's what Primrose calls it. Then, out of that Prim takes her own wages, and an amount for household expenses. Miss Weston signs cheques with her good hand, and Prim always explains what they're for." Kemp remembered how the old lady had signed her Will, firmly and without a shake. "Apart from these withdrawals," Mary went on, "the cheque book's hardly used unless there's a larger item of expenditure – as happened when they needed a new kitchen cabinet because the old one fell off its hinges . . ."

Kemp was studying one of the statements. "H'm, I see there's TV rental, but nothing for electricity, gas or water, nor for council tax."

"According to Prim, they're all paid for by the Property Company."

"Very generous of them. What's this debit of five pounds?"

"It's not on this one." Mary held out the other slip.

"Looks like some kind of quarterly payment. I've got it – it's due to the bank itself."

"What for?"

"Well, most banks now make a charge if they hold anything on deposit for you."

"Like what?"

"Your title deeds, for instance, when you don't have a mortgage."

"That certainly wouldn't apply in Miss Weston's case . . ."

"Or a safe deposit box. People often used to keep a deed box at their bank. It might hold share certificates, or jewellery. They might think a bank a safer place than their home, and because of good client relationships the banks did it for free."

"But no longer?"

Kemp shrugged. "Changes in the attitude of your high-street bank. Lack of space in their buildings. They make a minimum charge. That could account for this five pounds debit."

"Scarcely minimal for someone in Miss Weston's position.

I do wonder at it . . . Could you enquire? You're her executor, aren't you?"

"But that only applies when she's dead," Kemp objected.

Mary looked again at the bank statements. "Why should she have me bring them out from the desk? Why does she draw my attention to them?"

"You're racked by curiosity . . ." Kemp hesitated. "But it's a weakness of mine as well. You'd better return those slips to Miss Weston's desk as soon as you get the chance, and in the meantime I'll make some excuse to raise the matter with the bank."

If you are known, if you are trusted and if you are a solicitor but preferably if you are all three, then information is not too difficult to obtain.

"Nothing particularly secret about it," said Mr Ferris who was on the point of retiring from the relevant bank. Kemp had telephoned him. "Miss Weston has had a deed box here since her father's time. In those days we held the firm's account as well as the family's. Sorry about the charge . . . Head Office policy, you know. We needed the space. Miss Weston would have been given the option of removing the box. Is she complaining?"

"No. But she's not very well off."

"Look, Mr Kemp, I'd have had a word with her if she hadn't had that stroke. The deed box has been here a long time and it's never asked for. She left it at the time of George Weston's death and said it contained nothing of value, just some of the old office books. To tell you the truth I thought she was only keeping them out of sentiment. Now we have to charge it's a bit embarrassing. Do you act on her behalf?"

"In a manner of speaking . . ."

"Then perhaps you can persuade her to have it picked up. Is the old lady capable of making a decision for herself?"

"Oh, yes. I'll speak to her, Mr Ferris, and it may well be that we can take the deed box out of your hands. But of course I shall first get her authority."

The conversation ended amicably, the manager grateful for any move that might rid the bank of an irritating anomaly.

Kemp duly reported back to his wife.

"You mean Miss Weston has a box in the bank for which she has to pay house room?"

"Well, she would have been told when they began to charge, and she doesn't seem to have objected. Perhaps she didn't understand."

"Oh, I'm sure she did. But for some reason she didn't want that box around the house. Now she's drawing my attention to it . . ."

"Why not Primrose Sutton? After all, she's the one deals with her money matters."

"Perhaps its not to do with money. Could you be getting at that box?"

"Only with Miss Weston's authority."

"I could be getting that . . ."

"Not you," said her husband, firmly. "I shall have to see her and find out if she really does want it out of the bank. As for opening it, that would have to be done in her presence. We must be very careful, Mary, we must not be seen to be meddling . . ."

"Meddling, my arse!" It was rare for Mary to revert to the language which had been the everyday coin of her girlhood. It had surprised her to find how easily shocked middle-class English ladies could be, and that Nixon's language on those off-the-record tapes had damned him to them far more than his conduct. Political skulduggery was all very well if couched in tasteful diplomatic prose, but not when scattered with colourful expletives best kept in the gutter where they belonged.

Seeing Kemp's quick frown, she hurried on: "I just know it's what Miss Weston wants. Wouldn't we be doing her a favour, and her not able to get to the bank herself?"

"Perhaps you're right. I could just drop in one evening and say Mr Ferris wondered if he was still to retain the box as they're pushed for space. You do get me into telling falsehoods, Mary . . ."

"Pooh, it wouldn't be the first time. You are a lawyer . . . Seriously though, it might be better if Prim was out, otherwise she might take umbrage. But if Miss Weston had wanted her to do it then she'd have asked her. There's a big dinner coming up at the Castle Hotel soon and Prim has been offered a waitress job again if she wants it. It's the first time since the murder and she's unsure of herself, but she can't resist the extra money. She asked me if I'd sit with the old lady, and I've already agreed. You could come in then and ask about the deposit box, and I could make myself scarce. I do think we're doing the right thing, Lennox. There is something Miss Weston is trying to tell me. She's clearer in her mind than she was, almost as if recent events have made her more determined. And the appeal has been to me – I can't walk away from it . . ."

Seventeen

It is astonishing how quickly the public forgets – or, to put it more accurately, the media allows them to do so. Now that an accused man was in custody, and his trial months away, the death of Blanche Quigley had passed into a kind of limbo land. But Mary Kemp could not free her thoughts from the family most affected. She knew from Primrose that Jasper still occupied the flat next door. As she returned from shopping she met him in the passage between the two houses.

"I'm sorry," she said, "we must clear this gate away. It was only put there when the reporters . . ."

"Its all right, Mrs Kemp," Jasper pulled the old wooden structure to one side. He had surprising strength for one so willowy in appearance. "Shall I just lay it back against your house wall?"

"Yes, thank you, Jasper." She decided to be frank. "I don't know your parents and anyway there was nothing I could say . . . but, Jasper, I did care for your sister, and I think the greatest loss is yours. You'll not be wanting words given you by strangers but if it's to talk about her you need then I've the willing ear . . ."

She knew she had caught his attention by the way he stopped and looked at her, and then seemed at a loss.

Finally, he said, with a sigh: "It's too complicated . . ."

Mary nodded. "I thought it might be," she said, "but when you're ready . . ."

He turned away and trudged down the path towards the staircase leading up to his flat, but she sensed that she had given his thoughts a turn. Up till now he was in her mind simply the other half of Blanche, and she had never considered him a character on his own. Perhaps now was the time to do so.

The events which had happened to the people in the house next door had disturbed Mary more than she liked. After all, they were neither kith nor kin to either she or Lennox and their lives should not have impinged on them so deeply. Was it that there was an emptiness in their late, almost middle-aged, marriage which needed to be filled? Or was it simply that she, Mary, had looked outside her own cosy home for the excitement hitherto inseparable from her life?

It was not that she found her adopted country so dull – certainly not in these months running up to an election. Switching on the television that evening there on the screen was the Right Honourable Stephen Durward-Cooke pontificating on the high moral values to which his party, it seemed, held the sole rights.

Pink and white, like a well-scrubbed pig with his hair sleeked back and a curl to his lip, he sounded the very soul of sincerity since he obviously believed every word he uttered. There was an air of absolute confidence about him which reminded Mary of Elmer Gantry type preachers she had heard in small churches out the mid-west, men to whom all copyright in the texts of the Lord had been graciously given . . .

"Why's he got it in for the Germans?" She asked her husband. "He doesn't much like the French – though I bet he drinks their wine – but I thought the war was over years ago."

"There's a certain age-group he's aiming for. The ones who fought and didn't get quite the country fit for heroes they expected. And that goes a long way back. He'd like to strike that bitter chord."

Mary looked at the screen a moment. "Please can I turn it off?" she said, eventually. "Perhaps I'm prejudiced, but I just don't care for him."

Kemp did as she wished. He sighed. "I'm afraid we're going to have a lot more of the same in the next few months. If you've never experienced a British election before, you've never lived."

"Why? Are they worse than ours?"

"Just different." Mary could see that he was, if anything, faintly cynical when it came to politics. Well, that suited her. She could not herself show much interest, although intrigued by the Honourable Member for – what was it? Welchester West.

"The two cousins," she said, referring to Durward-Cooke and Simon Quigley, "don't look like one another but they do have that same haughty manner, and implacable confidence in themselves."

"That need not be a family thing. More the result aimed at by their education. It's supposed to have won us the Empire . . ."

"It may have won it," said Mary, tartly, "but it didn't do much good keeping it. And the young don't have it, thank goodness. Jasper for all his private schooling seems to me an uncertain kind of fellow . . ."

"You've seen him lately?"

"Yes. I think he wants to talk . . ."

"What about?"

"Well, there's only one subject, isn't there? He's caught up in conflicting emotions: sadness for the loss of a sister, and what should he feel for the friend accused of killing her?"

Kemp shifted uncomfortably. They were sitting after dinner, drinking coffee. He had not had an easy day. There were other problems at Gillorns besides mounting some kind of defence for Gregory Venn, but after several interviews at the Lea Prison Kemp was beginning to feel up against a brick wall. Perhaps it would clear the air somewhat if he talked over the case with Mary. She was a good listener, and she had known the persons concerned before the tragedy. He asked her outright whether she thought Gregory capable of such a crime.

"Not when he was sober," she said, after some time, "but drink can do terrible things to a person, and it seems he'd had a lot."

"The prosecution will say so – secure in the knowledge that drunkenness itself is no defence . . . but a few bottles of wine? And some of that was in the stomach contents of Blanche. It's not as if they'd been drinking all day. Gregory drove them to the wood, and I think he was sober enough then. I don't think he could have been drunk enough not to know what he was doing."

"Did the scene of crime officers do their job properly?"

"No doubt of that. I've read the reports. The ground was covered meticulously, they even went deep into the surrounding woods."

"I only ask because once they'd got Gregory they might not have bothered."

Kemp shook his head. "They didn't bring him in until the Saturday night, and even then John Upshire wouldn't be sure they'd got their man. No, the scene was thoroughly searched for signs that others might have been involved. Remember, it's a favourite spot for local lovers. There were tyre marks of other cars in the nearby wood. They put out an appeal for witnesses, anyone who had seen or heard anything – but it came to nothing. Not surprising when you think of it . . . Courting couples – to give them an old-fashioned name – aren't likely to come forward when they've been snogging in the back of cars, and as for those with adulterous partners they'd be the last to want publicity. No, Mary, I have to take it that the whole police operation was properly conducted, and I've been out and looked at the place myself. As I said, it's a popular spot after dark."

Mary turned the corners of her mouth down.

"H'm . . . just the kind of place that would suit Gregory. He's not got a lot of imagination, that one. And if it was Blanche who suggested it, he'd go along with all the zeal of schoolboy love."

"He's no schoolboy, Mary, he's halfway through a law course."

"I think it's overturned completely he's been. It had come suddenly, this feeling for Blanche; there was no inkling of it earlier when he and Jasper were just fooling around."

"Was it Blanche, then, leading him on?"

"I don't think so. I think she was surprised too. Sometimes it happens that way with the young." Mary was silent for a moment. "Perhaps that was the trouble," she said, eventually, "it coming so sudden on both of them, for there'd be things behind that would come to the surface."

"You mean what they quarrelled about?"

She nodded. "It wasn't the sex thing . . . That had already

happened. But say something out of the past came up and set them at loggerheads."

Kemp considered the idea. "Must have been serious enough to send young Venn striding into the darkness – if his story's true, of course."

"Oh, I don't think it was trivial . . . And from what you tell me of his present mood, it still bugs him. Can't you get it out of him, Lennox?"

Kemp sighed. "Whatever it is, he's hanging on to it. Of course I want to know, and so will his Counsel. I agree with you that Gregory at that stage wanted to make their relationship more permanent, he wanted some commitment on her part. It must have been her answer that brought them both to the sticking point. Something she said then . . ."

"Maybe the reason for her uncertainty?"

"Perhaps. Could it simply be the class thing?"

Mary had a long think. "I doubt it," she said. "Blanche was well on the way to throwing off the last shreds of her parents' influence. She liked being part of the student thing, and was beginning to see herself as liberated from middle-class prejudice. Dating Gregory Venn might have started out as part of that liberation, but I think she found herself genuinely in love."

Kemp could only take this as feminine perception but he had to agree that, given present fluctuations in values, there could not be anything particularly incongruent in a match between Blanche Quigley and Gregory Venn, especially if one took into account the future career he might have had as a rising young lawyer.

Even middle-aged, well-established lawyers had their problems, and the one at present on Kemp's office desk was the file purchase of Deloraine Court. According to the last letter from Roberts, the vendor's solicitors, 'family matters' were causing the delay in signing contracts, and the forbearance of the purchaser was requested until the matter could be resolved.

"It's all too vague and airy-fairy," fumed Charley Copeland, "and not the kind of language our Mr Brinscombe understands."

Kemp had to agree; forbearance was not something that came naturally to the son of a dodgy East End trader. "I'll try and advocate patience," he promised Charley, who left the office with raised eyebrows in an expression of 'rather you than me, mate'.

Fortunately, Lennox and Mary Kemp were entertaining the Brinscombes to dinner that weekend.

"It's the election, of course," said Kemp to Alan, over the sherry. "All prospective members are keeping their powder dry, their little white socks out of the mud, and their business dealings out of the public eye."

"How's it affecting the Deloraine Court deal?"

"Search me . . . but for some reason I think it does. Could be Stephen Durward-Cooke simply doesn't want people to know he's selling till after the election . . ."

Alan snorted. "That's rubbish. It's not over the odds, the price I'm paying. He was asking too much years ago; at least the depression's brought him down to summat reasonable."

"You and I know that, but the general public don't, and it's the general public that all candidates are keeping well in their sights. The man in the street has only to hear the word million and he's all in a twitter – particularly if it's going to a Conservative MP."

But Alan Brinscombe was shrewd. "I don't go along with that, Lennox. I think Durward-Cooke's stalling for another reason, and it's got to do with that cousin of his . . ."

"Certainly Quigleys were the first to put a stop on the deal – which I find interesting, since they'd be taking a hefty commission on the sale."

"Family matters, my arse . . ." Alan did have the grace to turn round to see if the women were safely out of earshot. He wasn't bothered about his own wife, but Mary Kemp looked as if she might have a prim side to her. He needn't have worried; both women had heard him and giggled.

"Will he hang on then for the property?" asked Mary. "He's not got the reputation for patience . . ."

"Oh, he'll hang on." Brenda Brinscombe knew her husband to the core. "He wants that property and he can afford to wait. He's right about Quigleys being the stumbling block for all that they were so anxious to get the property off their hands at the start. I've got a niece works there, and she says the order to hold things up came right from the top."

"Meaning?"

"The high and mighty Simon himself. Do you know him?"

"A very brief meeting. What's he really like?"

"Everybody who works there respects him. I don't think he's the sort to be liked exactly. Olive's been at Quigleys since she left school and now she's on a good salary with prospects. The original firm was just auctioneers and surveyors, but once Simon Quigley took over from his father and branched out into property-owning he built up one of the most prosperous businesses hereabouts. Of course he had to eat up a few small estate agents on the way, but that's business, isn't it?" Dennis Brinscombe had eaten up several struggling builders, too, in his time.

"Simon Quigley's never married?"

"No – which is surprising, for he'd be some catch, the money he's got. Lots have tried, according to Olive. Of course he's always been very thick with that cousin of his, him that really owns Deloraine Court. We don't get to see much of him these days in Newtown, now that his constituency's down in Hampshire. Don't like what I see of him on the telly – what's he know about single parents, I ask you?"

Mary recounted with delight the tale of Stephen Durward-Cooke's inauspicious opening of the college library, and she and Brenda were still laughing about it when they went to inform their husbands that dinner was at last ready to be served.

They had reached the pudding stage when the subject of the Deloraine Court property came up again. Alan remarked that if he and Brenda did decide to give up on their Spanish retirement they might well come home and live in one of the houses on his new development – that is, if this present pesky deal ever got off the ground.

"Of course it'll go through eventually," Kemp assured him, "if I have to tackle Cedric Roberts and Simon Quigley together on the reason for the delay . . ."

"Did you know we have a spy in the enemy camp?" said

Mary, innocently, leaving Brenda to explain the position of her niece, Olive. Mary was intrigued to find what a small world Newtown was, and she was aware that underlings in offices tend to be surprisingly well informed.

Eighteen

Having to attend to the needs of the young and the elderly, both helpless without her, seemed to have brought Primrose Sutton back from the wobbly edge to which Mary thought she might be heading. Now the brightness had returned to her eyes, along with their habitual wariness, when she called on Mary one morning.

"Come in for a coffee, Prim?" Mary held the door open.

"I've come to ask another favour, if you don't mind." Prim's words tended to come with a rush when she wanted something. "The thing is, there's a get-together at Liza-Jane's play group this afternoon. All the other mums seem to be going. Only an hour or so, bit of a tea-party . . ."

"And you want me to sit with Miss Weston? Of course I will. It's my afternoon off college, anyway."

"Trouble is, Dr Parks said he might call in this afternoon, he can never say a time, poor man, he's so busy. He doesn't stay long. Auntie Gwen's fine just now. She'll be in her room, and he usually sees her in there . . . it's just somebody to open the door for him. He knows his way round the flat. Thanks ever so, Mary . . . don't know what I'd do without you." She gave a little, nervous laugh.

She's almost back to the old, lively Prim, thought Mary. Possibly there had been other crises in Prim's life before this one, and whether shaken by them or not, she recovers fast. Perhaps it helped that her nature was essentially superficial, her way of life haphazard. It might even be that her very lack of attachment to the people in her immediate vicinity cushions her against the hurts and confusions that assail those of deeper feelings in the wake of tragic events.

Mary remembered how quickly Primrose had disposed of

even the memory of Grace Juniper by simply never speaking of her again.

"Have another cup, Prim?"

"No, but thanks. Must be on my way. I've got to tidy up Aunt Gwen's room – although the doctor is in and out so quick he'd never see any dust."

She hesitated on the doorstep. "I don't suppose there's any news?"

Mary shook her head. "Lennox is doing all he can for him. If only Gregory would do more to help himself . . . How is Jasper taking it?"

"I hardly see him these days. I think he'd rather live somewhere else – I can't say I blame him. He's well in with that uncle of his so perhaps he'll get him another berth. Thanks again, Mary. Me and Liza-Jane we'll be back before five I reckon."

"Take your time. I don't mind how long I stay."

Which was the truth. Mary was only too glad of the opportunity to be alone at 4 Albert Crescent with Miss Weston, and even Dr Parks' visit might prove informative.

It warmed her heart to see the delight in the old lady's face when she entered the bedroom where Miss Weston was sitting in her chair by the window. It looked out on the back garden and the view of grey-green bushes and long, uncut grass was not inspiring. When the boys were about, they used to take turns with the old mower and kept the lawn fairly tidy, but of course that was weeks ago, and neglect had showed up all too soon.

"I've brought that anthology you asked for ages ago," said Mary, wheeling the chair into the sitting-room which was lighter and where there was a fire.

Back in the days of normality the old lady had indicated a liking to have poetry read to her, and by turning the pages herself she pointed to those she wanted. To Miss Weston these were obviously favourites, for sometimes her lips would move as she listened to the words, but to Mary Kemp this was jungle territory hitherto unexplored. Never had she heard poetry spoken, and little enough had she read until she began her college course. At first she had not known how to speak the lines, the language so strange, the images so outlandish, the meaning so elusive. She had lived her life in a hard factual world which had no room for imagination, so this form of creative thought had been denied her – indeed she had scorned it as useless. However, on raising the matter with her mentor, the Mancunian Bradshaw, he had said that a good dose of poetry was just what she needed, and recommended Palgrave's *Golden Treasury* which happened to be one of the books from Miss Juniper. Mary had begun to practise at home – much to the amusement of her husband, for her voice was flat and her sense of rhythm and metre rudimentary. Gradually she felt the pull of the words and, almost like a child hearing for the first time sounds and rhymes not used in every day speech, she was becoming entranced by this new world of music, myth and magic. "But I don't understand," she had wailed to Mr Bradshaw, who assured her that meaning would come after, just to enjoy the buzz.

When the bell rang they were on the last verse of 'Lepanto', and Mary went to the door singing to herself 'But Don John of Austria rides home from the Crusade', while her mind was telling her that this old woman, Miss Weston, knew who he was, and what the battle had all been about, whereas she, Mary, knew nothing.

Her feelings of inferiority were further stressed by recalling how much of her working life had been spent opening doors to doctors.

"Go right in, Dr Parks," she found herself saying as she followed him through the hall. "I'll take Miss Weston into her room."

Mary herself went off into the kitchen to make tea, and wondered just how many such kettles she had put on to boil in the whole of her days. It must be the poetry that's doing it, she muttered, it makes you reflect on space and wasted time.

Dr Parks was not long with the old lady. "She's resting now," he said when he came back into the sitting-room where Mary had a tray ready on a table by the fireside. "Would you be having a cup?" she asked. "I know you're busy, but . . ."

He was middle-aged, ruddy of face but overworked and tired. "The very thing," he said. "I wish all my stroke patients were as good as Miss Weston. She handles her disability well, doesn't try to fight it, and apart from the effects of the stroke, she keeps in excellent health. Surprising that, in view of all that's been happening round her."

Mary handed him tea, and a buttered scone. He seemed very ready to sit for a while and talk, perhaps simply a respite in a busy schedule.

"Is it wrong for me to be dredging up her memories?" She asked. "There are things she's desperate to remember. It won't hurt, will it, her trying to get them back?"

"A lot of rubbish talked about repressed memories, Mrs Kemp. Of course it won't hurt someone like Miss Weston. She's always been a sensible woman and having a stroke doesn't change basic personality. I've noticed that in fact she seems brighter when she's got a person face to face. Miss Juniper was good for her, so are you."

"Has she been your patient long?"

"She and her father were on our practice list when we started. Miss Weston herself never needed our services much until Mr Weston was dead, and it was only when she had a couple of minor strokes and then a large one that she needed treatment. She was in hospital for a time, and then was most fortunate in being able to return to the family home."

"I understand the property company who own it have been most generous."

"Ah, that's because Simon Quigley is behind it . . ."

"Now, I'd not be knowing that," Mary observed.

"Few people would. Old Simon tends to hide his philanthropic side. And I should imagine it was he who found someone like Primrose Sutton to come and live in to look after the old lady. The practice wasn't too keen on that in the first instance because she had no professional nursing experience, but she's done a good job."

Mary agreed, and after a few more minutes of conversation she discovered why the doctor, despite being hard-pressed by home visits and still with an evening surgery to face, was nonetheless inclined to linger. Like everyone else, he was human and infected by curiosity about the household in which he had a peripheral interest.

"I don't think I ever met young Venn," he was saying, "though I'd heard him spoken of. Do you think he did it, Mrs Kemp?"

Mary had found that medical men could be forthright – so long as they were not themselves being asked for their professional opinion, when they were more likely to hedge. Well, she could be equally forthright.

"No," she said, firmly. "And I can tell you no more. It's my husband's duty to help the young man, that's all I can say . . ."

"Of course. Of course. I quite understand. A terrible business. And Miss Quigley a relative of that MP . . ."

"Does that make it somehow worse?" Mary responded, tartly.

The doctor laughed. "I only meant it was something for the Press to pick on. Stephen Durward-Cooke's no great favourite of mine – though doctors are supposed to be non-political animals . . ." He got to his feet, reluctant to leave the fire. "Must be on my way. Thanks for the tea and chat, Mrs Kemp. Don't worry about what you call dredging up the old lady's memories. A mind needs exercise as much as a limb – and I don't think you'll find any dark secrets in Miss Weston's."

She followed him to the front door.

"Puzzles me a bit, Doctor Parks, you saying how Primrose Sutton might have come here . . . Why should Simon Quigley – if indeed it was him – know someone like her?"

"Oh, probably she was one of the squatters. His company bought a lot of semi-derelict properties down by the railway three or four years ago, and cleared them out. It's quite likely that Mrs Sutton and her little girl were homeless. She'd have jumped at the chance of a roof over her head."

When the doctor had gone, Mary repeated the phrase to herself; it was one often used by Primrose.

If the circumstances suggested by Doctor Parks were true, it would explain Prim's deliberate vagueness on the subject of her previous life, and the various tales spun about as to why she had ended up looking after Miss Weston: she was no relative, and there had been no advertisement in any magazine, no agency had introduced her to the job.

Homeless. And with a new baby . . . Mary gave a shudder. Even that shack in Vineland had been a sort of home when she left. But she had been unencumbered, glad to leave and full of resource. If you had a child and were without a roof over your head, to what lengths would you go, what would you not do?

Mary went back to Miss Weston, brought her into the sitting-room for tea, and then resumed the poetry, reading the invalid's favourite – 'The Lady of Shalott'. Not a word of it did Mary understand; she could only guess in what faraway century the poem was set, but as she stammered over 'God in His mercy lend her grace' she saw Blanche Quigley's shining fall of hair as if it was she who had lain down in the boat to die. She too had had a lovely face . . .

Mary choked, and could not go on. "I'm sorry," she told Miss Weston, "I don't know what's come over me . . ."

The old lady put out her good hand, and closed the book herself. She nodded several times, and briefly closed her eyes.

She understands more than I do, thought Mary as she cleared the tea things. Those words in poems are wakening something in me that I never knew existed. Is it what they call imagination? I've got along well enough without that up till now . . .

Any further revelations as to other hidden depths of mind were prevented by the arrival home of Prim and Liza-Jane. Mary found herself following her usual habit of getting answers to anything that puzzled her as soon as practicable.

"Prim," she said, when they were in the kitchen, and Liza-Jane fully occupied giving Miss Weston a blow-by-blow account of events at the tea-party, "how did you actually come here to this house?"

Primrose kept her head over the sink, and her hands busy in the soapy water. "Why d'you want to know?"

"Sure and there's no harm in talking about it, is there?" Mary planted the ball firmly in Prim's court, and waited.

"Well, the job was going . . . wasn't that the money was anything . . . But it was a roof over our heads, me and Liza . . ."

"I meant how did you hear there was a job going? Were you already in Newtown?"

Prim turned and wiped her hands dry on the roller towel. "I suppose someone's been gossiping. If you really want to know, Mary, I was in a bit of trouble . . . Liza-Jane's dad went off, like, back on Merseyside, and I had a friend down here but that didn't work out either . . ."

"You were in a squat?" Mary put it bluntly.

"Nothing wrong with squatting," said Prim with the pugnacity she brought to any question of social justice.

"I'm not saying there is, and anyway I'm the last person to question it . . . It was something Dr Parks said about Simon Quigley's properties that made me ask you, Prim."

Primrose finished drying her hands which had taken longer than need be. She slumped down on a kitchen chair. "No reason why you shouldn't know now, with so much happening. I was desperate, we were getting thrown off the site where I'd been about six months. It was good at first, we all chummed up and they were great about the baby. A right little community we were, about half a dozen of us . . ." Prim's voice had a note of prideful nostalgia as at some lost paradise which Mary guessed had never been but had slotted into Prim's vagrant memory like a glimpse of Utopia.

"And then the property you were in got bought up by one of Quigley's companies?" she prompted.

"I've never even met Simon Quigley." Prim turned belligerent. "I don't know him at all."

"Well, who was behind this offer of a job?"

"I didn't know it was him. The Social Services were after me because of the baby. Said it was their duty to house us . . . that rotten bed-and-breakfast stuff. I wasn't having any of that . . . so when this man came from the Quigley estate agency and said his boss was sorry about everything, like turning us out, and he'd a special interest in me because of the kid, and there was this old lady needed looking after . . . Well, it was a roof over our heads, wasn't it?"

"So you keep saying, Prim. Could you be telling me how the arrangements were made?"

Primrose shrugged. "They never asked for references if that's what you mean. They took me to see Miss Weston, and we got on like a house on fire, so it was all right, and I

162

just moved in. I told the doctors when they came that I'd done a bit of nursing . . . Well, I'd helped out at an old peoples' home when I left school, and I'm not thick." She stopped and glared at Mary who burst out laughing so heartily that Prim laughed too.

"You're far from thick," said Mary. "In fact you're a very responsible person, and you're doing a good job here with Auntie Gwen, as you call her."

"That was their idea, that I might be some sort of relative. They said it would reflect badly on the old lady if people thought she'd just taken in someone off the street. I only hinted, mind you, I never told anyone direct I was kin to her."

Mary was more intrigued than ever. "You keep talking about 'they' – who do you mean?"

"After I got settled in I never saw the man from the estate agency again, and all my instructions started to come by letter – no heading, simply marked 'Private and Confidential'. It set out my pay, and the arrangements for Miss Weston's cheques and banking and all that. It was all very straightforward, as if it was from solicitors or accountants, so I took it they were the people who had Miss Weston's best interests at heart. After a while I never really thought about it. I was so blessedly thankful to have a job and a roof . . ."

"Over your head. Did any further instructions come?"

"From time to time . . ." But Prim seemed reluctant to talk further. "Best be getting back to Auntie," she said, in her abrupt, dismissive way. Mary had no option but to follow her back to the sitting-room.

Nineteen

"People say 'they' when they talk about employers, authorities or the Government – usually when looking for somewhere to plant the blame." Lennox Kemp had listened with growing interest to his wife's detailed account of her afternoon.

"In Prim's case it would be her employers," said Mary, "whoever it was sending her instructions from time to time, and they seem to be the faceless ones. Wait now, I'm remembering something else . . . the morning Prim was at her most unsteady, just after Blanche was killed and Gregory was already being held. I wondered what she was talking about. Just let me get her words back: 'Nobody told me what they were doing here . . .' and 'they said for it not to happen'. And more about the old lady not being allowed to get upset remembering, but then Prim was always going on about that. I've had it straight from Doctor Parks' mouth that there's no harm in it. Oh, and Prim did say; 'She got too close . . .' and I'm thinking now she meant Blanche." Mary paused.

"Do you think both the Quigley youngsters – and Gregory Venn for that matter – were all aware that Primrose had instructions to watch over Miss Weston? Do you think they were all of them in it?"

Mary's face suddenly lit up. "Of course. Now I see it, what I only felt before. It was always there between them, some kind of understanding. I'd maybe not be exaggerating if I said conspiracy. And I was always an outsider. I thought it was because they were all young and I wasn't . . . but there was more to it than that." Mary was frowning now with the difficulty of putting into words the blurred impressions that had floated in her mind. "Their jokiness," she said, slowly, "their larking about, they were all very much at home with each other like you get when people share a secret and have fun at the expense of those outside their circle . . . I'm not putting this very well . . ." She ended, lamely.

"You're doing all right. At least with you, Mary, I know you don't imagine things." He himself was more perturbed by what she had told him than he would allow her to see. In his own mind he was building brick upon brick, the interlocking pieces of a sort of framework, fitting in vague facts which had up till now seemed irrelevant. For instance, the so-called mystery of how Primrose Sutton had come to work next door, the relationship of the younger Quigleys to the property tycoon, Simon, and the recent advancement in their careers of both Jasper and Gregory Venn. And did any of this help the lad now languishing in the Lea Prison? Kemp said nothing of this speculation to his wife except to murmur: "Perhaps when we get that box of Miss Weston's from the bank all will be revealed." Privately, he doubted it.

As if reading his thought, Mary said: "She signed the letter you gave me." It was short.

To the Manager
Southminster Bank Ltd
Newtown

Dear Mr Ferris,
    I hereby give permission for the handing over to my solicitor, Mr Lennox Kemp, of the deed box marked 'Weston' at present in your safekeeping.
                                        Yours faithfully
                                        Gwendolyne Weston

"I explained what it was," Mary went on, "and let her read it for herself. She seemed glad to sign it. She got a bit flurried about having the box in the house so I said you would only bring it to her when she was quite alone. She indicated that she did want it opened and that you were to do it. Now, that dinner at the Castle Hotel, it's this Saturday evening and Prim is going to wait tables. I told

165

Miss Weston you would come in then, and she smiled and nodded agreement."

Kemp was not altogether at ease with what they were doing. He put his hesitation down to a lawyer's natural caution, born out of experience of seeing the most innocent of actions misconstrued. On the other hand, it did look as if the old lady herself was aware that she was under some kind of watchful eye in her own home, and was taking steps to avoid it over this particular possession. And, of course, Kemp did not lack curiosity.

In fact, the deed box turned out to be just a nondescript container of the old-fashioned sort, black tin, somewhat scratched over the years and with the lettering "G. Weston" almost indecipherable. A key was attached to the lock by an ancient piece of string when the box was handed over by the bank manager.

"Thank goodness for that," said Kemp. "I did wonder if Miss Weston might have mislaid the key and I didn't fancy having to break the thing open." Honesty was called for in case his action ever came into question so he had explained to Mr Ferris that it was Miss Weston's wish to have the box opened in private at home.

"Quite right," said Ferris, "she'll be tidying up her affairs before she goes so as not to trouble her executors . . ."

"Invalid she may be," remarked Kemp, drily, "but Miss Weston has no intention of leaving us just yet. I understand her general health is good."

"Sorry . . . I didn't mean . . . I'm afraid we tend to get into the habit of thinking people with stroke are on the brink of . . . Please give her my good wishes . . ." Still apologising, he hurried Kemp to the door.

About the same time that morning, Mary was leaving her house to go shopping when she saw Jasper Quigley in the drive of Number Four carrying two hold-alls.

"Are you going from us, Jasper?" She called over.

He hesitated, dropped the bags and came across. "Just putting a few things in the car," he said. "Yes, I've got another place." His face was haggard, its pale beauty – for he still had that – smudged as if it had been wiped

with a soiled rag. His eyes looked heavy from want of
sleep.

"Are you not well?" Mary was sorry for him and it showed
in her voice. "Would you like to come in a minute for a cup
of something warm?"

The young man stood irresolute, then with an air almost of
resignation, he said: "I wouldn't mind, Mrs Kemp . . . I'm a
bit cold, actually. It's rather chilly up there in the flat."

"Put your stuff in the car, then, and come in," said Mary
briskly. "I think there was a touch of frost in the night . . ."
How useful is weather-talk, she thought, as she went back
indoors, how it bridges those awkward moments. She turned
up the thermostat in the kitchen, and bustled about with coffee
pot and a couple of mugs so that by the time Jasper came in
the setting was cosy and welcoming.

They talked at first of trivial things until Jasper had relaxed,
the pallor of his cheeks warmed by the atmosphere and the
hot drink.

"You really were cold out there," said Mary, keeping up
the pretence that that was all that was wrong with him. "You
should be wearing a thicker jacket."

"I've not got round to thinking about clothes," said Jasper,
ruefully, "there's been too much going on . . ."

"And no one to share it with. Is that the trouble, Jasper?"

"I can't sleep. I keep on thinking about him . . ."

"That's only natural. He's your friend."

If Jasper caught the intent behind the tense used he didn't
respond. He sat in silence for a few minutes, absent-mindedly
picked up a biscuit and munched it; he'd already demolished a
plateful. As Mary suspected, he'd obviously had no breakfast,
and young men like him were not in the habit of going
for long without eating. Sleepless nights and foodless days
combined with the sudden drop in temperature had reduced
Jasper Quigley to a state he probably didn't recognise as
unhealthy, quite apart from the emotional strain recent events
must be having on his mind.

"Can I tell you something, Mary?" He said, abruptly. She
had already admonished him for not using her first name,
saying it made her feel older than the hills.

"Yes, if you want to, Jasper."

"It's about Greg." Only Jasper ever called him that – a relic of their schooldays.

"Ah, well then I must be careful. Is it something you'd be wanting Mr Kemp to know?"

"Yes, I think so . . ." Jasper paused. Then he could scarcely contain the flow of words that followed. "It was me who told Blanche that night they went out for the picnic, the thing they quarrelled about. I didn't mean to . . . well, yes, at the time I probably did . . . I was feeling – oh, I don't know what I was feeling. I missed the nights down at the pub with Greg once he began going out with Blanche, and I suppose I missed her too in a different way. There wasn't any other reason for telling her, I just thought it might put her off getting serious about him . . ." Jasper stopped to get his breath.

Mary allowed a moment to go by, then she said: "Whatever it was you told her, would it have made any difference?"

"I just don't know . . . But if I hadn't said anything they wouldn't have quarrelled and he wouldn't have left her like that."

"What do you mean, like that?"

"Going off into the wood, leaving her there . . ."

Mary had not seen any of Gregory Venn's statement to the police, and had only her husband's conversations with her to go on, but she went hurriedly through her mind for what she could remember of Jasper's part in the matter before she spoke. The Friday night of the murder Jasper had been at his parents' house where he was looking after their dogs while they were in Spain. A neighbouring couple had been in and they had all watched television together. On the Saturday, he had been found there by the police and told of his sister's death, and he had accompanied them to the morgue. He had gone back to his own flat from there but Mary didn't know whether or not he could have seen Venn before he was arrested.

"What you told Blanche before she went out with Gregory on the Friday evening, that's what's bothering you, isn't it? Tell me, Jasper, what it was?" Mary could be very persuasive when she tried.

"What really happened to Miss Juniper . . . what we'd all

done. I thought Blanche must have half guessed anyway that it had been a joke which went terribly wrong . . . which it was, of course. But I don't think she'd known Greg's part in it till I told her. And I swear I didn't know everything at first . . . it was only when Greg began telling me the facts. I'd been ribbing him about his promotion, how it had come sooner than expected. It was then he told me why . . . and I realised how serious it was, Miss Juniper's fall that night. I swear I hadn't known, and by the time I got it out of Greg it was too late . . ."

The facts. What I am about to hear, thought Mary, is going to shock and hurt me. She braced herself. "Go on, Jasper, you have to tell me."

"Primrose started it by saying Grace Juniper was upsetting her patient, talking to her about things she shouldn't. Someone outside was saying the same thing to Greg. I knew all about how Greg got the flat through his firm – it was a condition he kept an eye on things downstairs. Someone had an interest in the old lady. We treated it as a bit of a joke, actually. But then he was told the new tenant in the middle flat was becoming a nuisance. Word had got round. It was hinted perhaps it would be better if she left. Greg thought a little accident . . ." Jasper heard Mary's sharp indrawn breath, and stopped. "Only an accident," he muttered, "nothing serious . . ."

"The facts, Jasper," Mary prompted, softly.

"It was one of the times when Prim would be out all night – that had happened before but we weren't supposed to say anything, and she would have Miss Juniper on tap, as it were. Gregory was to watch a late-night film on the TV while Liza-Jane and the old lady were safely asleep. I never asked how he did it . . . Probably called Miss Juniper from the foot of the back staircase . . . something about Liza-Jane needing her."

Mary flinched. I don't want to hear any more of this, she thought, but I must.

"Her torch?"

Jasper's fist went over his mouth. His voice choked on the words. "It was meant to be a joke. That day I'd offered to put a new battery in it for her. I made sure I put in a dud. All we meant was for her to have a little fall, just enough to make her leave . . ."

"Gregory said he wasn't there that night? He came back at ten the next day."

"That's what we arranged. He says that when he heard her fall he never even looked, just got in his car and came over to our house. I was to say he'd been with me all the time. No one ever asked."

Of course they didn't, thought Mary bitterly. Just as no one ever checked Prim's story that she'd been home. And Prim must have known. She said it aloud.

Jasper shook his head. "I don't think Prim knew anything, though she may have guessed a lot. She picked up the torch and made sure it disappeared. I think she probably tried it to see if it worked. Greg said she should have left it for the ambulance men to find, and it would have gone to the police as another reason for an accidental fall . . . I don't know . . . I don't understand the way Prim's mind works. And she'd seen me put in that battery."

So she'd keep the torch to use against you if need be, thought Mary, grimly. What a parcel of rogues they all were! Prim was more victim than the others; they'd used her and there was nothing she could do about it. She could hardly come out in the open and admit leaving the old lady and the child all night.

"You know this is very serious, Jasper," she told him, "I shall have to tell my husband."

"But no one else," said Jasper, eagerly. "Don't you see? That's why I've told you, so that Greg's defence can use it."

"I don't see that it's going to help his chances that he's already responsible for someone dying," said Mary.

"Because it's that he's feeling so much guilt about, not for killing my sister!" Jasper got up and pushed his chair aside. "I was behind the police when they went up to his flat that Saturday. They barred my way in but Greg looked at me over his shoulder, and that's what he said: 'I'm guilty of one thing but not of this . . .' He was speaking to me, Mary, he wanted me to understand. Then they closed the door and I didn't see him again."

Twenty

It was Friday and Lennox Kemp was on his way to the Lea Prison. It would likely be the last time he would visit without Venn's Counsel, for the brief would soon reach Quenton Spence. Kemp curled a rueful lip when he thought of the word: a succinct recital of facts to be put to the court in defence of the accused, straightforward, sober facts that a jury could understand, nothing too abstruse or difficult for the man in the street to comprehend and, if possible, sympathise with. No room here for airy speculation or abstract theorising – apart of course from what might be skilfully introduced as possible alternatives to the prosecution's case, just enough to blur the issue if the going got rough, and plant seeds of reasonable doubt in the combined heads of those in the jury box.

And then, with the verdict against you, the mitigating circumstances: hard-working young man from decent but underprivileged background; brilliant career till this tragic event; a culmination of drink he was not used to, sexual passion he could not control, and the misery of rejection by the girl he genuinely loved . . .

Kemp sometimes felt he could do it all himself, but the system was the system, the unchanging face of institutionalised law. On the other hand he knew he hadn't the talent, the touch of theatricality which exudes sincerity in the voice of a good barrister as it does with an actor. Kemp's own *métier* lay rather in the building-up of a case, the foundations, the footings, the infrastructure, knowing which bricks to use and which to leave out. These things were occupying his mind fully as he drove.

He had listened and taken notes of Mary's account of her talk with Jasper, and been as frustrated as she with its ending.

"Of course I wanted to know who was behind all this

watching of Miss Weston, but every time I asked him that he clammed up on me. At first he just muttered that it was all a joke. They called it the secret she didn't know she had. When I went on about it, he got angry – really angry. Out of what seemed to me utter misery he suddenly jumped into a fury. Not hot anger but something cold and nasty. He would deny everything, he said, if this got out, it was to go no further than you and me, and he'd only told me to help Greg, so's you'd know Greg's state of mind – why there was guilt there that was not for his sister's killing. When I pressed him about the others, the ones behind Miss Juniper's suggested accident, he shouted not to touch them, and was out of the door like a whirlwind."

But in Kemp's mind these faceless others loomed large. The connection with Simon Quigley's property company was too obvious to ignore and must involve the man himself, not any underling, for there was power behind the seemingly casual way people had been manipulated. First, the grant of a favour, then the hint of some harmless-looking task in repayment, small misdemeanours noted but a blind eye turned until such time as they could be used as probes and prods once the fish was firmly netted.

Primrose Sutton had been carefully picked. Not content with that roof over her head she would want just a little bit extra, and, being naturally agin the system, she would see nothing wrong in a fiddle at the benefits office, nor bother to hide what she was doing. When the net closed on her she would be utterly vulnerable. Any shift in the tiles of that sheltering roof or even the threat of it would panic her into submission. She would say she heard nothing, saw nothing, knew nothing, and she was just smart enough to get away with it. Had she known beforehand that something was to happen to Grace Juniper? Was she out deliberately that night or did the others simply take advantage of her moonlighting, knowing she could not admit to it for to do so might be seen as the action of a negligent mother?

As for the two young men, each had been rewarded. Gregory had been given his articles by Cedric Roberts – as a favour to Simon Quigley. This seemed to be a small world of favours handed out and, maybe, recouped later, or were they gathered in from some past association? When local people said that Roberts, solicitors, and Quigleys, the estate agents, were in and out of each other's pockets they usually meant no more than the buying and selling of houses. Kemp thought the mutual back-scratching probably went deeper. At any rate, young Gregory Venn had come out of it rather well; he had been a clerk in Roberts' office with a long way to go even if he'd aimed only at being a legal executive in time. Suddenly he'd been given articles and was well on the way to becoming a solicitor.

What had Jasper gained in all this? Kemp had done a bit of delving into that young man's career. Until these last few months it had not been brilliant. On his father's money and a vague job in the City, it looked as if Jasper would play the young man about town for ever. But Father, John Quigley, fell on hard times financially speaking, and it looked as if Jasper's City job had been dependent on his investing money in his employers' firm – when his own money dried up so did the job. And there in the background was Uncle Simon with the big teeth . . . Come under my wing, dear nephew . . . and another fish was landed.

Kemp gave up, he was too mixed up in his zoological metaphors to make much sense.

He found Gregory Venn looking rather better than could be expected in the circumstances, but Kemp had already noted that the young man fitted his new background in a surprising way. He seemed far more at ease in prison, not only as if resigned to it but as if it answered a need. Kemp wondered if indeed the key to Venn's behaviour now lay in his hand; it was guilt that fuelled it from the moment during the picnic in the woods when something went horribly wrong, to his subsequent arrest and questioning.

Facing Venn now across the bare table, a better, more coherent picture of the young man was forming in Kemp's mind. Gregory was no villain, whatever he had done, but he had been tempted by ambition and the desire for a different kind of life, while his strict upbringing and perhaps something of his father's sense of duty opposed the conduct he had allowed himself to fall into. He must have been told often enough in his

173

boyhood that retribution follows swiftly on bad behaviour, that any deviation from the straight and narrow brings inevitable punishment. And so, when he himself slipped it had come as no surprise that he must pay for it. What Kemp had to find out was just how grave that slip had been.

He decided to come straight to the point.

"Jasper told his sister about your part in Miss Juniper's fall. Was that what you quarrelled with her about that Friday night?"

Taking Venn by surprise had been a good ploy. He had no time to compose his features, turn away his eyes, adopt any of the poses he had hitherto been hiding behind. As if struck in the throat he could not even find the breath to answer. In exasperation his fist drummed on the board between them.

"How did you . . . ? How did Jasper . . . ?"

"Perfectly simple, Gregory. He's your friend and he doesn't want you to suffer more than necessary. But just answer my question. Was this what you and Blanche had a row about?"

Venn nodded.

"She hadn't known beforehand that you and Jasper had anything to do with Miss Juniper's death?"

"Of course not. She . . . she . . . knew nothing . . ."

"But what Jasper says is true?" Kemp asked, gently. "Take time before you answer, Gregory. Did you in fact have something to do with Miss Juniper's fall?"

"It wasn't meant for her to die." The words were blurted out, but there was relief too. "It was only to be a small accident, nothing worse . . ."

"And what was your part in this so-called accident?" Kemp's voice was stern and it was perhaps to that note the young man in front of him had a natural tendency to respond in full. Once the drain was unblocked, the dirt flowed non-stop.

Venn had told Primrose Sutton that he wanted to watch a late night movie on her television. It was on a night when both he and Jasper knew she would be out till the early hours, perhaps not even back till morning. It had happened before after a big dinner at the Castle.

About one o'clock Venn opened the staircase door, and turned up the television sound to full volume. It was a very noisy film. He heard Miss Juniper come out of her room, obviously concerned at the noise. All he had to do was simply close the door again so that the stairs were plunged into darkness. He turned down the sound, and he heard her fall. He turned off the television, went out to his car and drove over to Jasper's house where they continued to watch the same film.

Throughout this whole sorry recital it was as if Gregory was slowly reliving the event, and by the end he was as white and horrified as his listener. When full realisation came, he buried his head in his arms and sobbed uncontrollably.

Kemp gave him a moment to recover.

"And when did you learn Miss Juniper was dead?"

"Prim phoned Jasper's house next morning after the ambulance had left. She guessed I'd be there. She was upset. She wanted to know why I hadn't been home as arranged. I just said I'd decided to watch the film at Jasper's house because they'd a bigger screen . . . I'd thought it wouldn't matter because Miss Juniper was upstairs, and anyway I expected Prim would be back before midnight."

Kemp felt a sick disgust for all of them; they'd played on each other's weaknesses just as someone else was playing on theirs.

Now he must tread carefully. At least this young man couldn't dart off like Jasper had done.

"Who was it wanted an accident to happen to Miss Juniper?"

Venn turned bleared uncomprehending eyes on him. "It was just meant to be a joke . . . She'd got on our nerves a bit, always hanging round Aunt Gwen like she did. We only wanted to take her down a peg. Jasper said she reminded him of one of his teachers at prep school, and he'd like to trip her up . . . thought it'd be a bit of a lark . . ." His voice trailed off miserably as he had another look at what had been done, and he was forced into silence at the enormity of it.

Kemp's time at the prison was nearly up. He could see that Gregory was exhausted, and even if he did know more about the whisper to get Miss Juniper out of the way, it wasn't going to come out now.

175

"Let me get this right," he said. "That Friday night after you'd had a picnic and sex, did Blanche confront you with the truth behind Miss Juniper's accident?"

"Yes. I'd asked her . . . I wanted us to get engaged. I thought she loved me the way I loved her . . . She said . . ." He stopped.

"Go on."

"She said she wouldn't because of what Jasper had told her . . . what I'd done . . ."

All the more reason for killing her, thought Kemp, unwillingly.

"And then?"

"I had to think. It knocked me for six, her knowing . . . I felt awful . . . I had to get away . . . take a walk to clear my head. I had to think, there was so much on my mind . . . the guilt of it . . ."

Venn suddenly looked up, his pinched white face a mask of misery. "But after I'd walked around for a while in that wood, I'd made up my mind. I knew what I was going to do. I was going to tell her I'd do anything for her, even confess if it would make her love me again. But when I got back she was dead."

Those bleak words held the ring of truth – like the sound of iron striking bedrock. Gregory Venn had reached bottom.

Kemp got to his feet. Partly to cut through the heavy atmosphere of despair, partly because he really wanted to know, he said:

"Before I go, Gregory, tell me one thing. It's got nothing to do with this business. Could you cast your mind back to when you worked on the sale file of Deloraine Court at Roberts . . ."

It was like dragging someone out of the ocean onto a foreign shore. Venn stared as if he'd never heard of Roberts, as if his working life had been on another planet.

"What I wanted to know," went on Kemp, "was who called off the sale. You and David Roberts must have been surprised . . ."

Venn was struggling to retrieve his mind, which had been a fairly alert one before its overturning, and bring it to bear on the question Kemp was asking.

"Yes," he said, eventually, "David Roberts had it first from
Quigleys and he went straight in to the old man. I'd some recent
stuff to put in the file and went in a bit later when old Roberts
was obviously on the phone to the MP. I heard him say: 'Well,
he's your cousin, Stephen, you'd better ask him yourself . . .'
It was Simon Quigley who put a stop on the sale."

"And Jasper's the only key we have to turn the lock at
Quigleys." Kemp had just finished telling Mary what he had
learned from Gregory Venn.

She shook her head. "We haven't even got him," she said.
"Prim tells me that Jasper's being sent over to Spain on urgent
business in connection with his dad's villa there. Prim of course
is gleeful as ever she is when any of the rich have to sell up.
Jasper's flying out from Gatwick this morning."

"Damn. Somebody's whisked him away fast as soon as he
started talking to you. Did you get anything out of Primrose
Sutton?" Kemp's attitude to the housekeeper next door had
changed, and it showed in his voice.

Mary sensed it, and was on the defensive.

"Prim is a victim as much as anyone. So, she was moonlighting as they call it. I guess it never brought in more than
peanuts. And her sleeping over at the Castle once in a while
doesn't make her a bad mum – she always made some kind
of baby-sitting arrangements . . ." She saw her husband's
grimace, and went on, hurriedly: "Yes, there was a rep from
somewhere up north came down every few months or so, and
they'd meet up. What was the harm in it?"

"It left her open to pressure, a part in someone's scheme . . ."

"Simon Quigley or that nasty MP cousin of his?"

"It's only conjecture. We've really no idea who, or, more
important, why . . ."

Mary thought about it. "I'd sure like that Stephen to be the
villain – if only because he knocked me down."

"If he did. You couldn't prove it."

"Have you heard his latest views on unmarried mothers?
He wants them down at the benefit offices on a regular basis
as if they were criminals on probation. You should have heard
Prim going on about it."

"More to the point, Mary, did you try bringing Simon Quigley's name into your conversation with her, just to see her reaction?"

"She gets very wary when you mention him. And she throws you off the subject the way only Prim can. Yes, I think she knows something but she's saying nothing. She keeps saying she's never met him. She still hides behind that tale that it would be bad for Miss Weston's health if she was badgered – Prim's word for it – about her memories. We know now that these instructions didn't come from the obvious source, the doctor . . . so it's someone else has an interest . . ." Mary suddenly grinned. "Shall we know all," she said, "when we've opened the box tonight?"

Twenty-One

"Can you come in early?" Prim had said. "I've got to be there to lay tables by seven."

"Yes, of course . . ." Mary was all too eager.

"And I'll be back by twelve." In response to Mary's raised eyebrow, "It's not what you're thinking. My friend from the North, he's not here this weekend." Primrose looked ashamed as if already regretting what she had told, under pressure.

Mary was conscious of it. "I didn't mean to pry, really I didn't. It was just when Jasper told me . . ."

"Well, all right, then. Let's forget it, shall we?" It seemed to be part of Prim's easygoing philosophy that if something hit home, got nasty, needed a wash of thought or the tint of regret, then it should be cast into the bin of oblivion, plucked from the memory.

"OK," said Mary, docilely, "I'll come in before seven."

As it happened she was there to hasten Prim's departure. "You look fine," she said, "you've lost weight and it suits you." Both statements were true enough; whether the weight loss had been caused by worry and the trauma of recent events, Prim certainly looked at her best, bright-eyed if a trifle feverish, bronzed hair in a whirl, and dressed up to the nines – an expression Mary had recently learned.

When the outer door closed behind Primrose, Mary returned to the sitting-room, and was struck by its desolate air. It was not simply that its moving spirit had departed; the whole space seemed imbued by a sense of loss. It had moved on into the present while still retaining the poignancy of the recent past. All this of course did not come immediately to Mary's mind; what she was conscious of was the emptiness left in space by the people who had gone. There was the sofa where Blanche

179

and Grace Juniper had sat with the child between them, there the cushions by the fire where Jasper and Gregory had lolled and laughed and larked about . . .

Now there was only Auntie Gwen, Miss Weston in her armchair, smiling as Mary came in from the hall. She had expressed her wish to stay up when she knew who her visitor was to be, and Prim had fussed over the arrangements for her ultimate bedding down despite being assured by Mary: "You forget I was for many years a nurse, Prim. I know how to put an elderly person to bed, however disabled they are." Prim had had the grace to blush.

Mary took hold of Gwen Weston's good hand. "I'll be right back to you when I've read a story to Liza-Jane."

When Lennox Kemp rang the doorbell at half-past eight, Mary let him in and couldn't contain a giggle: "I feel like a conspirator," she said, "one of those hooded men in the Gunpowder Plot . . ."

He gave her a look. "Don't get carried away by that new imagination of yours. Just because it's never seen the light of day before doesn't mean you can let it rip."

Miss Weston beamed at the sight of him, and when he carefully laid the deed box on the table beside her she patted it with an air both proprietorial and affectionate. She let her fingers stray over the frayed string.

"Its not been opened, Miss Weston," Kemp assured her. "You should be the one to do it."

But she shook her head and gave a little laugh, showing the palm of her hand to him holding out the key.

"If you so wish," he said, taking it up.

It turned the cheap lock easily, and he raised the lid, tilting the box slightly towards her so that she should be the first to see inside. She nodded vigorously and put her good hand firmly on the red and black book which was all the box contained. Her fingers scratched gently on the leatherette cover as she tried to lift it out.

"Let me help." Kemp took up the book, an ordinary-looking ledger of the sort kept by firms in the days before computers, to record the buying and selling of goods, monies paid in and out, customer lists, or the day-to-day accounts of the business.

On the cover of this one the lettering read: 'G. Weston & Co. Day Book 1953–59'.

Miss Weston sank back in her armchair with an air of satisfaction. Lennox Kemp and his wife looked at each other. Whatever had been their separate expectations, only Miss Weston seemed pleased.

"This was your father's?" Kemp asked.

She nodded.

"Is there something in this book you want us to see?"

Another vigorous nod.

"I think I know how to do it," said Mary, remembering her success with the garden book. She came over to the old lady's chair, put the book in her lap and guided Miss Weston's good hand on to the pages she turned. At last they came to rest on one particular page. Mary smoothed out the crinkled paper and held the book up to Miss Weston's spectacles.

"Is that the date?" she asked, and after waiting patiently for a moment they heard the faint sibilant "Yes". "Good, good," said Mary as the old lady smiled at her small success in getting out the word.

But then, as quickly as the smile had come it faded, and the face crumpled, the keen blue eyes closing under their heavy lids.

"It's enough," said Mary. She put her arms around the old lady and hugged her. "It's tired out she is. And overwrought by the excitement. She has managed this far, now I must put her in her bed."

Before Mary took her to her room, Kemp raised her good hand in his own. "That was what you wanted us to find, wasn't it? I have the page you pointed out. Do you want me to keep the book and read it?"

Miss Weston nodded, and squeezed his hand in answer. When he let go her hand she gestured with it towards the book, then at the door.

"You want me to keep it safely?"

Again the great effort at speech, and the soft affirmation on an outgoing breath.

"Then I shall do as you wish, Miss Weston. Good night."

Leaving his wife to the rest of her baby-sitting, Kemp slipped away, taking the box and book with him.

Once in his own study and under good lighting, he went through the pages. George Weston at this stage had obviously been keeping his own day book, writing it up either daily or weekly but certainly meticulously, in a good copperplate hand he would have learned at school. He seemed to have taken on all kinds of work from the building of barns and outhouses to garden walls, and everyday repairs and maintenance. He had itemised and costed out each job as he went along. The restrictions imposed during and after the war were still apparent, and George seemed to have taken pride in improvisation, re-using bombsite materials as well as from army surplus stores in a way that would be an object lesson to present day builders.

When it came to the conservatory to be built at Deloraine Court there were many entries before the page on which Miss Weston's hand had rested. The first was a note: 'Col. & Mrs abroad; bldg to be finished by return, 3 mths. Queries to Mrs D.Q. in hse.' The Colonel's quite exacting requirements for the new conservatory were noted along with items of materials (the glass had indeed come from a big house up the county recently demolished), measurements and locations.

When he came to the page which Miss Weston's hand had creased, Kemp looked more closely, for the writing was cramped and George Weston's individual type of short-hand used more frequently. The date was 17th May and the year 1954.

"AM – dug up rose bed Sth side of hse. Memo: Samuels to replant in new bed.

PM – turned up bones. Told Mrs DQ & she came out. Dug further & found more bones. Mrs DQ sd it was ancient grave-site. Best not say anything. Not to worry the Col. I sd archlogical sites need reporting but Mrs DQ sd not necessary. the Col wld not want people tramping all over his garden. Wld make his wife ill. Re-bury bones, skull(s), say nothing."

The following day's entry read: 'Told Samuels to keep off site. Removed both sets of bones myself, put in wooden toolbox & re-buried.' There followed a line of figures difficult to decipher. Then: "Mrs DQ v.pleased. I wld never regret, she sd. I wld be pd & mine looked after."

Kemp skimmed quickly through the rest of the book but could find no further references to the discovery under the rose bed, simply the final accounting to Col. Durward-Cooke on completion of the work, and a note to the effect that Mrs Olga was well pleased with the building.

On the inside marbled cover of the ledger there was writing in capitals: 'KEEP THIS BOOK'.

Kemp closed it with a sigh. Was that all there was to it? The casual discovery of an archaeological site and its subsequent cover-up? It was hardly a serious matter these many years later, and if indeed the re-buried bones were still there it was not such an unusual event for them to turn up on a building site, it had happened to developers before and, though there might be some delay in the building of houses the discovery would not prevent it in the long run.

Kemp went through the entries again later that night with Mary who also felt the opening of Miss Weston's box, the finding of the book, and its revelation had merely led to anti-climax.

"Surely, it's no big deal," she said, "finding bones that have been there for centuries. And I can sympathise with people just wanting them covered up again. That Mrs DQ – she'd be Dorinda Quigley home from Kenya or wherever – looking after the house when her sister for once did the Army wife thing. Everyone speaks of Dorinda being the sensible one of the two."

"H'm . . . It sounds as if she was. If there really had been an ancient burying ground on the site and word got round, it's true that archaeologists would be tramping all over it in no time, and digging up Mrs Durward-Cooke's beloved garden."

"So nobody said anything. George Weston got money out of it. That bit about 'mine looked after', presumably that'd be wife and daughter. And I suppose you could say Miss Weston has been looked after. Do you think this has been a handed-down tale, the Durward-Cookes and the Quigleys all thinking Gwen Weston knew their secret and one day might spit it out?"

"But would it matter?" said Kemp.

"I don't know anything about archaeology but it must have been Miss Juniper got close – that's why she asked her brother-in-law about it. But . . ." Mary's eyes widened in speculation as she too said: "would it matter?"

Kemp shook his head. "It's hardly a hanging offence. I wonder where old George re-buried the bones. Those hieroglyphics are probably measurements or directions of some kind, his own shorthand to show where he put them."

"Why not just shove them in the concrete foundations of the new conservatory?" Mary had heard the rumours of London gangsters' methods of body-disposal in the fifties and sixties and, although she considered the Krays cuddly boys compared to criminals bred in the States, there was a lot to be said for the solid permanency of concrete.

"Dear me, you sound as brisk as Mrs DQ. She obviously wanted them out of the way so that her precious sister's conservatory could go ahead, and leave the rest of the garden safe from prying eyes. But it was old George who had disturbed them in the first place and he might well have thought they deserved proper burial."

"Simon Quigley thinks they're under the conservatory," said Mary, decisively, "that's why he's taking a crowbar to it."

"Not so fast . . . If both families knew all about this secret, why wait till the place is being sold? It's been empty for years, they could have had the conservatory razed to the ground before this, and disposed of the bones again if they were a problem. It just doesn't make sense. I'm beginning to wonder if Miss Weston, and now ourselves, are the only ones in the know."

"It was her secret, Lennox, there's no doubt of that. When I took her to bed after she let you know she wanted you to take the box and the book out of the house, she was happy and relieved. It was as if a weight was gone from her, and by the time Prim came home she was sleeping peacefully . . . even those lines from her forehead smoothed out . . ."

"A secret she didn't know she had . . ." Kemp mused. "Weren't those Jasper's words to you?"

"I thought he meant she didn't know because of the stroke, but the secret was hers before it, I'm thinking."

"H'm . . . could be . . . But it sounds to me as if Jasper was repeating words said to him by someone else."

"Who had been told that Grace Juniper was talking to Miss Weston about archaeology . . ." Mary caught her breath. "Oh, my dear," she said, "it's the awful thing I can't get from my mind, how she fell, and died there . . ."

"Misadventure," said Kemp, grimly, "or death by suggestion. Wouldn't be the first time. The murder of Becket, now there was an early contract killing."

Mary was bewildered, and not much the wiser when the reference was explained. "I thought it was only the Mafiosi who hired hitmen for their dirty work. Anyway," she objected, "this King Henry of yours, he said he wanted revenge on a turbulent priest, he didn't say kill him."

"Ah, but it's the way it's said, and in what company. It's all innuendo. Up to a point, I believe Gregory Venn. I don't think Grace's death was intentional but his actions nevertheless were wilful, that is careless as to their consequence. It may be all that was required of him was to put her out of the way for a time . . . while something got sorted out . . ." Ideas were moving at the back of his mind, and they were all to do with time.

"To hell with it," he said, suddenly, "look at the hour. High time we were in bed."

But the ideas running in his head had prevented sleep, and the next morning he found his curiosity sharpened and needing exercise. He spent the morning in the County Record Office, looking up local land deals – but stopping short of the feudal period which had so intrigued him when he'd done his Land Law, now quite irrelevant to present students. And a good thing, too, he thought as he closed the last book and returned to his office. What price ffeoffment now and the seignorial rights of the manor, when gazzumping and dry rot in the attic were what mattered?

He was no sooner at his desk than Charles Copeland came in, triumphant. "We're on the move with Deloraine at last," he announced, "but there's one condition . . ."

"Let me guess," said Kemp. "That the vendor demolishes

the residence, and the purchaser doesn't get on the site till that's done."

Charles glared. "How did you know?"

"Never mind. Let me have a look at what you've got on title."

"There's just a copy abstract before the land was sold to the Durwards in the early 1870s because prior to that it was all part of the great Seldon Park estate. But that's a good enough root of title, surely?" Charles was ready to take offence.

"Of course it is, I'm not bothered about title, Charlie. Let's have a look. I know the whole Seldon Park estate had to be broken up, I suppose it was to meet death duties at the time. All I'm interested in is what kind of land Deloraine Court was built on. Ah, here it is described in the conveyance . . . a nice acreage, including a bit of woodland . . . meadows, coppices, water courses, etc. etc. – those Victorian clerks left nothing to chance. Ah, here's a map, and we can see where it fits in with the plan of the house when it was built."

"Most of that land would be arable," said Charles, peering at the plan on the conveyance of 1870, "it's close to what was the Home Farm at Thornton. That too went under the hammer before the end of the century and it's now the council estate. They'd never do that nowadays," he went on, "take good farming land, and build on it."

"Don't be too sure," Kemp retorted, but absent-mindedly, his thoughts elsewhere. "So, the land on which the Durwards put their late-Victorian gentleman's residence was farmed land, and probably had been for centuries." He caught Charles Copeland's enquiring look. "Oh, yes, I've checked. It would have been well ploughed over the years. The underlying soil was clay – fine for Olga Durward-Cooke's roses – with a topsoil of our good old Lea Valley gravel. Thanks, Charlie." He handed back the folder. "Is our client happy with the new condition in the contract?"

"Not what you would call happy . . . Mr Brinscombe was raring to go and now he's got to wait. There'll be an adjustment to the price, of course, and a rather later completion date. But, otherwise, yes, we go ahead." Charles eyed Kemp suspiciously. "And you're not going to tell me how you knew about this fresh condition?"

"Not yet, Charlie. What date have they set for completion?"

"Six weeks ahead. They say that's to give them time to demolish the residence, and clear up afterwards. Mr Brinscombe offered to lend them his equipment but Roberts have said the vendor will get his own team in."

"I'll bet," said Kemp. "Two men and a boy . . ."

Twenty-Two

Mary Kemp was sitting on the garden seat she had just bought. "I've the very place for it," she'd told Barry Samuels, "where my husband and I can enjoy the evening sun . . ." It made her think of the evening of their days, and she laughed, transforming her rather sedate features so that Barry looked at her with a new interest. Business was slack in late autumn when the occasional night frost deterred the buyers of plants, and he was enjoying the company of this woman.

"Gwen Weston understood when I told her you were asking for her. She did remember you, I'm sure of that, Mr Samuels."

"My dad had nothing against the daughter. Once she'd come home she kept a tight rein on her old man whilst she nursed her sick mother."

Mary, who in her youth had had a similar experience, felt a rush of empathy with Miss Weston.

"What was the nature of George Weston's trouble?" She enquired, innocently.

"Got above himself." To Barry Samuels the worst that could be said of anyone in the top layer of the working class (from which he himself had emerged). "That, and too much money slipping through his fingers . . ."

"How did he come by that?" Mary sounded, as she was, genuinely interested.

"Well, there'd be a bit of a building boom in the fifties and old George Weston should have benefited, but his business was already on the skids through his drinking and gambling. That made him unpopular . . ." Barry thought back to things that had been said, indeed had been a constant, bitter refrain in the Samuels' household.

188

"Folk said he was overpaid for the Deloraine Court job. I mean, it was only a conservatory after all, but to George Weston it could have been the Crystal Palace the fuss he made of it. Aye, and the money he got out of it . . ."

"'Tis a fine piece of building," said Mary, but added, sagely, "for its time, of course. But, costed out, it couldn't have been that expensive for folk of the Durward-Cooke quality."

"You're right there, Mrs Kemp," said Barry, earnestly, "but the way old George boasted about it, and the way he said he'd got in with the nobs because of it, that's what got people."

Mary laughed; she had been studying Victoria and Albert and had caught the allusion to the Crystal Palace. "As if he was Paxton and they the royal family?"

"You've hit the nail on the head, Mrs Kemp, that was just the way he talked down at the local when he'd had a few. My dad would hear him and come home furious . . . 'Weston's got something on the Durward-Cookes,' he'd tell my mum."

"Scandal?" asked Mary, hopefully.

Barry Samuels shook his head. "Weren't no scandal about that lot," he said, decisively. "That was just the drink talking in George Weston. It's not like them at Deloraine Court were real gentry like the Courtenays at Ember; the Durward-Cookes were dull folk. The Colonel and his wife, they lived quietly, the son – the one who's now an MP – was away at Harrow or Eton. Maybe Mrs Durward-Cooke was a bit on the nervous side, but folks round here liked the family. No, there was no truth in old Weston's talk. And anyway, when the chips were down and he nearly went bankrupt, it wasn't the Durward-Cookes who bailed him out – it was the property company, Quigleys."

"And they are still looking after Miss Weston, I understand . . ."

"Are they now? That'll be Simon Quigley – he's a philanthropist in his own way, that man. Done a lot for the town. Funny you should say that, though. Rumour was that it was Quigleys who paid George Weston off. And he got nothing under the Will of either the Colonel or Mrs Olga when they finally died."

Mary looked her surprise.

Barry shuffled his feet. "Mum checked," he said, rather shamefacedly, "she'd never forgotten George Weston was the cause of Dad losing his job. I suppose she was suspicious because of the rumours being spread by George himself. She went to the Record Office herself and checked. I think it satisfied something in her to find that George had got nothing out of the Durward-Cooke family in the end . . ." He brooded for a moment; it had helped his mother in her declining years that the old enemy had not prospered.

"I've wasted enough of your time," said Mary, rising, "but I have enjoyed our chat."

"It's been a pleasure, Mrs Kemp. I'll give your bench a good thick coating before I deliver it, seeing it's to stand out in all weathers."

"She doesn't look any the worse for it," said Mary, with a nod towards a stone nymph among other garden ornaments at the side of the path. "She looks like one of these archaeological finds you read about being dug up in ancient burial sites."

Barry laughed. "Not a chance," he said. "I've got a local mason turns them out by the dozen. They used to get put in graveyards, now people have them in the garden and light them up at night."

Not a flicker of a connection made, not a suggestion of anything taken as underlying her pure facetiousness; Barry Samuels was as open a man as she'd met and a look on his face would have betrayed him. Whatever rumour he had heard through his folks about George Weston's desecration of the old rose bed at Deloraine Court, there had been no mention of bones.

She would have liked to tell her husband straight away about the conversation with Mr Samuels, if only to prepare him for the future arrival of a garden seat which would otherwise be unexpected – and possibly unwelcome, for Lennox was not the kind to sit of an evening contemplating sunsets. But there was the remainder of the day to get through first. Her afternoon was already booked for a visit to Louisa Channing in the Eventide Home to which she was by now resigned. Such visits had been intermittent until put on a more regular basis by the matron who liked to have her charges well visited, and had seen in Mary Kemp a patience and a professional skill with the elderly which made her an ideal visitor.

Mary, aware of Matron's prescience in the matter – which was accurate enough – nevertheless deplored the pigeonhole in which she was being placed, for it was an image she was trying to live down as much as her other background of dire poverty and a feckless family. Matron's wish had prevailed, however, and Mary found herself visiting Mrs Channing once a month. Today's appointment having been made, and Mary being punctilious in such matters, she must keep it, although on this occasion unwillingly for she had much to think about and was not in the mood for idle chatter.

Not that Mrs Channing would regard her own conversation in that light; she was spry for her age, and still took a lively interest in matters beyond the confines of the Home. Which was just as well for the hobby of most of her fellow residents was complaining about its inadequacies. Complaints about the meals, the furniture, the heating, the plumbing, and of course the manifest failings of their fellows were forever winging their way into Matron's office where they were carefully filtered through the fine veil of her experience, and shown the door.

Mrs Channing, on the other hand, had had the benefit of an Edwardian upbringing and the inbred good manners of her class, so she kept a stiff upper lip – a tenet learned in girlhood from her bullying brothers – and made no complaints, but she liked to talk and was pleasantly disposed towards Mrs Kemp who was a good listener.

It was scarcely surprising with the election looming that her subject today was politics. Her conservatism could be taken for granted; it was as much part of her as the ash-blond hair, now grey, and the high-bridged, narrow nose which tilted its tip ever so slightly to the right.

Mary did not have to lead the conversation round to the MP, Stephen Durward-Cooke, he was in the fore of it from the start. "A fine man, and of good family. There are too few of his kind left, and the country's the worse for that . . ." Louisa Channing put her cup down hard in its saucer so that it rattled – a gesture of what she might like to do with all opponents of her dear Conservatives.

"Did you know his family when they lived hereabouts?" asked Mary.

"I knew of them, of course, but not personally. My sister Caroline was for a while friendly with Olga Durward-Cooke, and Dorinda. But Dorinda went abroad when she married, and I don't think Olga would have moved in Caroline's circle . . ." Mrs Channing wandered off into reminiscences as she tended to when the name of her sister cropped up.

Mary had heard about Caroline Sumner; she had married into the Diplomatic Service, and thus had entry into a higher level of society than was open to Louisa who had merely wed a City banker: Louisa remained in Newtown, whereas Caroline had lived a more glamourous life, in the capitals of Europe and in Washington, DC.

"We visited, of course," Louisa went on, "and took the children. Do you know, Mrs Kemp, Caroline was at the Embassy there when the Burgess and Maclean affair broke?"

Interesting though that tale was, Mary had heard it before from Mrs Channing so she gently interrupted the memoirs with a fresh slice of cake. "You said your sister and Olga Durward-Cooke were friendly," she prompted.

"Oh, I wouldn't say they were close. I suspect Caroline found Olga a bit dull, really. She was of a neurotic disposition, and rather shy . . . never went out much, adored that garden of hers . . ." Mrs Channing gave a light laugh. "Not exactly Caroline's cup of tea. I think, looking back, they only got to know one another because Caroline got some domestic help for them at Deloraine Court at the end of the war when it was impossible to get servants here. Bernard Sumner was on Sir Ivor Kirkpatrick's staff, and Caroline went out there with him . . ." As her listener didn't seem to know what she was talking about, Louisa kindly explained. "Deciding the future of West Germany, you know. And what to do with all those poor things without papers, and all those refugees running from the Russians . . ." She paused as if suddenly overcome by the enormity of the tasks her brother-in-law had faced.

Mary should have been impressed but international affairs had never meant a great deal to her, getting from one day's end to the next had been enough at that time in her young life.

"She got two of them out of that displaced persons' camp." Louisa Channing had resumed. "Irmgard – now there was a sweet girl . . . Caroline eventually took her with them when they were posted to Washington."

"And the other?" asked Mary, catching on. "She went to Deloraine Court? It must have been nice for the two foreign girls at least to have each other as friends . . ."

"Not at all. They had nothing in common – well, apart from being refugees, that is. Irmgard came from a good family, she was young and pretty. The other one, Helga – I've no idea of her other name – was older, homely-looking, I understand, and rather plump. She was only a cook."

Oh, dear, thought Mary, class distinctions still count even among displaced persons. "It must have been useful," she said, "her being a cook. Did she stay with the Durward-Cookes?"

"I believe not. Dorinda sent her packing in no time. From what she said, the woman was barely house-trained." Mrs Channing could have been speaking of one the labradors she used to breed. "Now, Irmgard, she was a great success, she became part of the Sumners' household in Washington."

Lucky old Irmgard, thought Mary, her face just happened to fit.

"Dorinda Durward," she said, "sounds a much more forthright person than her sister."

"Caroline always considered her the better of the two. She was more Caroline's sort, of course, a go-ahead girl and clever . . . But as soon as she was married, she was off to the Colonies – Kenya, I think it was. Ran some sort of mission school, and was very popular with the natives . . ." Louisa looked at the observation she had just made as if she found it incomprehensible. "A pity . . . she and Caroline had a lot in common . . ." She was tiring.

She folded her napkin carefully, and put it beneath her plate. "They are all gone now," she said. "I miss my sister, Caroline. She had such tales to tell . . ."

Mary said as she quietly cleared the table: "You remember her, Mrs Channing, and you speak about her to me and so she lives now in both our memories . . ."

The old lady reached out and took Mary's hand, but only for a moment.

She understands, thought her visitor, but of course she won't admit anything has passed between us, she's too much of a lady to have such sentiments.

After a few moments Louisa Channing asserted herself; she was not to be thought of as one living entirely in the past.

"Your neighbours, Mrs Kemp . . . I am so sorry for poor Miss Weston, the trouble she has known and now this . . ."

"She has taken it well. After all, those concerned are not kin to her."

"But in her own house! The house indeed of her father and mother . . ."

"She can cope with that, I think."

"Indeed. But to have your home made into flats and let out to strangers – look what comes of it. This young man, it seems he has murdered a niece of Durward-Cooke's. Did you know her, Mrs Kemp?"

"It's for the court to decide whether he killed or not," said Mary, steadily. "And, yes, I knew Blanche Quigley. I thought her a nice girl."

She could tell from the pursed lips that in Mrs Channing's book nice girls didn't go into the woods after dark; the press had made much of that out-of-season picnic. However, the old lady was intent on getting her relationship record straight for this had always been an important part of her life.

"She'd be one of the Newtown Quigleys, then . . . the family into which Dorinda Durward married. It doesn't seem long ago that I saw the obituary in *The Times* of her husband, Daniel. He was in the Colonial Service, you know . . ." She felt she was in danger of repeating herself, a trait in the elderly which she deprecated. "Of course the Newtown branch of the Quigleys were in trade," she added in a tone which effectively dismissed them, leaving Mary to wonder how the late Mr Channing had reached the upper levels of banking without at least some contact with commerce.

Mary went into the supermarket on the way home not only to get something for supper, but also to get back into the real world where trade was no longer a term of opprobium but rather, if one was in the producing end, a road to riches.

At the check-out she met Brenda Brinscombe, who said immediately: "Let's go and have a cup of tea." Mary, feeling the need for down-to-earth company after the rarified atmosphere of the Eventide Home and the conversation of Louisa Channing, agreed.

Sitting comfortably in the cafe, Brenda Brinscombe was eager to share her news. "Funny that it's the vendor going to pull down the house, but that's the way they want it." As Mary looked blank, Brenda went on:

"Alan is over the moon. Oh, haven't you heard? The Deloraine Court business is on again."

"I didn't know."

"We've only just heard ourselves. You know what men are like, tell them they can't have a thing and they want it all the more. Alan wasn't all that keen at the beginning. Just something to do with his time, he kept telling me, but soon's Simon Quigley put a spanner in the works it was like an obsession; Alan simply had to have the Deloraine estate . . ."

"Well, I'm glad for him," said Mary. "What was all the mystery about, then?"

Brenda shrugged. "Nobody knows, except that it was Simon himself, not the MP like people thought."

"How can you be so sure, Brenda?"

"Ah, a little bird told me. No harm in you knowing, Mary," she leant across the small table. "Our Olive . . ."

Mary grinned. "Your spy in the other camp."

"You'll meet her yourself in a few minutes. I usually see her in here for a cuppa when we've both done the shopping of a Saturday. Between you and me, Olive's looking for another job."

"Why's that? I thought she had a good one at Quigleys."

"Nothing wrong with the job, it's her boss that's the trouble. Secretary she was to him when she started, and then upgraded to personal assistant, and that was fine until recently when he seems to have changed. And his behaviour to her – well, to all the staff – got so overbearing and rude . . ."

"When did this change take place?"

Brenda didn't answer immediately. She had been in business long enough herself to know what confidentiality meant. "Olive's not one to gossip and she's always been loyal to her employers. But this change in his attitude, well, it seems to have happened so suddenly she had to remark on it. It was overnight, she says, and all to do with Deloraine Court. One day he's the same man she'd always known, next morning he's like a madman. And it was the first thing he did – Olive was to get Cedric Roberts on the phone right away. He took the call in his room, but she could hear what he said because he was shouting so – and him never one to raise his voice."

"He didn't need to," said Mary, remembering the high tone of the man she had only seen once, in the doorway of the doomed house.

"What Olive heard," went on Brenda, "was that the sale was off. No, the property was not being put back on the market, it was simply not for sale. There were a lot of telephone calls after that, and instructions in the office that all brochures and sale particulars were to be withdrawn, and there was a rare old row with the cousin, the MP. Of course there was a lot of pussy-footing by both sets of solicitors who didn't want to lose the business altogether, so it was quite a while before Alan was told. But Olive swears it was an overnight decision by Simon Quigley himself, no one else . . ." Brenda stopped, quite out of breath, and looked round the cafe.

"Here she is now."

A slight brown-haired girl was threading her way between the tables. She plonked her shopping bags on the floor, and sat down. "Thank God that's done," she said. "Hullo, Aunt Bren."

Brenda introduced them. "My niece Olive Meredith, Mary Kemp. I've been telling Mary what you told me. Is that OK with you?"

"Oh, I know all about you, Mary Kemp. You're the bad lad in welly boots that broke into Deloraine House and got clobbered by that MP." Olive was shaking with laughter. "I'm sorry, but it really was so funny, Mr Stephen Durward-Cooke striding into our office that day like a raging bull, and throwing his weight about—"

"Which is considerable," put in Mary, "I should know."

"He went on and on at Mr Simon – why was there no security, why couldn't Quigleys take proper care of the place, he couldn't do it himself, he had important duties elsewhere, he was a Member of Parliament, for heaven's sake . . . Well, we all listened with the right amount of awe till Mr Simon took him off for a drink to calm him down. When the boss came back he dictated a lot of stuff about strengthening security, but of course the very next day in comes Uncle Alan's offer and everything was sweetness and light."

"So it wasn't then that Simon's behaviour changed?"

"Oh, no, that came weeks later. Did Auntie Brenda tell you about it? It happened overnight . . . Have you read Dr Jekyll and Mr Hyde?"

"I've seen a film."

"Well, that was what it was like. It certainly wasn't the sale of the property. Mr Simon was pleased about that. In fact he said to me that it would get Cousin Stephen off his back, with the election coming up he was going to need every penny. He also said that it wouldn't matter any more if the council hooligans did break in. Hooligans was his normal term for folks living on the Thornton Estate, it didn't mean anything . . . just like anyone not born and bred in Britain was a wog to him. I'd got used to it – it was his way of speaking."

"Wogs," explained Brenda to Mary, "an old Army expression not confined to officers. I've heard Alan's old man use it – he's the Alf Garnett type . . ." This explanation mystified Mary further. She was in any case more interested in what Olive Meredith had to say.

"This changed behaviour of Mr Simon's, what was it like?"

"Started to get short with everyone, bad-tempered and moody. Well, when he got that way with me I'd just about had enough. He'd never been like that before, and I'd always had full access to all his files like a P.A. should. Then he turns all nasty and secretive, locking up the cabinets and holding on to the keys. Well, I thought, if he can't trust me any more, then blow him, I'll get a job somewhere else."

"How long have you been there?" asked Mary, and was

surprised when Olive said four years; she was older than she looked, and obviously efficient.

"Did you ever hear the name Weston in the office?"

"You mean the old lady lives next door to you? That was one of Mr Simon's confidential files I dealt with. He told me once it was a burden he'd inherited from his father when he came into the firm." Olive hesitated. "Damn it all, if I'm going to leave, what's the harm . . . ? There was never much in that file anyway, just a record of the money coming from Kenya, and being paid out. An annuity under a Will, I think it was, and there was a letter. But all I had to do was check the account and see that it went to your neighbour's bank. That would be Miss Weston, wouldn't it?"

Mary nodded. "Do you know whose Will it was, Olive?"

"I believe it was an aunt of Mr Simon's. The letter was written by her too with instructions about the annuity she was putting in the Will. Her name was so pretty that I remembered it. Dorinda Quigley. I did read the letter once, and found it very peculiar, the wording I mean, schoolmistressy with a lot of underlining . . ."

"I don't suppose you remember what it said, our Olive," said Brenda, hopefully. "Miss Weston is now a friend of Mary's. She's had a stroke and can't speak."

"Oh, I'm ever so sorry . . . Let me see, it was ages ago I read it. There was something about nothing would be said by Mr Weston that would hurt Olga – I'm pretty sure that was the name – but he might tell his daughter, so she must be looked after and kept quiet. That last bit was underlined, and made me giggle – it could mean left in peace or like they do in the movies, make sure she keeps her mouth shut . . ."

"I'm afraid the stroke has done that, Olive."

Both Brenda Brinscombe and her niece were silent for a moment, staring down at the teacups. Perhaps they were contemplating the awfulness of not being able to speak; they belonged to a family of cheerful, talkative women.

"Didn't Mr Simon's Uncle Daniel die last year? He would be the widower of this Dorinda Quigley," said Mary, her mind running in its own track.

"Yes, the boss was so relieved that the Will and everything

198

was dealt with by lawyers out there in Kenya. It's only now that stuff's started to arrive at his brother's and he's passing it on that it's become a nuisance. He joked about his uncle's black servants being honest wogs for once because they'd packed up the personal effects and shipped them home – as if the relations would want old uniforms and pith helmets . . ." Olive stopped, and giggled. "That Jasper, he came into the office one day wearing one of them, said he was taking the pith. Apparently his dad wanted nothing to do with all that junk, and a whole trunkful of moth-eaten old books was left in the boss's room for ages. He swore every time he stubbed his toe on it until eventually he had it carried out to his car, and he took it home."

Mary was recalling that conversation she'd had with Blanche in the pub. Tatty, the stuff was, she'd said. Ebony elephants. Mary felt that sudden lurch into emptiness which comes with thoughts of the recently dead – too early for them to have reached the light of memory, too late to see them in the flesh; the hiatus of purgatory. Blanche was there in front of her, the shining river of blond hair falling . . . but the figure was blurred, indistinct as if underwater. It sharpened when Olive spoke.

"That girl that was murdered – she used to come into the office sometimes to see her brother. I was just getting to like her. She and Jasper used to lark about – just to annoy their uncle, I think. There was that undercurrent, you could tell, but of course Jasper was dependent on my boss for his job so he tended to be careful."

"I too liked Blanche Quigley," said Mary. "Do you remember when she was last in your office?"

"Not for a while – but she did telephone on that Friday, you know she died that night?" Mary nodded, hoping that Olive would enlarge on the remark, which she did. "It was around four o'clock and the boss was out. She'd asked to speak to him, so I said I'd take a message. All she wanted, she said, was another read of Aunt Dorinda's book, she had a friend thought there might be money in it. Then she laughed and said, of course she hadn't read it – too deadly boring, but not to tell the boss that. Her friend was in publishing and was thinking of another Diary of an Edwardian Lady or something. She'd pick up the book at the weekend from her uncle's. Well, I did as I was bid, and left the message on his desk, just the first bit of course . . ."

"Did you see your Mr Simon after he got the message?" asked Mary.

"No, he wasn't back when we packed up for the day at five thirty, but I presume he got it. The typed slip of paper certainly wasn't there when I tidied his desk on Monday morning. Why're you so interested? Nobody's asked before about Blanche Quigley around our office. Well, they wouldn't, would they? They hardly knew her, except as Jasper's sister – all the girls were certainly after him."

"Do you think you could write down for me exactly the message you typed and put on Simon Quigley's desk?" Mary wondered if she was making something out of nothing; but she wanted more substance than idle gossip before she told her husband about this.

"Sure," said Olive, and reached into her bag. She wrote on the back of an envelope and passed it over to Mary:

Your niece Blanche Quigley called this pm. She wants another read at what she called Aunt Dorinda's book, she has a friend thinks there might be money in it, and she would like to pick it up at the weekend.

"There," said Olive, "I think that's exactly what I put down. I never thought it was important."

Mary hastened to reassure her. "Oh, I'm sure its not . . . Anyway, thanks for the chat, it's time I was getting home."

Twenty-Three

"**D**amn," said Mary. She was sitting in her kitchen looking at the day's entry on the memo pad she and Lennox kept hanging on the wall. "Damn," she said again. She had forgotten that this Saturday evening her husband was to be in London. 'Old Stafford's retirement do' he had written plainly against the date, and she now remembered he had told her.

"Been at Gillorns' head office for nearly forty years. They're getting up some sort of presentation which we've all subbed towards. I ought to go . . ."

And he must already have left by train, for the car was still in the garage. Mary glanced at the clock. She had not intended to be so late home nor would she have been had she not met Brenda Brinscombe.

Something was nagging at the back of her mind, something Brenda had told her before Olive arrived, about the house being pulled down. That was it. The vendor was going to do it, not the developers.

Suddenly it came upon her that there was far greater urgency than she had thought. If the decision had been taken to continue with the sale then a solution must have been found, and here it was. The property would be demolished, the greenhouse razed to the ground, and a determined search made before the building company were allowed in.

Could it be done over a weekend, she asked herself . . . would they hire the equipment and do the job themselves rather than risk outsiders coming across the burial first?

She went into Lennox's study where he had put away Gwen Weston's precious box. She took out the ledger and looked again at those hieroglyphics of George Weston's. They must mean something, although she knew her husband had already

201

been frustrated in his attempts to read them. "I'm sure they're directions of some kind," he'd said. "But I would be better mapping them out later on the site itself . . ."

Only there wouldn't be time. Not now. Not when others would get in before him . . .

Mary was not much given to theorising. In all the crises of her life – and there had been many – she had spared only a short time for thought before acting, and this practice had usually worked. Quick, decisive action was what counted with Mary.

It would soon be nightfall. She changed into black trousers and sweater, and put on the infamous dark hooded anorak and gumboots. She took a spade and fork from the toolshed; it was still too early for hard frost. I don't think it's under the conservatory, she thought, Lennox was right, George Weston might have been too sensitive about the bones for that. She carefully copied the day-book entry on to a large sheet of paper, checked she had a torch in the glove compartment, and drove off in the direction of Deloraine Court.

Her husband had indeed left Newtown on an early train but it was not because he wanted to be first with the champagne at Clement's Inn where Gillorns still had their Dickensian head office; that particular frolic could wait – or perhaps get along without him.

Instead, he was keeping an appointment made by telephone with an old friend at the Institute of Archaeology.

"Good of you to see me – and out of hours."

David Harwood shrugged. "I was here anyway. What's your problem, Lennox?"

Kemp told him, spreading out plans and maps of the area, but it didn't take Harwood long to give him his answer.

"Impossible," he said. "That was all part of the Seldon Estate. Had you never heard of Sir Algernon Percy who owned it in the middle of the last century? A bit of an amateur scientist he was, and dabbled himself in what was then the new hobby, archaeology. He even wrote a couple of monographs on ancient sites in another county. It was quite the in-thing with members of the nobility who had the time and the money for such diversions. Sir Algernon's great disappointment was that there was nothing found in his extensive lands, he would have dearly loved an exclusive archaeological site all to himself. So, every one of his tenant farmers must have known the score. If they turned up the merest fragment of bone, the tiniest of potsherds, they'd to report it to the lord of the manor – and likely as not, there'd be a reward."

"I see," said Kemp. "It's what I suspected, but I had to be sure."

"Well, you can be. Just look at the map. That was farmland the Durwards got, some of it even bits of the home farm when the whole estate was split up. Because Sir Algernon was so obsessed by his scientific hobbies he never got round to matrimony, and his inheritors were distant cousins who cared not a fig for the land, so people like the Durwards got prime sites for their country houses. I'd wager my professional reputation on there never having been an ancient burial site on that land."

"So . . ." Kemp looked his old friend in the eye.

"So . . ." David repeated, "It is not my problem but yours. How many people have seen these bones?"

"To my certain knowledge, only the builder who found them and one other, a lady."

"A lady, indeed. Not a woman . . . Would she be of the educated sort, then? I only ask because I wondered if she knew what had been dug up on this so-called ancient burial site."

Kemp considered what he knew of Dorinda Durward Quigley.

Yes, she would have been well educated. The stronger of the two, people said, and she must have had character – she had eventually run a mission school so successfully it had withstood troubled times. Yes, it was as likely as not that she would have known the difference between an ancient burial and . . .

"I think she must have been aware that it was possibly not what she said it was," he answered his friend, cautiously, "and the builder took her word for it." Along with money, and the promise of more.

"What reason could she have for getting him to cover it up – in both senses of the word?"

"It may sound facetious, but it's the truth; she didn't want her sister's beloved garden spoiled."

Harwood looked sceptical so Kemp went on: "Oddly enough, in the circumstances which I know, it's a perfectly good explanation."

"And now I presume the lady is no longer with us, nor is the builder, and the bones are going to be re-discovered?"

"Yes, that's about it . . ." Kemp sighed; he wasn't even sure they were.

"Another thing," said Harwood, "for them to have been really old, that was the wrong sort of soil out there for them to have been preserved enough to be recognisable immediately, even if the land had never been ploughed over. You said there were skulls?"

"It's only a very abbreviated note I'm going on . . . some ambiguity about it, but, yes, skulls are mentioned in the plural." Kemp rose to leave. "Thanks again for your time, David."

"Well, you now have the twin blessings of carbon-dating and DNA to help you when you get hold of the relics this time round," said Harwood as he went to the door. "Do let me know the outcome . . ."

It's not 'when' I get hold of the relics, thought Kemp, but a bloody big 'if' . . .

He decided then and there that he would have to miss seeing Old Stafford into happy retirement. Unfortunately it was the slack hour for trains to Newtown; the railway companies expected hundreds to throng into London on a Saturday evening for its varied pleasures, but at that hour who would want to be going in the opposite direction?

It was frustrating, but there was nothing he could do but wait.

The fading light helped Mary. By the time she had parked her car in an obscure corner of the council car park, it was almost so dark that she merged into the shadow of the wall as she walked along beside it. On both previous visits she had noted a gap where the local vandals had made the amazing discovery that if you poked out enough bricks from the middle of a wall, the top fell in. Now the gap formed a jagged V shape against the pale sky, and it took only a few minutes to climb up into it, and over.

The bushes in the shrubbery flickered in the wind, now

catching the remaining light, then losing it again to become solidly black objects in her path, but she need not have worried. When she finally rounded the last of them she saw the house was in darkness, and obviously deserted. She wasn't sure what she had expected, but at least she was alone. She stopped and looked at the conservatory – a poor thing, now, only the bare structure remaining. The bones of it, she thought, bereft of the wonderful plants, the sheltering glass that had fleshed them out – even the love Olga Durward-Cooke had had for the place. Mary was not usually given to such thoughts, particularly when out on a dark expedition like this, so she hurried over to the garden seat where she and Lennox had sat, and where there was just enough light to see. She took the notes from her pocket, and shone the torch on George Weston's writing. Lennox had said they were directions; she didn't need a compass, she knew where the sun had set. If she had long enough, undisturbed, she knew she could work it out. She had brought only the fork, but if she found anything she would go back to the car for the spade. She had enormous patience; long hours of night duty had seen to that. She had confidence in her own power to carry out a task; she only hoped she would be given the time.

Experience should have taught her not to have such hope. Because of the sough of the rising wind, she did not hear the unlocking of the gates but she heard the car engine revving up, and saw the sweep of its headlamps as it came up the drive.

Mary fled, but not to the gap in the wall and the safety of her car; safety was not in the forefront of her thoughts. If there was to be a showdown it would take place in the house, not out in the cold garden, so it was to the house she ran, skimming the lawn and arriving at the steps into the glasshouse before the car reached the front door, and the headlights were switched off.

Unfortunately the conservatory no longer provided any hiding place now that the great thick-leaved plants had gone, and the flooring itself had been hacked through to the concrete, that too already holed. Mary went light-footed, watching each step she took. The doors into the sitting-room were wide open, no need any longer for security as the glass was gone.

Mary peered desperately into the room. The dim light showed isolated shapes of a table and some chairs which she recognised as the cheap wicker furniture that had been in the conservatory. Otherwise, the room was empty. All that remained of its soft furnishings were the drapes which still hung on either side of the patio-type doors. As she slipped into the room she scrunched the fabric in her hand, giving it a gentle pull. She could feel the authentic stiff glaze of old-fashioned chintz against her fingers – the pattern would be of full-blown roses and hectic white lillies. The curtain she had touched was torn in places, where deep rents ran down the folds, frayed by years of neglect, but there was sufficient width in the material to pull round her as she squatted down on the floor just inside the door. It was a refuge of a sort – at least she could not be seen either from the conservatory or from the sitting-room.

She had heard the slam of the front door, and now there were voices so she knew that Simon Quigley had not come alone. There had been no mistaking the roar of his car engine on the driveway and she wondered who was with him this time – it could hardly be young Jasper, he'd been well and truly put out of the action . . .

Mary had not long to wait for an answer. There had been footsteps in the hall which had died away into the rear of the premises, now another door slammed and the footsteps and voices approached the door of the sitting-room.

"Stop wasting my time, Simon. I still want to know why you've brought me out here at this godforsaken hour of the night. You call me over from Hampshire where I've got a busy schedule, and when I get to your place you drive me out here . . ."

Even as Stephen Durward-Cooke spoke the room was flooded with light, its intensity contrasting sharply with the surrounding darkness. Looking out through a tear in the curtain Mary saw it was coming from a single bulb hanging where there must have once been an ornate chandelier.

"Just as well I kept the electricity on for the demolition men. Take a pew . . . might as well be comfortable. This bottle's one from the cellar – you know you left some?" Simon Quigley drawled, and there was the chink of glass-ware.

"I took the best of the stuff. Come on, get to the point of all this. You talk about demolition so I assume you've come to your senses at last . . ."

"Contracts have been exchanged, yes, and the sale's going ahead as you wish, except that you're doing the demolishing of this place . . ."

"What? I thought Brinscombe—"

"I have my reasons. And it's in your best interests. In fact I've been acting in your best interests all along, though you might not have appreciated it."

"Like hell I don't. Never mind contracts being exchanged, final completion should have taken place by now, and I should have had my damned money. Can't you understand, Simon, I've had to borrow against the money coming in from Deloraine Court because of what you've called delaying tactics – for which you had no instructions from me. I've a good mind to charge you the interest on my borrowings, since it was all your fault."

"Oh, for God's sake, Stephen, take your eye off the money for a moment . . ." Quigley's tone sounded world-weary. "Sometimes it seems to be all you politicians think about . . ."

"There's no need to be rude." There was the sound of a chair being pushed back.

"Sit down, and listen." This time it was the property man's voice which rose high, and peremptory. "I too haven't got all night. You want plain speaking? Very well, you shall have it."

There was a pause, the sound of pouring and again the clink of glass. To Mary it seemed as if both men had stopped for a breather, conscious perhaps that their being at odds was not helping matters forward. The listener felt much the same way, but had not the benefit of refreshment.

"I don't suppose you remember old George Weston who built that conservatory out there for your mother?"

"I knew there was such a person," Stephen Durward-Cooke responded, somewhat stiffly, "but I was away at school and the parents were in Singapore when the glasshouse was extended, so I could hardly know him, could I?"

"Your Aunt Dorinda was here keeping an eye on the property while your parents were away. It would be the year she married my Uncle Daniel and went with him to Kenya."

"I didn't come here just to listen to family history, Simon. Get to the point."

"Might have been better if you and I had listened to family history a bit earlier . . . But no, perhaps not. There was never much said about it so we assumed there wasn't any . . ."

"What has this Weston person to do with it?"

"Ah, Stephen, you may well ask . . ." There was more pouring of wine – or Mary presumed it was wine. Simon was obviously enjoying it, it was he who held the reins in this conversation, and although Mary was anxious for him to get to the point and impatient for more information, she could not help noticing the difference between the two men. Durward-Cooke was ill at ease, as well he might be having been apparently dragged from his home and important duties in a high-handed manner by his cousin who was relaxed and in no hurry to explain. At the same time, listening but without seeing she was also intrigued at how alike they sounded; both of them the products of upper middle-class homes, and public school education, their use of words the same, their pronunciation, their well-bred accents with just a hint of the equine bray they could produce if necessary.

"The Westons were a burden wished on me by my father when I came into the firm." It was Simon speaking. "'See that George Weston and his daughter are all right, old chap' was what he said to me. No reason given – he might have been a butler being pensioned off. I didn't think much about it but when the Weston business went under – I understand he drank and gambled – I did what I could, rescued some of his properties, and after George himself died I let the daughter live on in the family home."

"Yes, yes, we all know you like to think of yourself as a bit of a philanthropist in Newtown, Simon, but what's it to do with me?" There was a flicker of spite in his cousin's tone; he was getting his own back for the gibe about politician's greed.

"I'm coming to that. By Jove, yes, I'm coming to that, Stephen. I began to get hints in letters from Aunt Dorinda Quigley out in Kenya that I should keep an eye on Gwendolyne Weston – that's the daughter. She had become quite friendly with your mother after your dad died. Well, as you know your mother had been an invalid for some time, so I suppose she

208

was glad of any friendship. But I couldn't help linking the two, especially when Dorinda wrote in her very obscure style that Gwen Weston might have been told something by her father, but she wouldn't talk while Olga was alive . . ."

"I believe I remember a Miss Weston coming to see my mother – seemed a nice, sensible sort of woman to me. Is she still alive?"

"She is – but its no use asking her. She suffered a stroke some years ago which left her speechless. That's been the trouble . . . I was left with a lot of rumours flying about and nothing substantial to go on. But there was certainly an annuity left for the woman by our mutual Aunt Dorinda, and those cryptic messages from the same source about the Weston's knowing some secret of the Durward-Cookes. Oh, you may well stare, Stephen, because this is about your side of the family, not mine . . ."

"I don't believe you. I can't think why I've come out here to listen to such rubbish . . ."

"Bear with me, Cousin. At one time it got to my ears that before he died old George Weston talked of knowing your family secrets – boasting about it when in his cups in the local hostelries. Very distasteful . . ."

"I never heard any of this . . ."

"Naturally you didn't. You were never here. First you were at school, then up at Cambridge, then you married and went to Hampshire. I was here and in the business as soon as I came down from College. Your ma was pretty batty by then—"

"She suffered from neuraesthenia, we were assured by the doctors . . ."

"I'm sure you were. But she was round the twist all the same. When I heard these rumours first, I began to wonder about some indiscretion . . ."

Mary heard the scrape of chair legs again; it sounded as if Stephen had got to his feet.

"For God's sake, man, keep still. Here let me fill your glass. When I say indiscretion I don't mean anything serious, someone was always around to protect your ma – first it had been sister Dorinda, then your dad, and after that she had spells in nursing homes. I only thought perhaps old George Weston had seen her floating about naked in her garden, and was making the most of it. I didn't take it seriously until you put the property on the market."

It seemed that Stephen had decided to settle down and listen. This time he spoke his voice was calmer. "The family always knew I'd sell the place when Mother died. Even when Father was alive they had let it go. I was never going to live in it once I had my constituency. Anyway, I think it's high time you got to the point of all this."

"I kept an eye on Miss Weston – I went to a considerable trouble over that, but I reckoned if the thing was important enough to be remembered in far-off Kenya then it must matter to someone. I got a bit of a lead when a schoolteacher in the same house as Miss Weston evinced an interest in archaeology which seemed to spark off the old lady's memory. I did some metaphorical digging myself, talked to a couple of old-timers in the town who said that was what old Weston was gabbing about in the pubs, said he'd dug up a burial site. Of course no one believed him, he'd always been full of tales that he was 'in with the gentry', stuff like that. But the archaeology thing could have been a nuisance, the developers might have taken fright – there's always delays if something of historic interest turns up . . ."

"I still think this is humbug, Simon. If there'd ever been anything in the grounds of Deloraine Court, I'd have known."

"Don't be too sure of that. We've not yet come to the crux of the story. As you know, I stalled on the sale – just enough to give me time to do a bit of actual digging myself. If there was anything in George Weston's story, the burial must have been where he put up the new conservatory. I was beginning to put two and two together. The fact that Aunt Dorinda was the only member of the family who was in residence when the thing was built meant that if anything was found she'd be the one Weston would go to. And I'll bet she decided off her own bat simply to get the site re-buried – save everyone, especially your mother, a deal of trouble."

"You could be right about the aunt." But Stephen's tone was grudging. "Father used to say she was fiercely protective of my mother. But what if she did have the site covered up? It's no crime. Better than having a set of nosy-parkers tramping all over your property."

"That would be our Aunt Dorinda's view entirely, not the most civic perhaps but understandable. If only that had been all. Look here, Stephen, I'm going to get another bottle – you're going to need it."

There was some kind of muffled protest but it quietened down as Mary listened to the other man's footsteps fading. She took the opportunity to stretch the cramp out of her legs. How long was this tête-à-tête, dialogue, whatever, going to go on for? It was certainly no meeting of minds; Simon had the upper hand and knew it. She found she was, in her mind, calling them by their first names as if she were on familiar terms.

When Simon returned she heard the glug-glug of more wine being poured. That's half a bottle each so far, she noted, not a lot between gentlemen of their class. In her collection of fascinating facts picked up in recent reading was the amount of port wine Palmerston had drunk before putting pen to the paper which effectively opened the Crimean War; just as well there were no nuclear buttons in those days.

The silence in the room was long enough for them both to have a good swallow. It was going down faster now.

"I'm getting tired of this charade," Stephen's speech was slurred. "In a minute I shall call a cab."

"The phone's cut off."

"I've got a—"

"Shut up, dear boy, and take a look at this." There was the sound of a case being put on the table.

"What have you got there?"

"Aunt Dorinda's diary – the most tedious piece of reading matter since Gibbon's *Decline and Fall* – except for the last two pages."

"Where'd you get it?"

"Well, now, there's a curious thing . . . It was never meant to see the light of day. I think it was meant to be buried with her – and how ironic that would have been. You and I would not be here this night discussing it . . ."

"And what's it got to do with me, may I ask?" The drunker the Member of Parliament got the more grandiose became his manner of speaking.

"Oh, a great deal, Stephen, a very great deal. First, I shall tell

211

you how it came to my hands – luckily for you I may add – and then I shall read the relevant passages. As I said, I believe the book wasn't ever supposed to surface. Dorinda wrote in it right up to a week before she died, which was some years ago, as you know. Uncle Daniel never read it – well, who would? – the wearisome world of a missionary lady set down in the most turgid prose, lists of names of native children, little homilies on the Bible, notes of hymns and texts and all in a crabbed handwriting like a Chinese laundry list. But somehow it got preserved – perhaps her native servants considered it precious, I don't know. Anyway, when Uncle Daniel died last year, the bungalow at the Mission where they'd lived all these years had to be cleared out, and what do you know? They packed up the books and one of them was Dorinda's diary. A trunk of them was dumped on my brother John who was moving house at the time and he in turn dumped it on me . . ."

He paused for breath. There was the sound of a bottle being pushed across the table.

"Has anyone else read this – this diary?" The words came thick and treacly.

"One . . . but don't worry, Cousin Stephen, she has been silenced."

It was only then that Mary began to be afraid. Up till then she had been intrigued – intrigued and amused by the clash of the two men, their demeanour, the seeming absurdity of their behaviour – but now as she took in what Simon Quigley had said it came home to her with chilling sharpness: this was not a game, this was not a stage-play about to reach its climax, this was about murder, a cold and calculated killing.

The atmosphere too in the room seemed suddenly charged with foreboding. She heard Simon Quigley clear his throat. Either he had not consumed as much wine as his cousin or he held his drink better. "I shall now read from the first lesson . . ." he declaimed. "As I said it was written a week or so before Dorinda died: 'Daniel is good as are the nurses so I am in no pain, and Dr Macfie has told me I cannot last out the month. So be it. I must write now, not in expiation and not in confession either; I do not believe confession is good for the soul. I want to write it down for my own sake. At the time it was such a reasonable thing to do, to protect Olga. When I have written it down it will be off my conscience, but I don't think it was ever on it. I am a rational being and have so lived but I believe in a just God and I think He would want me to write it down. No one will ever see it. Daniel has never been interested in my diary, he believes in actions not words. But I must begin. In the year I married, the bones were dug up, but Mr Weston was easily misled. I told him it was a prehistoric burial site and asked him to re-bury the remains. I did not ask where. It was the sensible thing to do.'"

Simon stopped reading. "Then it was just an archaeological discovery. That's all there is to it?" Stephen Durward-Cooke stumbled over the words and the rising note of hope in the question was a feeble thing.

"That was written on one page, then there is a gap of about two days. I shall now read the second lesson: 'I shall never forget that awful winter of the snow. Percy and Olga were overjoyed with the hope of the child to be born in January. Percy had been posted to the Middle East but would be home for the birth. There were still wartime shortages in 1947, power cuts and now the snow that came in December, and the black frost that froze the roads to Deloraine. We were lucky to have help; Caroline Sumner had seen to that when she brought us Helga.' There are some lines here that are scribbled through," Simon Quigley went on, "but appear to be the writer's opinion of Caroline Sumner, not altogether complimentary. Strange that . . . our Aunt was writing of unmentionable things yet she had crossed out her derogatory remarks about a friend. Such delicacy . . ."

"What unmentionable things, what d'you mean?"

"Have patience. I shall continue my reading: 'It would be in Caroline's nature to keep the best girl for herself. Irmgard is presentable and of good family whereas Helga . . . But I am wrong to judge her, her situation before coming into Caroline's hands was indeed pitiable. She was from Konigsberg in East Prussia, having survived the siege, and fled from the Red Army across the Baltic into the British Zone. I should have compassion for her but cannot for she deceived all of us. The Sumners would not have brought her had they known, and because she was well built and always wore the full black skirts and white aprons which were the only clothes she had, it was some time before I realised. It was a freezing night in December just before the snow came that I saw her clutch the kitchen sink as she washed up after dinner. I went to her immediately but got the usual sullen look for she was of an ungrateful disposition and brushed off any gesture of friendship. I heard her go upstairs. Because there were only the three of us in the house we had given her a decent bedroom, not the usual servants' quarters. Olga had retired early for she was near her time and fatigue overcame her in the evenings. I was in the sitting-room when I heard the crying. I could not believe my ears, it was the crying of a baby. I rushed up to Helga's room. She had delivered her own child, the child she had been carrying. She was calmly cutting the cord with scissors. It is at moments like these that all one's womanly instincts take over. I got Helga into bed, washed the child and laid it beside her, not a word between us – her English, as Caroline had forgotten to warn us, was non-existent. I tried to telephone the doctor in Newtown but already the lines were down.'

"There's another gap in the writing here but it is resumed some days later: 'I am getting so tired. I must write fast. Two days after Helga's boy was born we were still isolated from the world when Olga went into premature labour. I had told her nothing of Helga's deceit and Olga never heard the baby cry – I made sure of that by making her keep it in her room or in the kitchen by the stove where she had it in a wicker clothes basket. I shall not speak of that terrible night with my poor sister, and I thank God that the delirium she was in kept her from knowing. When the child was born it was a female, and it was dead, the cord tight round its throat, but as if that was not enough it was deformed, its spine unfinished. Even Helga wept at the sight. I am coming to the end now. I gave Olga a sleeping draught and took the dead baby away.

'At eight o'clock the next morning I went into the kitchen. Helga's child was in its basket, the back door was open. Helga was out bending over the wood-store getting logs for the stove. There was an axe lying on the block. The snow was soft and she did not hear me. I hit her to the ground, and once again when she lay there. I made sure she was dead, then I left her. I went in and took the boy from the basket and carried him up to my sister's room. I put him in

214

her arms. She was just waking. The joy on her face I cannot describe.

'Time to write is short now. It thawed a little that day, enough for me to bury Helga and the female child deep in the rose bed. Days later, when the doctor could get through he was relieved that we had coped, too busy to do other than take a quick look at Olga who remembered nothing and wished for nothing but the feel of the baby next to her heart, and the joy of feeding him.

I phoned Caroline Sumner and said Helga was unhappy and wanted back to Germany. She sent me the necessary travel document and I went myself to Kings Cross. No one has mentioned Helga since.

It was a rational decision I took. It saved my dear sister from madness. I do not ask God's forgiveness but I hope for his understanding . . .' Here endeth the last lesson . . ." But even Simon Quigley's flippancy sounded choked as his voice faded, and a terrible silence filled the room.

It was that very stillness which made Mary give herself away. Listening was one thing but now she had to see, she wanted to know what the effect would be on the face of the man who had just heard such appalling revelations. There was a tear in the curtain in front of her and she pulled at it gently but was unprepared for the result. The drapery moved and dislodged a curtain ring on the pole above the window; the noise had both men on their feet.

"What the devil . . . !"

She knew it was Simon Quigley who was striding across the room towards her. She could not bear to be caught crouching on the floor, she might as well take the initiative. She was on her feet and had pulled back the curtain before he reached her. Stop him in his tracks, she thought, catch him off-guard, so she said:

"You needn't have killed Blanche, Mr Quigley, she'd never read the diary." As she listened, she had realised how it had happened: after he'd seen that message he'd found out from Jasper where she was going, or he'd followed Venn's car – what a chance that foolish young man had given him . . .

But the past had gone, only the present mattered as Simon Quigley reached for her as a tiger claws its prey.

Twenty-Four

S imon Quigley forced Mary's hands behind her back as he marched her over to the centre of the room. He was a strong man and there was no point in her struggling. His initial fury had cooled to a hard, sustained anger, making his voice shake as he addressed his cousin.

"The interfering bitch heard it all. God knows what she's doing here, but we can't let her go. You and I haven't come this far, Stephen, to have everything ruined by a snooping wretch like this." The scathing contempt in his tone clipped the words short as if they came through closed teeth.

Stephen Durward-Cooke was standing with one hand on the back of his chair to steady himself while he leaned forward and peered into Mary's face. "Why, you're the one who broke in . . ." He stopped. The process of sobering-up was still taking time but he had a quick mind and it was starting to work. "What did you say about that girl's death? Hasn't there been a man charged?"

Simon tightened his grip on Mary so she twisted round and spat him in the eye.

In blind, disgusted fury he nearly let her go as she cried: "He murdered Blanche and he's going to let someone else take the blame!"

The back of her captor's hand caught her full on the mouth, and she tasted blood as he renewed his hold on her, and spun her round. "Blanche deserved it, the blackmailing bitch . . ." He dropped his voice. "She had read the diary, Stephen, and she thought there was money to be made out of it. Don't you see, she would have sold the story to the Press, and ruined you? I had to stop her – for your sake . . ."

I haven't a chance, Mary was thinking. There are two men

216

here with motive enough to kill me. The only question is, how are they going to do it?

Simon Quigley had conquered his anger; when he spoke now it was softly, and in a reasonable tone as if he saw his way clear: "Yes, Stephen, this is the woman who broke into your premises once before. You took her for a thief and you hit her. Now she has again entered your premises illegally. Hit her again, Stephen, hit her hard . . . Then we'll take her outside and leave her under that collapsing wall and pile bricks on top of her . . . A terrible accident, they'll say, but only what trespassers deserve. And there was no one else here when it happened for nobody will ever know we were at the house tonight . . ."

He was back in control, he was very plausible, very persuasive. As he pushed Mary nearer to his cousin, he whispered: "Hit her, Stephen, hit her hard. By the time she's found we'll be long gone. Tomorrow morning we bulldoze the conservatory to the ground and destroy the bones. Knock her out, Stephen . . ."

She was less than an arm's length from Stephen. She saw him clench his fists. He had huge, beefy hands, the knuckle bones on them white and shining against red flesh. She turned her head away, and shut her eyes so that she would not see the coming blow.

She felt a rush of air go past her cheek, and she heard the crunch as Stephen's fist crashed into Simon's jaw and the crack that broke it.

She was dragged to the floor as he went down. When she got to her knees he was lying still.

No one helped her to her feet. When at last she stood, shaking, Durward-Cooke pushed her into a chair, not particularly gently. "Sit there," he said, "while I think . . ."

He slumped down, and put his head in his hands.

Mary knew better than to speak. The minutes passed – slowly. A lifetime for him, she thought, looking at the down-bent head. It's more than I can take. What's it like for him?

Finally, with a long, shuddering sigh, he sat up and fumbled at an inner pocket. Oh, no . . . he couldn't have . . . For one other moment of terror, Mary froze. No, this couldn't happen . . . Members of Parliament in England do not carry guns . . .

He had taken out a mobile phone and was jabbing at the digits. "Police," he said, "Deloraine Court, Thornton Village, Newtown. Come at once."

He threw the instrument on the table.

Mary met his eyes, the tears welling up in hers. "Stephen," she said, "will your wife support you in this . . . in the troubles to come?"

It was out of her Irishness she spoke. It caught him as probably no other voice could.

"I think so," he said. "Elizabeth is a good woman . . ." Only then did he break down and he sobbed.

Nothing I can say can comfort him, thought Mary. Out of wells of her being, untouched for years, came the words: "Your mother loved you. She loved you enough to go through hell for you, put herself at the mercy of strangers, suffered their contempt in a language she didn't even understand, just for you, just to give you a decent birth . . ." Even as she spoke Mary was wondering where the words were coming from; it was only months later she knew they had come from the poor Irishwoman spurned by her native land because of the bastard baby in her womb, sailing in terror to an alien land. Mary Blane's Mother hadn't prospered either in that new country, the odds were against her from the start.

They were both sitting in absolute stillness when Lennox Kemp burst in through the conservatory doors five minutes later.

"The Fifth Cavalry are supposed to get here before the end of the film," said Mary to him, before she fainted for the first time in her life.

Some months later, her husband read out the announcement saying that the Conservative member for Welchester West would not be standing as a candidate in the coming election. "Wants to spend more time with his family," Kemp quoted.

"A good idea," said Mary. She could not but think of the sorry little heap of bones in the rotted toolbox, and the pitiful skulls found nearby when Kemp had led the police to the burying place, underneath that ivied bench. "I hope the Durward-Cookes weather the coming storm."

"I don't know whether you mean in the political or the personal sense. If it's the latter, it should not be too bad, now that Simon Quigley has made a full confession."

"Why did he do it?" Mary still could not understand.

Kemp shrugged. "Mixed motives . . . the family honour . . . money, prestige. He owed a lot of his own success to his kinship to someone as successful as Stephen. Simon Quigley was a rational creature – he genuinely thought he acted for the best."

"But Stephen was not your typical rational Englishman," said Mary, thoughtfully, "and he saved our lives."

"Your life, you mean . . ."

She gave him a long, cool look. "Two lives," she said. "I'm pregnant . . ."

Kemp stared, grinned, then couldn't help himself: "You went on that madcap spree with those two potential killers!"

"No. No. At that time I didn't know or I'd never have taken the risk."

"And from now on you're not going to get the chance," said her husband, grimly. "I'm going to lock you up and throw away the key . . ."